Final Chance

An Alternate American History

Time Travel Novel

Book 3

By

Michael Roberts

Final Chance

Want updates and more from Michael Roberts?

https://www.subscribepage.com/k8e0d9

Final Chance	1
Prologue	7
Chapter One Happy Birthday	17
Chapter Two Back At Sea	27
Chapter Three Nightmares	37
Chapter Four Bait	57
Chapter Five Homecoming	71
Chapter Six A Long Ride	79
Chapter Seven Setting the Trap	89
Chapter Eight Bird Whistles	103
Chapter Nine Two Monsters Meet	113
Chapter Ten The Wedding	125
Chapter Eleven Spies	141
Chapter Twelve Fear and Suspicion	165
Chapter Thirteen Change of Plans	183
Chapter Fourteen Old Friends	201
Chapter Fifteen A Bundle of Nerves	213
Chapter Sixteen Mother's Advice	223
Chapter Seventeen Three Years Later	241
Chapter Eighteen One Last Favor	255
Chapter Nineteen Good Guys Wear White	263
Chapter Twenty The End of a War	283
Chapter Twenty-One A Visitor	289
Excerpt from Aden's Chance, the next book in the exciting Second Chance series!	293
Excerpt from Book 1 *Chain and Mace*	297
About the Author	301
Also by the Author:	302

Final Chance

Prologue
February 8ᵗʰ, 1778
Windsor Castle

King George the Third sat in his throne room, up high on the dais in his oversized royal chair, sneering down at the incompetent men before and below him. He wore his deep red silk pants, large golden coat, and thick, flowing crimson robe. The sleeves at the ends of his magnificent coat folded back in huge, exaggerated cuffs. A soft, brilliantly white fur sat on and around his shoulders over the coat and robe. A decorative gold sword was secured around his waist. The sword's value in gold was equal to its worthlessness as a weapon. He didn't care much for wearing it, except to show people and let them know when he was disgruntled or displeased. The fingers of his right hand drummed on the armrest of the revered chair. The room was silent, everyone waiting for him to speak first.

Ten hard-looking and experienced soldiers lined the walls, loaded muskets in hand, bayonets fixed. The king had not gone anywhere since the assassination of his trusted Prime Minister without these soldiers. Two soldiers stood next to his bed as he slept at night, when he was able to sleep at all. His wife had taken to sleeping in another room. She refused to lie in bed with two armed soldiers standing so nearby. He wondered absently if her departure was really because he woke up every night screaming.

"The French have joined the war in America," the king announced, breaking the silence, eyes boring down on them.

The four men who stood before him didn't respond. It was not a question, nor was the king informing them of something everyone in the country didn't already know. He was letting them know what was on his mind. He was upset, displeased, annoyed, and yes, very angry. Several of his highest ranking naval and army officers now rotted in prison, stripped of their rank and property, soon to have their necks stretched, their families forced into a life of destitute exile. No one in the palace was safe from the king's swift and unpredictable wrath.

The king had forgotten names and dates before, but since this Pale Rider criminal had sacked not one but two of the king's ships, he'd been acting . . . well, crazy. Waking up in the middle of the night screaming. Running around the palace in his underwear. In days gone, late night talks with his trusted advisor Lord North had been the only way to calm his anxiety.

Since the assassination of Lord North, the king had become completely unhinged. There were rumors that the king had seen and actually yelled at the assassin the day before the criminal had killed Lord North. The king was one of the few people to come across the killer and live to talk about it. Since the murder, the king had sealed himself off in the palace, afraid for his life. He'd sworn to not rest until the criminal had been captured and killed.

Plenty of chairs littered the room, but the king had not given them leave to sit. In the mood he was in this morning, sitting right now without the king's leave might cost the person sitting his head. So, they stood, unmoving and speechless, until the king let it be known he so desired.

The king himself had declared war on France two days before. The same day King Louis, the king of France, had signed the Treaty of Alliance and the Treaty of Amity and Commerce.

"Our own Prime Minister, Lord North, was murdered," the king said, raising his voice and tapping the index finger of his right hand against the arm of his chair. "Right here, in this palace. In *our* palace. Not a hundred yards from where you now stand."

The four men readied themselves for an outburst of anger and profanity from the king. It seemed like any mention of the murder of Lord North or of the assassin known only as the Pale rider was enough to throw the king into a fit.

Two of the four men standing there were in the service of the king—George Germain, Secretary of State for the American Department, and George Collier, Vice Admiral in the Royal Navy. Neither man had stood at attention in over a decade, but now they stood as stiff and straight as they could manage. The two civilians were finely dressed merchants. The fact they were allowed in the palace at all meant they were either men with power or men with something to offer the king.

The king focused his anger at Germain and Collier, as if this situation was their fault.

"How did you allow this tragedy to happen?" the king asked in a horrible whisper, shaking his head.

Neither man opened his mouth. There was no right answer, only answers which would get a man hung. They had not even been *in* the palace when Lord North was killed. Worse than killed, he had been targeted and assassinated. None of this was on them, but to voice that opinion might sound as if they were saying it was the king's fault. A costly and fatal disaster.

"Why haven't you captured the assassin yet?" the king screamed, his hands balling into fists.

"My king," Secretary of State, George Germain said, stepping forward. "I've already ordered a dispatch to deliver a messenger to Joseph Brant. The message will leave with the next ship to Canada."

"Joseph Brant?" the king asked as he tilted his head to the side.

"Yes, your majesty," Germain answered. "Captain Brant. With the Mohawk Warriors, in Canada. Your majesty has met him once before. He leads a mix of Mohawk warriors and colonial loyalists. They are known as Brant's volunteers."

"Is he the Native they call Monster Brant?"

"Yes, your majesty. Among other names. He's of the Mohawk tribe, fierce warriors, and loyal to your majesty."

"And what orders are you sending him?" the king asked in a calmer voice.

"To travel south," Germain told him. "Track down and kill the Pale Rider and anyone who has ever given aid to him."

"Washington's Assassin," the king spoke each syllable slowly while his left hand touched his forehead as if he had a headache, "is not in America. Is he? No. He's in France."

"Yes, your majesty," Germain said quickly. "He is now, at this moment, but our spies tell us he'll be sailing for America soon."

"Your plan is to let him sail away free, out of our reach and hope to catch him at a later date, in America?" the king asked, eyebrows furling with anger. "What logic is that?"

"No, your majesty," Vice Admiral George Collier countered. "We have five of our ships ready to sail and sink any ship he sails on."

"How will you know what ship he'll be on?" the king asked.

"I shall supply this information, sire." The older of the two merchants spoke up for the first time.

"And you are?" the king asked.

"Freiherr Bartolomeo de Testa, your majesty," the middle-aged, finely dressed merchant answered. "I'm at your service. I'm also the father of two innocent young boys this man has killed. Murdered. Like you, I, too, seek revenge."

"Revenge?" the king asked, pulling back in surprise at the word. "I seek justice, not revenge. Revenge is petty. Revenge is for common people with common lives. We are the King of England. We are the embodiment of righteousness. We bear a burden you could never understand. We seek justice for Lord North and for

England herself. The empire has been molested by this man, and he must pay the price."

"Yes, sire," Testa responded, dipping his head. "I misspoke. I also seek justice. I have a fleet of merchant ships and crews to serve them. Every ship in every harbor in France is being watched right now. If he gets on a ship, any ship in France, I will know it."

The king's eyes shifted from the older merchant to the younger one. He didn't expect to have to ask the question. His one eyebrow rose in the unspoken query.

"May I introduce my man, Robert?" Testa asked. "He's my eyes and ears and very capable. I'll return home, and he shall coordinate with the rest of my people. He'll send word as soon as this assassin is located."

Testa had intentionally left out the simple fact that Robert once had this killer tied up in front of him. If Robert and Testa's son, Jacob, had killed this assassin instead of keeping him alive for extra coin, they wouldn't be in this situation now. It wouldn't be fair to blame Robert for Testa's son's mistake. His son had been the one to make the fatal decision.

"Your majesty," Germain interrupted with a slight bow, "on the high seas or back in America, it makes no difference. The man will be just as dead. Your majesty's justice will be served."

The room fell quiet when the king raised a hand. Pensively, his head rotated from side to side, possibly looking for unseen threats in the shadows. Then his eyes stared off to the corner, as if he was listening to someone no one else could see or hear. A bead of sweat rolled down the side of his doughy face. The king didn't seem to notice it and made no attempt to wipe it away. The king's fingers stop their drumming. After a long minute, the king mumbled something to himself, then cleared his throat. He focused his attention back on the four men before him.

"Send your message to this monster in Canada," the king commanded Germain. "If the killer makes it back to the colonies, I'll be very displeased, but we should prepare for it. He has, after all, out witted you every step of the way. Perhaps it takes a monster to kill a monster."

No one in the room mentioned the fact these men themselves had not yet gone up against the criminal, and he'd not in fact outwitted them at any time.

"If you manage to capture or kill the criminal, then the only thing lost is the monster's time," the king continued. "The monster's time matters not to me. We want a ship sent to Canada today."

The king swung his gaze to the Vice Admiral. "Assign your best captain to coordinate with this Robert fellow."

The king waved a hand in a flipped wave towards Robert.

"And set up a blockade immediately," the king demanded. "Every ship within a hundred miles of England shall be reassigned and added to the blockade. Block off both sides of the channel completely. Sink any ship trying to leave France. We want the assassin dead, one way or the other."

"Every ship, your majesty?" the admiral asked. "We have five standing by for this hunt. Most of the ships in the area are already committed to important duties, some of which are vital to the Empire."

"Every ship!" the king screamed, his face turning as red as a turnip.

"Yes, sire," the admiral retreated. "As you say, every ship."

The king waved them off. The four men bowed deeply as one, then turned to leave the room. As the doors shut behind them, they took several more steps, then stopped to face one another, shocked they'd made it out with their heads still fastened to their necks.

Testa faced the Admiral and Germain. "The king is upset. I'd heard rumors, but I was informed his condition was not *this* noticeable. I fear this has now changed. This assassin seems to be pushing the king's emotions over a cliff. Between the stress of this war, his advisers arguing, and his fear of this one single man, I would suggest swift action before he . . . "

Testa was trying to choose his words carefully, but his next words might be going too far.

"I would caution you, sir," Germain interrupted before he came up with a word. "Voicing those kinds of thoughts could be considered treasonous and punishable by death."

"Admiral," Testa said, changing the subject. "Take Robert with you. Keep him on your flagship. My men know to signal if this killer tries to flee France. We have several ships sailing up and down the coastline. If any of my crews on shore spot the assassin, they'll light a signal fire built with dyed cotton. If he goes north through the channel, the smoke will be blue. If he heads south, the smoke will be red. My ships trolling the coast will see the smoke and follow whatever ship is leaving the harbor. They'll in turn run up a large solid blue flag. Let your captains know the ship with the blue flag is following the ship they need to attack. My ships have been provided with these flags."

Testa pulled out two pieces of paper from the inside pocket of his coat and handed one to the Admiral. It was a drawing of a man in his late twenties or early thirties, clean-shaven, with close-cropped hair. One part of the drawing drew the eye, the scar on the man's head. Even with the pencil drawing, the scar made a wide cut through the hairline.

"One of these has been passed out to every ship I own," Testa said. "Robert will provide you with several more of these to pass out to your captains, so they know who we're looking for. Remember, he has posed as a British officer before. He can seemingly blend in anywhere. No one can be trusted, not even your own soldiers, until you verify that they are *not* this man. If you sink the French ships trying to escape your blockade and search any merchant ships, including English ships, he will not slip from our grasp."

"Thank God you didn't show the king this drawing," the admiral said, wiping the sleeve of his arm across his fevered forehead. "We may not have walked out of there alive."

"How long can you man this blockade of yours?" Testa asked.

"First, I need to order several of our warships to wherever they're needed most," the admiral answered. "Then I need to send a few ships somewhere else. More than a hundred miles from here. The rest I'll order to man the blockade."

The admiral blew out a lung full of air and ran his fingers through his hair, thankful he'd elected to leave his itchy wig back in his quarters.

"As for your question," the admiral continued, "how long? Two weeks before we fall behind on commerce, exploration, supplies to our troops, and shipments of tea around the world. We're at war with the colonists, now France, and soon Spain. Our ships will be blocking the channel when they should be patrolling the high seas. We have a shortage of ships already. We can't afford to have a dozen sitting out there."

"And after two weeks?" Testa asked.

"Unless you want to go in there and tell the king he's wrong, the blockade will stand, and the empire will suffer."

Testa handed Germain the second copy of the drawing.

"You can send this off with your messenger," Testa told him, "to this Monster in Canada. In case he somehow gets through our net. your monster will know who he's hunting."

"Captain Joseph Brant doesn't appreciate that name," Germain warned. "Don't let him hear you say it. He may not like it, but there are reasons people call him the Monster. He's a very intelligent and ruthless individual who does whatever is necessary to win a battle. If the assassin is to make it back to America, he'll wish we had sunk him here. Death by drowning is a slightly better death than one at the hands of Captain Brant. There are rumors he staked men naked on top of ant hills. Brant isn't a man I would want hunting me. His men are some of the best trackers in the world, and his loyalists are devoted to him. Make no mistake, Brant and his warriors are very good at what they do."

"Which is?" Testa asked, already knowing the answer but wanting to hear it.

"Tracking, terrorizing, and killing enemies of the king," Germain said.

Final Chance

Chapter One Happy Birthday

March 18th, 1778
Paris, France

I sat at the table across from Benjamin Franklin and John
Adams. Lafayette was to my right, and Captain John Paul Jones sat
on my left. The restaurant was one I had not been to before – high
class and upscale, even for Paris.

I'd let it slip that it was my thirty-first birthday, and
Franklin insisted on taking us out to dinner. Last year for my
birthday, my best friend and boss, Aden Steel, had taken me out for
pizza and beer in 2021, before I traveled back in time to change
history. This year, I had pheasant, small white potatoes, bacon-
wrapped asparagus, and mussels cooked in red wine. I decided if the
king of England ever caught me, I was going to ask for this exact
meal before I was hung. Did condemned men get a last meal in
1778? I doubted it.

The fact Adams was here meant this was more than a
birthday dinner. Adams hadn't been comfortable around me as of
late. He treated me with courtesy and was always friendly, but I
think my presence reminded him of the part he played in the

assassination of the Prime Minister of England, and that guilt weighed heavily on his conscience.

Franklin, on the other hand, always seemed affable around me. He seemed to like me, almost treating me like a grandson at times. He had a way of treating tools like friends and friends like tools. He went out of his way to make me comfortable, but only because, as far as tools went, he saw me as a sharp scalpel. I was an attack dog he fed steak, hoping to buy my loyalty. Or in my case, pheasant and mussels, but his desire was the same. I didn't mind as long as I knew what was going on behind his smile and those thin wire glasses.

His kindness didn't buy loyalty or anything else from me. I was loyal to the idea of beating the British and winning the war. If helping him helped me or, more importantly, helped General Washington win the war, then so be it. If it didn't, then I had no desire to do his bidding. Tonight, he either had bad news for us or he had a favor to ask.

Marie Lafayette had spent the last six weeks with his family and took the time to introduce me to them. His wife, the dark-haired and full-lipped Adrienne, seemed to adopt me into their family, like an older brother-in-law. Considering I thought of Lafayette as a little brother, I guess it was appropriate. Adrienne offered to let me stay with their family, but I was too big of a target. I was probably the most wanted man in at least three countries, four if you counted Canada. Putting them in danger was not an option.

King Louis had arranged for me to stay in one of the rooms at his palace. He was now at war with England and no longer cared if the British found out that I was his personal guest. He and I would often discuss the world and the decisions he'd have to make concerning his country that he loved with a passion. Even so, I still found myself pushing a chair under the doorknob of my bedroom door every night, to slow any spies or servants looking to make a quick fortune for themselves.

Today was the first day I didn't have a sling on my arm. I had been shot in the shoulder almost seven weeks ago by a British officer. He didn't survive the encounter, but I somehow had. His bullet ripped through my shoulder muscles, but my scapula bone – my shoulder blade – had stopped the bullet. The king's personal physician had been taking care of me and said my shoulder blade was not broken but may have been fractured.

The doctor also said my shoulder seemed healed, stiff from lack of use, but fully healed. I had started stretching it every morning for the past few weeks. The hole in my shoulder had healed up, leaving yet another puckered round scar on my body. My strength had returned, but the doctor insisted I take it easy for a few more weeks here in France.

Lafayette, however, was ready to go back to America and fight at General Washington's side. Washington was ready to enlist Lafayette and give him his own command and the rank of Major General.

Jones told us his ship was prepped to sail and had received word that upon returning to the United States that he was going to captain the USS Ranger. His face lit with animated excitement about the opportunity to command her. She was a sloop of war, built in Maine, and one of the first American-built ships for the Continental Navy. He had learned he would be pirating against the British Navy. He'd pirated before, years before we'd met, and against his objections, he had gained more experience while sailing with me.

Lafayette and Jones erupted into laughter at a joke Franklin had told and brought me back to the here and now. Franklin finished his wine and pushed his plate away. He wiped his mouth with a red linen napkin, his signal that he wanted to talk about the real reason we were here. The others at the table took the hint and pushed their plates away, giving Franklin their full attention. I wasn't done eating, so I sure as heck wasn't pushing a plate with food still on it away from my hungry belly.

"The British are still blockading the channel," Franklin said as he set his napkin down on the table. "They are still attacking every French ship they come across. Stopping and searching every merchant ship."

"We can't sail back to the United States until the blockade is over?" Jones asked, hands now clinched into fists. He was aching to return.

Franklin produced a piece of paper from his coat pocket. He unfolded it and laid it on the table, face up. Running the flat of his big fatty hand across it twice, he smoothed out the folds.

"How long do you think they'll keep this up?" Jones inquired. "They must need those ships elsewhere in the world. They don't have so many ships for them to continue this indefinitely."

As in answer to Jones's question, Franklin slid the paper over to me. "Madam Fournier sent a messenger with this. I'm afraid the blockade is for you, Thomas."

I wasn't surprised. What did surprise me was the parchment. The paper was a drawing of me that included my scar. It wasn't like looking in the mirror or anything but good enough for anyone looking at me would know I was the one they were looking for. I groaned around my mouthful of food.

"Does King Louis blame us for the blockade?" Jones asked.

"No," I answered for Franklin, swallowing a bite of pheasant. "The king talked about it with me several days ago. He seems to think it's funny. Most of the French Navy is out of the channel, so only a few ships are stuck. For their part, the English have half a dozen warships and a dozen frigates stuck here conducting the blockade. The blockade is worse for the British than it is for the French."

"The British will tire of waiting for you on the ocean," Lafayette said. "It's only a matter of time before the British start sending in spies to find you."

"I'm sure they sent spies weeks ago," Franklin commented, waving his right hand around the room, as if one of the other patriots in the restaurant might be a British spy. "Thomas has been staying at the palace protected. But Thomas, the king has expressed concern you'll be seen in the palace. Not for his sake or France's, but for yours. He's afraid you'll be a target. We need to get you out of France soon."

"How do we do that?" Lafayette asked. "The channel is blocked."

"You'll need to buy passage," Franklin said.

"Again, how?" Jones asked. "They are searching every ship."

"You three must ride south to the most southern tip of Spain," Adams broke in. "From there, you'll buy passage to America."

"Over eight hundred miles on horseback," Lafayette lamented. "With spies. The Testa family sent killers after us."

"We need to get you out of France. It's the only way," Adams repeated.

"No," I said, putting another mussel in my mouth. The whole table stopped talking, and every head turned to me as I chewed.

"No, what?" Franklin asked.

"No, we are *not* riding to Spain," I said after swallowing the mussel.

"You can't stay, Thomas," Adams countered, picking up his glass of wine.

"I know. I didn't say we were staying. I said we're not riding for Spain. At least I'm not. Lafayette and Jones should go. It would be safer for them to ride without me. I have different plans."

Adams pouted as if insulted. "What plans?"

"I don't know. Yet. But I'll be leaving the way I came. By ship and from the same port."

"This is your pride speaking, Thomas," Franklin scolded, holding up a hand to calm me. "You're smarter than that. You can't let your emotions dictate your actions."

"My ship is at your disposal," Jones added, ignoring Franklin. "If you want to fight our way out, we are willing."

"No," I said. "Thank you, John. We wouldn't survive a direct naval battle against the British fleet. No, I have a few ideas

21

not involving direct battle. I'll need to figure a few things out, but I'm not running from these assholes. I'll be leaving for the harbor in the morning. I don't want to spend my birthday on the road. Let's eat and enjoy the company of our friendship tonight."

I turned my attention back to Franklin. "Will you send a message to Madam Fournier for me?"

"Yes," Franklin answered.

"Whatever you're planning, Thomas, you're not alone," Lafayette said. "Tonight, we eat, drink, and laugh. We'll celebrate your birthday as comrades, but tomorrow, I'll ride with you."

"We both will be going with you," Jones added in.

"Very well," I said. "Then we'll need to send several messages tonight."

The next morning, I needed to pack and prepare to leave Paris. I laid out my belongings to take an inventory. Six months ago, I came to this century with the help of my best friend, a brave pilot, and some alien technology. A broken spaceship, to be exact. My goals, our plans, were to change history, to create a new timeline, one where the British Empire didn't rule most of the world, and where my wife wasn't raped and murdered.

In 2021, I had been told by a historian named Dr. Rock, if I saved General Washington's life, preventing him from being hung in the streets of Philadelphia, made sure the colonists won the battle of Saratoga to ensure the French joined in, and then secured a victory at Yorktown, the colonists would then win the war.

So far, I had saved Washington's life and helped the colonists win the battle of Saratoga. In doing so, I had changed history in good and bad ways. The late and now very dead Lord North had convinced the king to double down and send twice as many troops to the colonies. By killing Lord North, I had put things back into balance, but I was learning there was always a price to pay. Always unforeseen results, which couldn't be predicted. I still needed to ensure the battle at Yorktown ended in victory, and as of yet, I had no idea how to accomplish this. In my history, the Battle of Yorktown was nothing more than the final straw to end what I had grown up knowing as the Great Rebellion.

I did have two significant advantages – knowing history and the equipment I brought back with me. I had a finite amount of equipment, and my knowledge of history was less and less important as the timeline changed.

Now that I had time to breathe in France, I realized I needed to keep better track of my twenty-first century toys. Besides my pistols, swords and knives, I had forty-six 30-30 Winchester rounds left for my Thompson Center contender. I also had nine fully loaded magazines for my Tec-9, 9mm pistol, half of a first aid kit, one antibiotic shot, two morphine shots, one full bottle of pain killers, one fully charged smart phone, a range finder, two grenades, and my night vision goggles, which I was shocked I hadn't lost yet.

I had used my only two C4 charges, four of my six grenades, half of my ammo, most of my medical supplies, and all of my portable phone batteries. The next time my smart phone fell to zero percent, it would never turn on again. And once my ammo was depleted, I was going to have to learn to carry a real flintlock pistol and not the mockups I used now. In hindsight, I could have packed better weapons and equipment, but we were in a rush with only a few days to plan, equip, and execute, and no real assurances of what would work best in the 1700s.

As I dressed, I chose to wear my new sword, given to me by the King of France. My other sword was an English cavalry officer's sword that I had pilfered from a real bastard of a captain named Bonifield. I had killed him months ago, and though my new rapier was a much finer weapon, I could not bring myself to part with my old one.

With everything I owned either strapped to my body or in my leather satchel, I stepped out of my room, and I froze in place when I found the king in the hall with a broad smile on his face. King Louis the Sixteenth wore a simple gold outfit. Although it was finely made and cut, he only wore the pants and shirt and small-heeled gold shoes to make him appear taller. This was the first time I'd seen him without a formal coat. He stood there by himself, without guards or servants. There was an undeniable meaning to this – I just didn't understand what it was.

"Thomas," the king greeted me.

"Your majesty," I returned, with a small bow.

The king reached up and clasped me on my shoulder with his left hand, then motioned for us to walk with his right.

"Your friends are outside waiting with the carriage," the king told me. "We wanted to walk you out alone. Our last chance to talk as it is."

We started walking down the long hallway towards the stairs that led to the ground level.

"If you ever return to France, you are always welcome here," the king said in a serious tone.

"Thank you, your majesty," I responded. "But I fear I may never return to France. I want to help the colonies win the war, and then fade from history."

"We've had many talks, Thomas," the king said. "Yet we still don't know who you really are."

"I'm who you see, your majesty," I answered. "No more, no less."

"The most wanted man alive, and all you want to do is disappear?"

"Makes sense to me. Don't all wanted men try to disappear?" I reasoned.

"Most wanted men aren't called the Pale Rider."

"True. But the Pale Rider is no more. I will lose my vest and guns. Take up a new name, shave my head and grow a beard. You won't hear about the Pale Rider again. England now offers one hundred thousand gold pieces for my head."

"We understand your reasons for wanting to lose the name," the king said with a sad look on his face. "But we fear you'll be unable to."

"Why do you say this?" I asked.

"Because we understand the value in the name," he explained. "And we understand men like your General Washington. He's a great man, but we fear this war is everything to him."

"And to me," I added.

"*Oui*," the king said. "Don't be too hard on the General when he pushes for the Pale Rider to kill again."

"The General has already given me leave to hang up the vest and bury the Pale Rider."

The king nodded in understanding. "Then we shall talk of it no more. *Vive le cavalier pale.*"

Two servants opened the wide, ornate double doors leading from the palace to the large courtyard. Lafayette, Jones, Franklin, and Adams stood next to a black carriage. When the king and I walked out, they bowed to the king. Lafayette and Jones climbed into the carriage, leaving the door open for me. When I turned towards the king, he grasped my arms and pulled me in for a stiff hug. He kissed my cheeks and then pushed me back arms distance away. I bowed again and surprised him by thanking him for his friendship. I imagined kings aren't normally spoken to so honestly, nor do people make assumption of friendships with them.

Climbing into the carriage, I asked Jones and Lafayette if the arrangements I had asked for had been completed. They grinned at me as the carriage door shut, then jerked against the seat as the driver flicked the reins.

The next day, we pulled in front of Madam Fournier's place. She had information, new clothes, and a special item for us. Jones took the carriage and the *special item* ahead to prepare the ship.

Lafayette and I paid a coin for a second carriage to take us to the harbor. After one quick stop, we walked onto the Ariel. As soon as we set foot on her, Jones ordered the ropes cast off and the sails lowered.

The crew had repainted the masts from white to black last night in the dark, including painting over the ship's name. They had painted the ship with a Turkish name that I didn't know, but it didn't matter enough to ask. What mattered is we blended in with the other ships. I only hoped no one saw us board. The last thing we needed was for one of Testa's actual ships to come after us as we sailed out of the harbor.

Chapter Two   Back At Sea

Captain Charles J. Brownrigg stood at the bow of his two hundred-five-foot-long warship, the HMS London. She was a beautiful Rodney class ship with three masts and ninety guns. Despite such a fine ship, he was tired and bored and found himself walking up and down the length of the ship over and over.

He'd been sailing in the same area of the channel for five weeks now. How did he find himself here? This was a warship for Christ's sake! Yes, she was considered a second-class warship but only ten guns short of a first class. He should be in India or the colonies, enforcing British rule, making a name and fortune for himself. Not here looking for a ghost.

Not for the first time, he considered bringing his protest directly to the king. But also not for the first time, he thought about the rumors he'd heard regarding the king's mental state and unprovoked anger. No, he wouldn't go to the king. He would do his duty, no matter how worthless his duty was. He and his crew had done nothing more than stop and search any and every merchant ship trying to leave the channel. And found nothing.

Since England was now at war with France, they could attack any French ships they saw, but the French seemed content with letting the British tie up their fleet, sailing in circles. He'd hoped the French would come out and challenge him, give him a reason to fire, but he knew they would not. From their point of view, it only made sense to leave the Empire alone and let them waste resources. So far, he and his crew had stopped and boarded one or two ships a day.

The merchants knew the drill. They would drop sails and wait to be boarded and searched. Then, after the search, the two ships went their own ways. The merchants headed south to Spain or points unknown, while the HMS London continued sailing in circles.

Captain Brownrigg ordered his crew to run battle drills twice a day to fend off the boredom. Unfortunately, boredom was the only enemy they would be fighting as long as the king had them chasing shadows. He walked to the wheel where Lieutenant Bell stood, steering the ship.

His only consolation was he wasn't the only captain stuck out in this folly. Ten other warships coursed through these waters. Half of them were sailing around the south entrance to the channel while the other half were sailing around the north entrance. HMS Ocean was in sight, sailing ahead of them on the port side, commanded by Captain John Laforey. Like the HMS London, the Ocean also had ninety guns. Brownrigg felt a sense of comfort at seeing other warships in the area. It was reassuring to know they were also chasing this farce, and he was not being punished. Captain Brownrigg and Captain Laforey were friends, but they held a more than healthy competition with each other. Whether they were competing for a particular bar maid's favor on any given night or for a better command, they were always trying to out-show each other. The brass ring was who would win the honor of commanding a first-class ship. The golden ring would be getting promoted first. To have John forced to offer a salute to Charles would be the greatest prize of all.

"Ship ho," the sailor in the crow's nest shouted out loud and long, bringing Charles back to the real world.

The sailor was pointing towards the harbor. Captain Brownrigg moved to the railing with his spyglass to study the next merchant ship they would be boarding. Not a ship – ships. Two of them this time, sailing in line. This was new; the ships typically sailed out one at a time. These were merchant ships, not warships. The first one had twenty guns. The second one didn't have any guns that could be seen. Captain Laforey saw the ships, too. The Ocean had turned towards them.

"Hard to port!" he yelled to the lieutenant.

He decided to stop one of the ships and leave the second ship for the HMS Ocean. Captain Brownrigg lifted the spyglass back up to his eye. The two ships were Turkish. Unfortunately, he didn't read Turkish and didn't know what the ships' names were. The second ship was raising another flag.

A blue flag.

This was it. This was what they were waiting for, why they were out here. This was his chance to turn this shit detail into a reward and promotion from the king himself. He was ready to lower the sails to slow the ship, but not now. No, they would not be boarding this ship. His orders were clear. Open fire and sink the criminal on sight.

The HMS Ocean's captain had also seen the blue flag and her cannons were being pressed forward. Captain Brownrigg ordered his own cannons loaded and readied. His drills had paid off. His crew moved with professionalism and grace. The cannons were loaded and pushed forward forty-five seconds after he gave the order. Captain Laforey had fully opened his sails to gain speed. He was racing to sink the Turkish vessel. Captain Laforey should match the London's speed, but he wanted to get off the first shot. He wanted to sink the Turks first.

Captain Brownrigg yelled out orders for a small course change to grab more wind. He needed to fire his cannons first, but if he fired too soon and missed, then the Ocean would sink the Turkish prize. If he waited too long, the Ocean would fire first and again sink the ship. It was a race to get off a full broadside first that had to

29

be timed perfectly. The lead ship was dropping her sails as if she expected to be boarded. The trail ship had turned to her starboard, maneuvering out of the way of the hailstorm to come.

They were in position.

"Fire!" Captain Brownrigg yelled.

Forty-five cannons screamed with deafening explosions. Then a matching set of explosions burst from the Ocean. There was no denying it – Brownrigg got off the first shot. A side smile passed across his lips. The victory would be his. Yes, he might have to share some of the credit with Captain Laforey, but his report would show he fired first.

The air between his ship and the blasted Pale Rider was filled with acrid black and gray smoke, but he could hear the victory. Then he was hit with over pressure as the small ship evaporated into a flash of light. He flung his hand over his eyes to shade them. Brownrigg had known what would happen if a ship's magazine was hit directly by a cannonball but had never seen it for himself. He started to yell for his cannons to reload, but it was unnecessary.

Wood rained down from the sky in a spectacle which could only be described as Biblical. If all the guns hit their target, then ninety cannons struck the small merchant ship almost as one. Six or seven good shots would have sunk her, ninety had obliterated her. It was a total overkill, but his orders had been crystal clear. They were to give no quarter, no time to surrender, and no chance of escape. Brownrigg hadn't believed the rumors he'd heard of this Pale Rider, but then again, only fools took unnecessary chances.

Earlier That Morning. . .

Captain Badem sat at his desk on his ship, the Ayla, eating dry flat bread and boiled eggs. A pitcher of water and a clay cup sat on the desk next to him. He and his crew had been here a week, doing nothing instead of moving merchandise. Every day that they sat here, they were not moving cargo. Every day was a loss of money. His crew still expected to be paid, of course, but instead of the money coming out of profits, it was coming out of his own pocket.

Testa owned the Ayla, but Badem was the captain. He and Testa shared in the profits with Testa taking the lion's share. Since Testa owned and provided the ship, Badem was expected to pay the crew from his portion of the profits. While Badem ate in his quarters, his crew marched up and down the docks, looking for the man in the picture. The disfigured man with the scar. The man with the black vest and two pistols. The man who had killed Testa's two sons. Baden understood Testa's anger, but his rash decisions were costing everyone money. The Ayla had relieved one of Testa's larger ships that had also sat in the water doing nothing for two long weeks. He would be here one or two more weeks before being relieved by a different ship.

Badem hoped they would find this man soon. They had the blue flag Testa had provided him. If, or rather when, they spotted this man, they were not to stop him. Testa's orders were simple: they would wait until this man sailed from the harbor, then follow him. Then they would raise the blue flag when any British ships came into sight and let them deal with the criminal.

Testa had been distraught about his sons, but he was still a smart man. He understood if these men were left here too long, they would grow bored and lose focus. To resolve this, Testa had set up a clever rotation system. Captain Badem was peeling another egg when a knock came at his door.

"Come," the captain yelled in Turkish.

The first mate opened the door and stuck his head into the room.

"Captain, two Frenchmen are here to speak to you. They say they are here with orders from Freiherr Bartolomeo de Testa."

"Send them in, you fool," the captain ordered, dropping the egg and eggshells onto the desk and dipping his hands in a bowl of water, then wiping them on his pants.

Two well-dressed Frenchmen walked into the cabin, pushing the door shut behind them as if this was their ship and not his. They didn't offer their hands in greeting or provide their names. They stood with their hands clasped behind their backs even as they walked. Badem assumed rich men did this so that their own soft, lotioned hands were not expected to grasp the dirty hands of real working men like him. They looked like lawyers; they walked like lawyers, and they even somehow smelled like lawyers. Testa had many lawyers on his payroll. Captain Badem hated lawyers, with their fancy suits, perfumed bodies, and holier-than-thou attitudes. He had no use for them, but if Testa sent them here, then he'd listen.

In a thick French accent, the first man spoke. "*Monsieur* Testa sends his greetings."

The bigger man was being nosy, looking around the captain's quarters with inquisitive eyes. He was studying one of the three maps on the wall. Only a rich lawyer would think it was acceptable for him to stand there with his back turned to Badem while they talked.

"*Monsieur* Testa," the first Frenchman continued, "he orders you to sail the Ayla to Spain."

"What?" Captain Badem asked, his attention snapping back to the speaking Frenchman. "Why? Are we being replaced?"

"*Oui*," the Frenchman said.

"I don't know you," Captain Badem said. "I'll need those orders in writing."

"I'm giving you his orders," the Frenchman said.

"Not good enough," Captain Badem countered. "I'll need some proof of who you are, and of these so-called orders. *Monsieur* Testa made it quite clear to me that we would be receiving all our orders from Robert."

Captain Badem squared off with the Frenchman, ready to hold his ground. He was wondering why the second Frenchman was still looking at the maps on the wall behind him when a man's strong hand slapped over Badem's mouth from behind and pulled him back. He didn't feel the knife go into the back of his neck at the base of his skull. Badem was dead instantly.

Lucky for me.

"Well, that didn't go according to plan," I said as I eased the captain's body to the floor.

"I hope not," Lafayette quipped, "because if this was the plan, then we need better plans."

He wasn't wrong. I had no guarantees that our subterfuge would work. "What do we do now?" I asked him, shaking out my fine blue jacket, looking for blood stains. It was clean.

"Sit behind the desk," Lafayette instructed. "Keep the knife out and look mean."

I sat down behind the desk and stabbed my knife into the wooden surface. Blood dripped down from the blade and onto the desk. Lafayette opened the door and yelled for the first mate. A few heartbeats later, a Turkish man in his late twenties came running into the room. He froze in place when he saw his dead captain on the floor.

"*Monsieur* Testa believes this dog has been taking more than his agreed share of the profit," Lafayette said, pointing to the dead captain. "We ordered this pig to sail back to Spain, and he refused. By order of *Monsieur* Testa, you're now in command. You'll sail for Spain immediately, and we'll follow you. *Monsieur* Testa will be wanting to question the whole crew. Do you understand?"

The new captain glanced over at me, his eyes fixed on the knife. His breathing increased. His chest heaved, and his hands grabbed at his chest as panic started to set in. Lafayette stepped up and slapped the new captain across the face.

"Do you understand, Captain?" Lafayette yelled.

The new captain was unable to speak but nodded as fast as he could.

"You leave in twenty minutes," Lafayette said as he stormed out the door.

I sat there feeling stupid, so I jumped up, yanking my knife out of the desk and followed Lafayette, knife still in hand. The new captain began yelling orders to ready the ship as we walked down to the dock.

We made our way over to the Ariel, whose masts were now black instead of white. The name had been painted over with a Turkish name I couldn't read. The cannons were hidden with crates, ropes, blankets, and barrels, and Captain Jones was ready to sail. As soon as I walked into the captain's cabin, I removed the stupid wig, hat, and the makeup I swore I would never wear. I left my vest and weapons in the cabin when I walked back out onto the main deck, as they'd be of no use in this fight. The ship was already on its way out of the harbor. We were about five hundred yards behind the Ayla, like an escort.

Two British warships at the far south end of the channel noticed us and started to turn our way. Captain Jones ordered the Turkish flag taken down, and the solid blue flag Madam Fournier had provided us run up the mast. The real Turkish ship was understandably watching the two warships and not us. Testa's ship started lowering their sails, slowing the vessel, expecting to be boarded and searched by the British. One of the ships was going to pass on the starboard side of the Ayla and the other ship would pass on her port side. The British ships had their cannon ports open and cannons pushed forward.

As they closed in on us, Jones yelled for the first mate to turn starboard, and we sailed on the outside of the mess. We pulled away from the battle to come, if that was what you wanted to call it. The British captains made no effort to halt or intercept us. They seemed fine with us getting out of the way of the slaughter. The Turkish ship had dropped its sails. None of their cannons were readied, and they made no effort to avoid the giant warships bearing down on them.

Ninety guns fired between the two British ships in a volley of steel hail consisting of nine, twelve, and eighteen-pound cannonballs. The smaller Turkish ship was torn apart. Two of her masts were ripped in half, with the top half falling onto the main deck and the men running on it. Her sides were ripped apart, turning the thick wooden beams and planks into splinters. One of the cannonballs hit the magazine locker, and she exploded in a bright flash of light and ear-piercing explosion. I cringed back and covered my face with my forearm. One minute, the ship sat in the water, being shredded apart, and the next minute, she was raining down from the sky in a million pieces.

For a handful of seconds, splashes could be heard around us as pieces of wood from inches long to the length of a dozen paces crashed back down into the water. Then cheers erupted from the sailors on the twin British ships.

As the smoke cleared and the water bled a reflective crimson, the seagulls and sharks came to feast. We turned our back sides to the whole bloody event and to Paris. I only hoped this voyage was less exciting than our trip here had been. Our sails were full, our supplies were plenty, and our course was set. Jones was happy to be back on the ocean with his ship under his feet.

The two captains would report their victory to the king and receive their rewards and accolades. Testa would undoubtedly report they sunk the wrong ship. We would be a week out to sea before they realized their mistake. With a smile on my face, I wondered what would happen when the mad king found out I was still alive. Would his captains survive the truth?

Chapter Three Nightmares

Captain Joseph Brant reclined in the grass under a tree in front of a small but fast-running stream. He'd been laying there for over an hour and hadn't moved once since he crawled into place. His right leg was starting to cramp up. He was only thirty-five years old, but those had been a hard thirty-five years. When he was younger, he could have laid there day and night without so much as a twitch in his muscles.

He was watching the group of men on the far side of the stream that he'd been tracking for the last three days. There were ten of them, colonists who had taken up arms against their king.

Four days ago, these men had taken part in an attack against the king's men. Brant and his men came across the king's redcoats, most of whom were injured. Then Brant and his men went after the attackers. The main faction had broken up into four smaller groups, and Brant had followed the group going south. It made sense, seeing how he was heading south, anyway.

Today, Brant and his men finally caught up to the bluecoats in Cherry Valley, near the center of the state the colonists called New York, about eighty miles south-east of Lake Ontario. These men were making camp and getting ready for the night to come. They'd chosen to camp near the stream so they would have fresh water, but it would make killing them easier. He was good at swimming under water, and the water crashing against the rocks would hide any noise he made. Not that he would make noise or give any warning.

These bluecoats may know how to fight the British, and he gave them credit for moving quickly through the forest, but they didn't have a good sense of their surroundings. Joseph narrowed his eyes as he studied the small party of men. They camped in a nice clearing that led from the stream to a rock cliff behind them. The clearing was good for comfort and convenience but was a death trap for someone being hunted. Especially when they didn't know they were being hunted. With the fast-running stream in front of them and a thirty-foot rock face behind them, the clearing made for a good ambush spot. He didn't have to lead them there. They chose to set up camp in the perfect spot for him.

His second wife had recently died at Fort Niagara. He liked hunting colonists now, more than he had before. The king approved and it took his mind off his wife's death. When he was home safe in his own bed behind the walls at Fort Niagara, sleep eluded him. Sleep was always out of his grasp on most nights, until he was so tired, he'd pass out, only to wake twenty minutes later. On nights he did manage to fall asleep, he then woke up drenched in sweat from several nightmares. He'd unjustly outlived two wives and a son. The death of his wives bothered him. He felt no guilt over their deaths, but he did feel sadness. His son, Isaac, on the other hand, had died at Joseph's own hands one night when the two fought. He regretted killing his only son and knew he always would. Most days, his mind lamented over that bloody night, reliving it over and over.

As much as he hated the nightmares, they were justified and well-deserved. He'd done many things that God would never forgive him for, nor would Joseph ask forgiveness. The strong survived while the weak died. It was the way of the world, always had been and always would be. His son should never have challenged him. He was not experienced enough to challenge Joseph.

Captain Joseph Brant was well-educated and not superstitious, but after you've killed your own son, you welcomed self-punishment, even if it came in the form of nightmares. The only time he was able to sleep at night was when he was in the forest. It made little sense. He couldn't sleep when he was safe at home but slept like a baby when he was on a mission and chasing danger. He enjoyed killing bluecoats, and it kept him sane. He sometimes took unnecessary chances with his life to help himself feel alive. The more danger there was around him, the better he slept.

If he couldn't find peace, he would look for distraction. Two weeks ago, a welcomed message had come to Fort Niagara from England, from the British Secretary of State, George Germain. Joseph had met the man when he'd traveled to England a short while ago. He'd also met King George himself. Germain and he had formed a friendship of sorts. Now Germain had sent a request from the king. Joseph was to go south and find a man only known as Pale Rider.

At first, he thought the directive would be a waste of his time. Then the letter continued to describe how dangerous this man was. He had killed Lord North in the king's palace and somehow managed to escape with his life. This was after he'd attacked and captured two of the king's warships. Killing bluecoats was distracting but too easy. They smelled of sweat and tobacco. They were slow and like children when they were not in a city. They knew nothing about the woods or the dangers around them. Maybe this man, this Pale Rider, would give him a challenge. Maybe he would put up a real fight. The messenger had spent weeks looking for Joseph before he found him to deliver the message. Joseph didn't know how much time he had before this man arrived in the colonies, but he wanted to be waiting when he did. Joseph thought of it as a bit of a race.

Joseph decided to start tracking this man from Philadelphia, the one place the letter said the man had been. He was halfway there when he had come across the tracks of these men. After he killed these men, he would start back towards Philadelphia. Joseph had two pieces of paper in his leather pouch. One was a drawing of the man he was going to kill, complete with the detail of a distinctive scar on his head. This singular detail told Joseph a lot about the man. This Pale Rider was not afraid to fight, and the fact he'd survived this long, no matter how he'd received his scar, spoke a lot about him. The fancier parchment was an order signed by the British Secretary of State, George Germain himself. The order commanded any British officer to assist Brant with all supplies, manpower, or assistance he needed. With this piece of paper, he could walk into any British fort and demand anything he wanted from anyone.

The letter also indicated that his prey was now in England but would be heading back to General Washington. Who was this man who served Washington but caught the notice of the king? This man who had been able to avoid capture by the British, forcing them to turn to Brant to slay the man they themselves could not manage to kill?

Brant's men were several hundred yards back, waiting for him to return. He would retrieve them so they could be part of this kill. He'd brought twelve men with him – ten British Canadian loyalists and two braves from the Mohawk tribe. Most of his men carried muskets, knifes, and tomahawks. Some of his Mohawks favored the bow and arrow over the musket. The musket was more powerful, but they could shoot a dozen arrows in the time it took to shoot and reload the musket.

He didn't bring any of his tribe members. He was going far south and into towns and cities to learn where his target might be. He needed members that would understand the colonists better. He left behind the more traditional members of the tribe and only brought the two who were the best shots with the muskets. Joseph liked to carry his long knife, hatchet, Mohawk warclub, musket, and a flintlock pistol. He didn't like the flintlock pistol. He preferred to kill with his warclub or knife, but he was a captain, and the redcoat captains carried pistols, so he would as well.

Slowly, and without disturbing a single crinkling leaf or snapping any twigs, he pushed himself backwards away from these men and towards his own group. He'd let these men settle down for the night and feel safe. Then, as most of them slept, he would swim underwater to come up and kill the sentry. It would be up close with his knife, quick and quiet. He'd then allow his men to kill the rest of the bluecoats and share in the victory.

April 10th, 1778
Atlantic Ocean

I walked down the winding concrete path, but I couldn't hear my own footsteps. A park bench sat in front of me, empty. I wasn't sure where I was going, so I sat down on the chilly iron and wooden bench to look around. I couldn't remember the name of the park, but I was sure I'd been here before. This was a large familiar park, huge with open fields of green grass and a children's playground. Where were the kids? The whole park was unoccupied. No people of any age could be seen.

As if on command, one family came trudging over the green hill. Three of them came my way. I squinted into the distance. No, not three. Four. The woman clutched a baby to her chest. Must be her husband walking next to her. He was yelling something at the child who ran ahead of them. Maybe saying to stay close or be careful. A little boy about five years old.

As they came closer, I could see the woman was my wife, Jenny. I wanted to get up and run to her, but I sat, unable to rise, watching instead. The man she was with was me, but not me.

This was another version of the same dream.

I tried again to get up, but still I was stuck there on the bench. The other Thomas looked younger than I and had longer hair. They appeared to be a happy family. I was wrong. He wasn't younger – he'd somehow managed to live an easier life. Was I mad he was with her and not me? Was I jealous he'd not lived the life I had to live? Did his father teach him how to throw knives? How to fight with his hands? Or did he teach him how to play games? How to love?

A different woman walked up to the bench from out of nowhere. She sat down next to me and stared off at the family walking our way.

Annie. She sat there and didn't say a word.

We watched the couple stop and sit down on the grass. I turned my head to look at Annie, who had stood and was looking down at me. She held out her hand for me to take. I kept looking from Annie to Jenny. Jenny was dead in the timeline I had been born in, and Annie was alive but here in this century. A century and timeline that I didn't belong to. Two worlds both calling to me. I felt like I was being pulled apart from the inside out. But Annie had showed me I could love again. She was now the woman I loved. Jenny was part of a past for me that no longer existed.

As if I had made a decision without knowing I had made one, I was suddenly standing next to the bench, holding Annie's hand. Annie was now smiling as if pleased with my decision. Out in the grass was my best friend, Aden, the man who had sent me here. Behind Aden was the blue extra-terrestrial ship that had brought me to this time in history. The ship just sat in the grass, idle, but Aden was pointing back towards Jenny.

Annie was walking away and pulling me with her. Another person emerged over the hill, straight towards Jenny and her family. I knew this man – Lieutenant Reginald Hargrave, the man who had killed Jenny. He was the reason I was stuck here in this century. He held a knife in his hand. Aden was pointing to him and yelling to me. No words reached my ears, but I knew Aden was yelling for me to save Jenny.

I tried to pull away from Annie and run to Jenny. Annie wasn't letting go. She wasn't squeezing my hand hard, but she wasn't letting go, either. Hargrave was getting closer to Jenny. Why didn't the other Thomas see him? He needed to protect her since I couldn't. I yelled to Jenny and to the other Thomas, but no sound came out. Hargrave moved closer to Jenny with every step, and I was being dragged farther away. I screamed as Hargrave stood right behind Jenny.

I finally understood what my mind was telling me. I couldn't be with Jenny. If I wanted to save her, I needed to stay here in this century and help win the war. I needed to let myself be happy with the woman I now loved.

A door slammed shut behind me. I turned around, but I didn't see a door.

My eyes shot open.

I woke up swaying in my hammock, sweat dripping down my forehead. Another nightmare. The room was pitch black, so it was still night. Jones was at the wheel of the ship tonight and would be until daybreak. I laid on my worn hammock, not moving and covered in sweat. I hadn't had a nightmare like this in weeks. Most of my dreams were of Annie. I had accepted long ago that I was stuck here and needed to make the best of it. Meeting Annie changed things. I *wanted* to be here now, with her and her girls. I shook off the dream, rubbing my damp head.

Five weeks out to sea, and so far, all had been quiet. No pirates or British ships trying to sink us. No crazy plans to rip our ship out of the jaws of death. All in all, it had been a very uneventful voyage, a welcome, uneventful voyage. Captain Jones had ordered the name USS Ariel painted back onto the bow of the ship, and we were once again sailing under the American flag. With his new sail design, we were making good time. We found ourselves watching the ocean, expecting to see the entire British Navy after us like an unforgiving armada. The price on my head had to have gone up again.

A creak of the floorboards caused my body to tense. I wasn't alone in the room. The door I thought was in my dreams was really the door to my room. If Jones had come in, he wouldn't be sneaking around. He'd have lit a lantern, not poked around in the dark. Why did the thought of the hundred thousand gold crowns pop into my head? Had I moved when I woke? Did whoever was in here with me think I was still asleep, or did they know I was awake? Scanning the room, I saw nothing but rough shapes in darkness. My pistol was on my stomach under the blanket. My hands were at my sides but outside of the blanket.

Could I reach under the blanket and grab my pistol before the stranger in the room killed me? Suddenly, the sound of running footsteps banged to my right. My hands shot up in a reflexive move, grabbing the hands coming down at my chest. Those hands held a curved knife, and the tip of the blade stopped an inch from the center of my chest. I couldn't tell who it was, but his breath stank of fish and decay, and he was larger than me. He pushed down as I shoved upward. Then he leaned forward, putting his weight above the knife. The knife came down and the tip poked into my skin, and I couldn't stop the knife. I wanted to yell out for Jones, but I'd be dead before he opened the door.

I twisted to my left and tumbled out of the hammock, pulling the assailant's heels over head with me. I hit the floor, followed by the thunk of my pistol landing somewhere closer to the window. The sailor, who seemed determined to kill me, landed hard on his side in front of me. He still held the knife, and I still gripped his hands. He released the knife with his right hand, still holding it with his left. I wanted the hand with the knife, so I let go of his right hand, grabbing the left with both my hands. He was lying on his right side, and though it was too dark to see him, I assumed his arm would be pinned under his body. At least, I hoped it was. If he was planning on punching me, he wouldn't get much power behind the swing from his position. I lowered my head, tucking my chin down on my chest. If he punched for my face, he'd break his hand on the top of my skull.

I pulled downward on his hand holding the knife and twisted it, trying to free it. The punch I was waiting for never came, and I realized why when he used his right hand not to punch me, but to lift himself up off the floor. He pushed off forward with his legs and he came down on top of me again. He still had control of the knife, but I had control of his hand. The blade laid flat between us, but he was trying to turn the tip downward into my stomach.

Now he was on top of me again, and the punch finally came. Being dark, he didn't see my chin still tucked in. The punch was hard, thrown with all his power. The crunch of bones against my skull came as a jaw-snapping jolt, and he shrieked in pain. I took advantage of his distraction and rolled to my left on top of him. Now I was on top and had two hands controlling the knife. The knife started turning towards his stomach. His foot found purchase on the support beam in the center of the room, and he pushed off from it. We rolled again, and I found myself back underneath him. I had two hands controlling the knife, but he had his weight pushing down. And my arms were starting to tire.

The door to the captain's quarters slammed open, letting in a little ray of dim light. A male figure stood in the doorway, and I hoped this guy didn't have a partner. I could barely handle this guy. Boots ran across the room, and one of those boots kicked out towards us. I braced myself for the impact to my head that thankfully never came. To my relief, the boot collided with my would-be killer's face. The body followed the head, and the man flipped onto his back several feet away. The weak light from the open door was enough to illuminate the knife that laid between us. I grabbed the handle and rolled away from him, coming up to my feet in a fighting stance. I was ready to attack, but the guy didn't move. Captain Jones stood over him with his own knife in his hands.

"He's unconscious," Jones said flatly, as if he hadn't just saved my life.

"Who is he?" I asked.

Jones sheathed his knife and walked over to the captain's desk and lifted the glass off the lantern sitting. Picking up the flint and iron next to the lantern, he struck them several times. Sparks flew when he struck the gray iron against the black flint. On the third strike, the lantern's wick came to life with a flame. First, he placed the rounded glass back on the lantern, then he hung the lantern from the peg on the support beam in the center of the room. He positioned himself to stand over the man on the floor, hands on his hips, looking down at the unconscious man.

"You have good timing," I said, wiping blood from my lower lip.

"It looked like you had it under control," he replied with a smile.

"Yes, completely under control. Like a ship in a storm."

. "One of you yelled out," Jones told me. "I shoved one of the new guys on deck to the wheel and came running."

"Who is it?" I asked again, tilting my head to the unconscious man.

"His name is Bulut," Jones answered. "He was one of the new men we took on in port."

"Let's tie him up before he comes to," I said a bit breathlessly as I got to my feet.

A few minutes later, we had him tied to the beam under the lantern, his hands secured behind his back. After shutting the door, Jones and I leaned against the captain's quarters wall and tried to figure out what had just happened. Under the dim, flickering light of the lantern, I examined the knife my would-be assassin had tried to kill me with. It was a common enough looking sailor's knife.

"Who else came on with him?" I asked.

"Three others," he answered. "But I don't think they were involved. I think it's safe to say if he had a collaborator, they would have been here as well."

"Not if the collaborators had different jobs."

"Like what?"

"How was this guy going to get off the ship after he killed me?" I asked. "They would need to take over the ship or steal a Jolly boat. But why now and where would they go? And how would they get off the boat without being seen?"

"As for why now and where he would go," Jones answered, "we are right off the coast of Saint George's. The Bermuda islands. He would have had to kill me, too, because I was at the wheel and would have seen him taking the Jolly."

Jones's mouth fell open, and he grabbed my arm.

"The new crewman I had ordered to take the wheel!" he yelled, leaping off the wall. "He was one of the men who came with this man. I didn't have time to wonder why he was up on deck this late at night."

"He was up there to kill you," I said.

And as if on cue, the door burst open, and three men rushed in. The room was still half dark with only the one lantern for light. I hoped those dark shapes in their hands were knives and not pistols.

On their second step into the room, the knife that was in my hand was now in the air. I was running straight at the second man before my knife sunk itself deep into the chest of the first man. The first man fell face first onto the decking as the second man and I crashed into each other, like two bulls locking horns. My left hand struck out like a snake, grabbing the wrist of the hand holding his knife. We bounced off each other's chests as well as colliding with our heads. My right hand went forward and grabbed his throat as stars filled my vision. I blinked to clear it, and his left hand grabbed my right, trying to pull my hand off his throat.

The third man ran past us and the sound of bodies smacking into one another, followed by the sound of two distinct grunts of pain, told me that he and Jones had collided, and most likely were now rolling on the floor. The man I was choking out couldn't break my grip on his throat and would be dead in another ten or fifteen seconds. He grunted and started punching me in the face in hopes of making me let go, but his strikes were weak and ineffectual. He was losing consciousness and his punches weren't powerful at all.

I turned my head, trying to avoid one of his punches to my face and saw Jones on his back with the third man on top of him. He was in the same position I had been in a few minutes ago, and I had an odd sense of déjà vu. The third man held the knife with both hands, pushing the tip down towards Jones's chest. Jones was also holding the knife and pressing up for all he was worth. He looked like someone trying to bench press a bar with far too much weight on it.

The third man started leaning onto the handle of the knife, and the blade obeyed his commands, dimpling the flesh of Jones's chest. I took two quick steps towards the fighting men, dragging my attacker with me. Twisting hard and fast, I let go of my attacker and threw him into Jones's attacker. He collided with his partner, and they rolled on the floor and off Jones. My guy laid on the floor, holding his neck and sucking in air. Jones's guy came up in a wide-legged stance, ready to fight. Jones laid on the ground, with the knife sticking out the left side of his chest. It was only in about an inch or so, but still painful.

This would have been a good time to draw my pistol and smile as I shot them both. Since my pistol was still somewhere on the floor and I'd never picked it up, I had to settle for drawing the knife behind my back.

The guy sucking in air finally filled his lungs enough to be able to stand up and rejoin his comrade in the fight. Placing my knife in my left hand, I reached down to Jones. He held up a hand, thinking I was going to grasp his arm and help him to his feet. Instead, I reached past his hand, grabbed the knife sticking out of his chest, and pulled it free. Jones screamed from the pain and the surprise of my action.

Now armed with two knives, I was in my element. I leaped forward at the two men who, up until a second ago, thought that they had the advantage and were gathering their courage to attack me. Their eyes widened as I faced them one on two instead of waiting for them to attack. Their eyes had widened when I pulled the knife out of Jones's chest, and his scream of pain seemed to unnerve them a little more. After all, what kind of crazy sociopath would rip a knife out of his own friend's chest, so that he could have a second knife? They appeared more surprised when I decided it was a good idea to charge them. From their point of view, neither of these actions were the acts of a rational or sane man. At that point in time, Jones most likely shared their point of view.

The man who had stabbed Jones no longer had a knife and tried back peddling. The knife in my left hand slashed at my attacker's knife hand as the knife in my right-hand bit deep into the side of Jones's man. I was sure I sunk my left knife into his kidney as my right blade sliced through his friend's arm, causing him to drop his knife, and both of them squealed like stuck pigs.

The one with my knife sticking out of his side fell to the floor, with blackish-red blood pooling on the floor next to him. His buddy backed away while holding the bleeding wound on his arm that I had flayed open.

Suddenly he dived to the side, grabbing something on the floor. Before he turned, I knew he'd seen my pistol and dived for it. As he rolled over to face me and bring my own pistol up against me, the deer antler grip of my knife appeared as the knife I'd thrown struck deep in his chest. His head and arm dropped to the floor, and my pistol fell out of his hand. His dead, glazed eyes were still open, staring at me. I bent down and picked up my pistol. Walking over to his friend, I found he'd died in a pool of his own blood, along with the first guy through the door.

When I turned around, Jones was holding a rag against his chest. The attacker tied to the beam had awakened and stared at me as if I was a demon. He pushed back into the beam as if he was trying to get farther away.

"My god, man," Jones griped at me, still holding the rag to his chest. "That hurt like hell. Did you have to pull it out like that?"

He was right. It was a dick move.

"Sorry, John," I said, moving toward him. "I needed another knife, and you had one I assumed you didn't want. So, I just appropriated it."

He lifted the rag and opened his shirt to look at the wound.

"It isn't deep," he said. "Sliced the muscle. I think my ribs stopped the blade."

"Get in the hammock," I said. "I'll get Doc to come stitch you up."

Doc wasn't by any meaning of the word a real doctor. But he was the closest person we had to one. I wouldn't want him taking out my appendix, but he was good at sea sickness, blisters, and sewing up cuts. I once saw him sew a man's finger back on, so I figured he could easily handle Jones.

"What about him?" Jones asked, pointing to the man still tied to the beam.

I helped Jones into the hammock. "He can wait."

"Check on the wheel," Jones called out as I walked out the door.

I found the wheel abandoned with no one manning it. At least our little assassination team had taken the time to tie the wheel off, so it didn't spin out of control. Kind of like an eighteenth-century autopilot. I went to the first mate's quarters where the first mate Lieutenant Task and Lafayette slept. I woke them up and ordered Task to take the wheel and Lafayette to go below and get Doc and six sailors. After all, I had killed three men; I didn't see any reason why I should have to carry or drag them out of our quarters, too.

Then I returned to Jones, who was waiting patiently, not that he had a choice. Doc was the first one to make it to the quarters and had his doctor's bag with him. The bag looked more like a piece of sail that had been sewn into a bag. With his dirty hands, he pulled Jones's shirt open and looked at the laceration to Jones's chest. He didn't look impressed or worried. Lafayette was next through the door, with half a dozen sailors. The sailors dragged the three dead bodies out of the room. I told them to leave the bodies on the main deck. I had plans for using them in the morning.

Doc pulled out a long, curved needle and a single strand of horsehair. Threading the horsehair in the needle, Doc sewed up

Jones's chest while Jones grimaced with each poke. Doc finished, and one of the sailors threw sand across the floor to soak up the blood. We needed to question the one living traitor. He refused to talk and made it clear he'd die before telling us anything. It was about two hours before sunrise, so I had two of the sailors drag him out to the main deck and tie him to the railing.

Jones readjusted his stained shirt and insisted he was fine. I didn't argue. Unless he lifted anything or decided to do some pushups, the laceration wouldn't cause him too much trouble.

"He won't talk," Jones said. "He's too afraid of Testa to tell us anything."

"Want to make a wager?" I asked him as I started for the door.

"I'll not torture anyone," Jones said, pointing an accusatory finger at me. A strange statement from a man who helped me blow up several ships and their sailors. I shrugged at him.

I was tiring of people trying to kill me. I'd have answers one way or another. These men were afraid of Testa? Well, I'd give them something to be more afraid of. If Jones wanted to take torture off the table, then fine – I'd get the information in other ways.

"I'll bet you one gold British crown I can make him talk without hurting him or even asking him any questions," I said, holding my hand out to him.

"One gold crown?" he asked, clasping my hand in a shake. "It's a wager. No torture, and no questions."

I left him in the hammock and went out to talk to Lieutenant Task.

"Lieutenant," I called out to him.

"Yes, Major," he responded, turning his head to me while holding the wheel.

"As soon as the sun starts to show itself, drop sail," I ordered. "And I'll need a pulley and a coil of rope."

Task yelled for one of the men to get me what I had asked for. When the sailor returned, I fed the rope through the pulley, and asked him to climb the main mast, and tie the pulley at the end of the fore main yard.

As the golden sun came up, heating the ocean's waters and the ship's stiff, white sails came down, and the ship slowed to a crawl, drifting in the water. When we stopped moving forward, small white caps crashed against the hull of the ship and echoed back into the sea air. Seagulls flew overhead screaming at us, like clairvoyant scavengers that knew something bad was happening. I ordered the three dead bodies thrown overboard where they bobbed in the ocean like bloody corks. Bulut's hands were tied in front of him, then a sailor tied one end of the rope to the rope tying his hands together. Bulut tried to hang onto the railing with his one good hand, but with three sailors pulling on the rope, Bulut lifted into the air and his hands wrenched free of the railing. He screamed as his body was pulled out over the railing. and he hung over the open water, feet dangling and kicking.

Task, worried about my intentions, ran to get Jones and Lafayette. Jones was the first to reach my side, still wearing his blood-stained shirt. He stood next to me, not saying a word. He stared out at the human piñata, who was screaming for help. I looked down into the water where the first of what I hoped were many dorsal fins circled the three lifeless human corks.

"What exactly are you doing, Thomas?" Jones asked in a low voice.

"Not asking Bulut any questions," I answered.

The single dorsal fin soon became six. I recognized four of the slick torpedoes cruising under the surface of the water, with their flat noses and stripes on their bodies, as tiger sharks. The other two might have been makos, guessing by their blue bodies and pointy snouts. The tiger sharks circled the bodies like underwater vultures, while the makos bumped into the lifeless meals, making sure the food was safe and wouldn't fight back.

The whole crew was now leaned over the deck, their brows scrunched in confusion. They looked from the sharks to the man suspended above them and then to me. Shock filled their eyes, and I could see that they were questioning not only my intent, but my sanity. I didn't care. I needed this guy to start talking.

After a few nudges, the makos began timidly biting at the limbs. A few slow bites and tugs quickly turned into a feeding frenzy. The violent ripping of flesh and splashing in the crimson-tinged water only attracted more aquatic killers. By the time Lafayette walked up on the other side of me, two dozen man-eating predators swam in every direction, bumping into one another. The smallest sharks were six feet long, and the largest had to be at least ten feet or more. As the water churned and started turning bright red, it became difficult to see under the surface.

"What are you doing, Thomas?" Lafayette asked, repeating Jones's question in that same cautious tone.

"Getting ready to talk to Bulut," I answered flatly, keeping my eyes on the man squirming above the feeding frenzy. "He says he'll die before answering any questions. I bet Jones a whole gold crown I could get Bulut to tell me everything I want to know without having to ask a single question."

I stuck my arm out, palm down and motioned downward. The sailors holding the rope let out a few feet, and Bulut sunk in the air. He was still twenty feet above the water, but his screams got louder and more panicked.

"Thomas, you can't do this." Lafayette said, grabbing my arm. After everything we'd been through, I was a bit surprised he didn't understand my motives. I was done with all this. I needed answers, and I was going to get them. I crossed my arms over my chest as I continued to stare at Bulut.

The men slowly lowered him down. When he was five feet above the violently churning red water, he started yelling about Testa.

There it is.

I brought my palm up, halting the sailors from letting more slack out. Bulut hung in the air, mere feet above the doorway to Davy Jones's Locker and certain, painful death.

"Pull him back up," Lafayette hollered to the sailors holding the rope.

The rope started to move back up until I turned around and glared at the men. They froze in place, not knowing what to do. After a few seconds of thought they decided it was better to piss off the Frenchman they liked, rather than the crazy fucker who was ordering them to lower a man into shark-infested waters. I let my stare linger on them a few seconds longer for emphasis.

"Bulut! Remember when you said you'd rather die than tell me anything?" I yelled out to the man. "I'm going to give you the chance to do as you said."

Lafayette and Jones locked anxious eyes, trying to guess whether I was really going to continue with this horrific act of lunacy.

"Thomas, don't do this," Jones said. "We are better than this, and he'll talk. Forget the bet, please."

Ignoring him, my hand lowered again. Nothing happened. I turned to the men holding the rope. Catching my meaning with a look, they started letting out rope again. Bulut slowly dropped, closing the distance over the sharks. I signaled for them to stop the rope when his feet were inches from the bloody, churning water. You might think a shark is a shark is a shark, but no. Though the name tiger shark sounds like a top predator, the makos seemed to corner the market on aggression under Bulut. They were much more aggressive about eating. One of the makos shot forward, its head coming out of the water, mouth open and razor-sharp teeth showing. Bulut screamed and bent his knees to save his feet. He screeched louder for mercy. I turned my back on the carnage below and walked away from the railing.

"Bring him up," I ordered the men holding the rope.

They didn't like fishing for sharks with human bait and didn't hesitate to pull on the rope as fast as they could. Bulut's dangling frame came into sight, and Jones grabbed the man, pulling him back over the railing. He fell onto the deck, breathing hard, and crying.

"See?" I said to Lafayette. "Not a scratch on him. I mean . . . other than what I had already done to him." Lafayette shook his head at my explanation.

Walking over to the man who tried to kill me in my sleep, I stood between him and the sun's warm rays. My body blocked the sunlight, and my shadow fell over him like a specter of death reaching for his soul.

The man physically cringed and scurried away from me until he collided with the wooden railing. Upon realizing he'd actually moved himself closer to the sharks swimming on the other side of that railing, he screamed and tried to get up and run toward the bow of the ship. After a few steps and the sailors pulling on the rope, he was reminded of the fact that he was still bound.

"I'll tell you anything," the man sobbed.

"You owe me a gold crown." I flicked my level gaze to Jones.

"Yes," he said in a hushed tone, "but I'm starting to worry about your soul."

"As am I, my friend," I lied.

I was more than willing to sacrifice my soul to win this war. If Jones knew what the future held for the world if King George won, he might not worry about his soul either. But I understood his point. I wanted to make the world a better place, not a worse place. I would need to keep whatever humanity I could. Annie deserved a man who was more than a monster. And this act was monstrous indeed.

But my plan worked. Bulut told us everything he knew, as fast as the words could pour out of him. He worked on a ship owned by Jacob Testa's father, Freiherr Bartolomeo de Testa. The father was a rich and powerful man who had sworn to see me dead, even if it cost him everything he had. Bulut and the others were only part of the first of two plans. He was part of the plan that involved killing me on the ship as I sailed back to the colonies. He'd heard his captain talking about a second plan involving an Indigenous loyalist from Canada. The king had sent orders for this loyalist to travel south, track me down, and kill me. Bulut's captain had only referred to this man as a monster or as The Monster.

Bulut said he had no idea why the Native was called that or anything else about the man. Bulut had not known anything about the blue flag or the British trying to sink us as we fled the harbor. I believed him. Why else would he have gotten on the ship if he had known? Testa must have forgot to mention that part to him. So far that made three separate individual plans that Testa and the King had put in motion to kill me. How many more did they have that I didn't know about yet? When he was done telling us everything he knew, a relieved Jones ordered him tied up below deck.

Handing me a gold coin, Jones then asked what I wanted to do. The king's messenger had a six or seven-week head start on me. He could be in Philadelphia already. Given the choice, I'd rather go after him, instead of waiting for him to come after me. But since I didn't know anything about the man or how to find him, I was going to have to wait for him to find me. The chances of him finding me had to be low. The entire British army had been looking for me for eight months now, and I was still no closer to being captured.

I wondered how many of the ship's crew would tell their friends about the day I fed a man to a school of sharks. I wondered what other rumors and stories would make the rounds after this.

Chapter Four Bait

Three weeks earlier, Captain Joseph Brant and his twelve men rode into Philadelphia with only one goal in mind – to search out any information about the man they were to kill, the man Joseph had taken to calling the *scarred one*. Rumors flew about his black vest and how he seemed to have it on always, as if he wanted people to recognize him. But vests could be taken off. Scars were forever.

Joseph knew people here wouldn't want to talk to him, being a Native man and not a white man. Some damn fool would most certainly insult Joseph, and he'd be forced to kill the man. This scenario had played out before in several towns. Redcoats would point their muskets and he'd be forced to show his letter from Germain and, by extension, the king. He'd get what he wanted, but gossip would start, and people would learn he was here to kill the man with the scar. If this man was as dangerous as people claimed, then he wanted to keep the advantage of surprise on his side.

The easier way was for him to send out the Canadian loyalists under his command to ask questions for him. While his men were talking to people in town, he reported to General Sir Henry Clinton, who was in charge of Philadelphia and the senior officer there. He gave the general the blue coats of the men he'd killed a week ago and reported the movements of the rebels.

The general was the only person Joseph had showed the letter to, and in return, the general had told Joseph everything he knew of the scarred man. He'd also given Joseph requisitions for fresh horses, food, and the supplies Joseph needed. The general then called for one of the city's loyalists, one Benjamin Tallmadge, who was a young man of about twenty-four or twenty-five years old. Tallmadge oozed with loyalty to the empire and was eager to help Joseph. Tallmadge also told Joseph everything he'd learned about the scarred one, and Joseph was silent as he let Tallmadge's stories fill his ears. While many British feared the assassin, this Tallmadge didn't seem to believe most of the stories. Tallmadge had walked Joseph around the fort and saw to it that Joseph and his men received the supplies they needed. Possibly the most important item Tallmadge gave Joseph was a detailed map of the state and the known farms in the area. Joseph tucked it away in his buckskin coat for safekeeping.

It didn't take long for his men to hear the same stories Benjamin Tallmadge had told Joseph. They heard about how this man had ripped General Washington from the jaws of death. No one in town knew how the man learned that Washington was in danger or where the man had come from. If the stories could be believed, then the man had ridden into town mere hours after Washington had been captured, and single-handedly saved the colonial general. Some believed he'd killed eight soldiers single-handedly that night, while others alleged it was more than a dozen. This also happened to be hours before General Howe was to attack Philadelphia, and the scarred one had then attacked General Howe's camp. Tens of thousands of soldiers at camp, and this one man had distracted all of them long enough for Washington to evacuate the city.

Joseph's men added details about the assassin – an interesting story about a farmer named Ben O'Neil. It seemed this farmer and his daughter had helped the scarred man when he was injured. At least one British officer was smart enough to take advantage of this fact and had taken the woman's two daughters as hostages. The scarred man had not only saved the two little girls but had killed almost all the soldiers by himself. Joseph wondered if there was something in that tale for him to use. Could the man be forced to save the woman or her cubs again? Did he still care about them?

So many rumors about the man. Too many. People claimed this man, like Joseph, preferred fighting with knives. Also, like Joseph, this man was said to be seen talking to his horse.

Some of the stories were impossible. Some of them, Joseph believed, *might* be true. Like how he'd killed a few soldiers to steal their wagon. That was a plausible tale.

Others stories he outright didn't believe. Like taking on whole companies of soldiers by himself. Or how he could see in the dark and shoot a pistol farther than any could shoot with a musket. The worst tale was that this man had been raised in the forest by a shaman and taught how to turn himself into an animal. These superstitious fools seemed to want to believe this man was some kind of ghost instead of what he really was. A hunter, a man who was good at killing other men.

Joseph's jaw clenched as the stories grew. The rumors had raised the scarred one to the level of myth, and Joseph knew something about myths. Most were invented. The rest were horribly inflated.

Joseph also knew the truth. He, too, was superb at killing. No one said it to his face, but he'd heard what they called him behind his back. *The Monster.* He was just like this man, and the stories about the man could be explained.

Maybe the man had dropped his musket after he shot it, and people assumed because they didn't see a musket, he didn't have one. Maybe he had good eyesight and could see better in the dark than the average man. Joseph himself preferred to attack in the dark.

Maybe the man commanded a hundred men who were well trained at hiding in the forest. These redcoats couldn't see the forest for the trees, and irregular fighting was not their strong suit. How would they know if he fought alone or with others? Add into that heighted fear . . .

No. This was only a man. Strong, smart, and skilled at killing, but only a man.

Just like Joseph.

Joseph and his men had trekked out to this farmhouse owned by this farmer named Ben O'Neil. The house and barn had been burnt to the ground. No dead animals were found, so whoever burnt down the house had also taken the livestock with them.

The next farm over was owned by a family of loyalists. They readily told Joseph that Ben O'Neil and his family were seen heading to the Cornel farm with two wagons filled with food and supplies. This Cornel farm was only about three miles west of the O'Neil farm. Joseph found the spot on Tallmadge's map where the Cornel farm had been marked.

When they rode onto the farm, they were met by the Cornels, who denied knowing anyone named Ben O'Neil. Joseph eyed them with a hard glare. He had learned to put everyone into two groups – loyalists and traitors. It was simple for him. If someone lied to him, then they were traitors. He ordered his men to hang the whole family from the large tree on the side of the house. He hadn't come by the title of *Monster* without reason, after all. By the time the first rope was thrown over the large branch, the wife had told him what he wanted to hear. She didn't know about the scarred man, but Ben and his family had left for Valley Forge.

According to the farm wife, Ben's daughter Annie wanted to follow the man she loved, and that man had told Annie he'd be at Valley Forge with General Washington. Ben, his daughter, and two granddaughters rode off for Valley Forge about four or five months ago.

Joseph had learned what he wanted and let the Cornels live. It served no purpose for him to kill them now. But he made a note to tell the British about them, and he'd let the redcoats deal with the family and their attempt at treason against the crown.

Now, for over the past week, Joseph found himself perched in a tree with his new spy glass, watching over Valley Forge from about a quarter mile away. He had never used a spyglass before, but when Benjamin Tallmadge offered it to him, he was excited to try one out. Maybe he could see as well and as far as the scarred one with it. The comparison made his tight lips press into a hard smile.

His men had made camp a mile behind him. None of his men were surprised when Joseph ordered them to make camp and wait. He might watch Valley Forge for a day, a week, or a month if need be. They would be patient and wait for his orders. Two of his men came to him every day with provision and asked about his progress.

Joseph spent days tucked in that tree, studying the camp and learning what he could. Valley Forge housed ten or fifteen thousand men in the ramshackle camp. Cannons were pointed in all directions. Scouting parties left every day, making sure to return before sunset. Empty wagons were driven out of the camp and full wagons returned in their place. Hundreds, if not thousands, of tents covered the field.

Only a few log cabins were in the middle of the camp. He had learned this was where General Washington and his command staff would be. There was no reason the woman or her family would be there, so he focused on the tents. They would put the woman to work, so he spent much of his time watching the groups of ladies washing clothes and cooking food. He disregarded the older ladies and the young ladies. His eyes followed the ladies in the right age group with the spyglass until he was able to rule them out.

Then, a few days ago, he spotted two young girls playing with a lighter brown horse that had a white stripe down its nose. The girls appeared to be of the right age, and the scarred one had been described as riding a horse matching this one. He'd seen hundreds of women and children, but these were the first two girls he'd seen near the officer's portion of the camp. Camp followers were kept farther away from the officers, on the perimeter, but not close to the officers.

Watching the girls play with the horse reminded him of his own daughter, Christine. She and her brother Isaac loved horses. While Joseph wished these girls no harm, he'd do whatever was called upon him to kill the scarred one. His thoughts drifted, and he wondered where his own daughter was right then, and if she was happy. Thinking of his own children and the physical loss of his son and emotional toll of his little girl's absence weighed on him.

He shook his head.

No, he thought.

He changed his mind. Mission or no mission, he'd not allow any harm to come to these two girls. He would do what was needed, but no harm would come to them by his hand or by the hands of his men. Myths of the *Monster* were only true to a point, after all.

Joseph wanted to get into the head of the scarred one, to understand him better. Watching these two carefree girls, he understood how flawless the British Captain's plan was in kidnapping them, and at the same time, how that would be the man's downfall. If Joseph's own children had ever been kidnapped, he would hunt the men down to the ends of the earth to retrieve them. He wouldn't pay any price to get back what was his. Rather, he'd take them back by force and kill all those involved in their abduction. By snatching the girls, the British officer had ensured the scarred one came to him. The flaw in the plan was, by taking the girls, the officer had ensured the scarred one came to him with a vengeance. Joseph laughed at the thought.

Not that the plan overall was flawed, rather the execution of the plan. The redcoat officer expected the scarred one to do as he was told, but this assassin listened to no one but himself. Joseph wouldn't make the same fatal mistake. He'd use the woman to bring the scarred one to him, but *not* expect him to do as he was commanded. No, Joseph planned to set traps within traps.

He patiently watched them most of the day until a woman in her thirties appeared and made them put the horse back in the barn. Joseph had to admit she was a beautiful woman. He hadn't noticed many women since the death of his second wife, but this one did have a strong beauty about her. Joseph could see why the scarred one would claim her as his own, and he could use this relationship against the man. He started to say to himself he would use it against his prey, but if he used that word, that idea, he'd be making the same mistake as the British officer. There was no prey in this game.

There were two hunters, but no prey.

Joseph couldn't hear them, but he didn't need to hear them to see the protest the children had offered, not wanting to put the horse back into the barn. The woman stood with her hands on her hips, and that was all it took to gain compliance from the two girls.

He kept the three of them in the center of his spyglass as they walked out of the barn and across the field. They surprised Joseph by walking into one of the log cabins. Joseph stiffened on his tree limb and focused his attention on the cabin. He had quickly learned that this particular cabin belonged to the great white hair, General Washington.

Had he presumed incorrectly and watched the wrong woman, the wrong girls? Was she Washington's daughter? More likely his personal maid and cook. He'd heard some officers brought servants with them on campaigns, although he didn't think Washington was that kind of officer. And those two little girls were the only two children he'd seen near the officer's cabin so far. Joseph couldn't imagine a general bringing his children or those of his maid into a military camp. Yet, the scarred one was also called Washington's Assassin – Washington seemed to have a personal interest in the family.

Joseph viewed these facts in a new light, a set of problems and no small obstacle to his objectives. Strangely, his smile widened at the new set of problems. The woman *had* to be the scarred one's woman. There was no other option. Washington must have taken a special interest in her and her children. His biggest problem was the woman and her children resided in the same cabin as Washington. Guards surrounded the cabin, as did a ring of tents, and another outer perimeter of sentries.

He would have liked to abduct the woman while she was alone, washing clothes at the river or walking around the camp. But he couldn't get near the camp in daylight. Even if he managed to get past the sentries unseen, too many soldiers milled around that made abducting her in daylight nearly impossible.

Now he knew where she was, Joseph looked for a routine in the soldiers' defenses that he might serve to his advantage. When his two men came to him that day, he ordered them to go back and gather the rest of his men. They'd expected him to order them to regroup at his location, but instead he ordered them to pull back to the stream where they'd killed the bluecoats a month earlier. He instructed them to set the area up for an ambush and explained how he wanted it done. He'd stay closer, watch, and plan. He could grab the woman in the next couple of days, and his men had a one-to-three-day head start and plenty of time to set things up.

He and his men had done operations like this before, so they knew the drill. Joseph referred to this kind of ambush as the snapping turtle. Early in the Seven-Year War, he had tracked some French soldiers for the British. The French had gone into marshy swamplands while Joseph sat next to a body of water, resting. A large snapping turtle drifted a few feet away, under the water, close to shore. The turtle opened his large, beak-like mouth and didn't move. Joseph first thought the animal was dead. Then the turtle's worm-like tongue came out of its mouth and wiggled around. Joseph watched as a large fish swam right into the turtle's mouth, thinking it would eat the worm that was the turtle's tongue. Then the turtle's mouth snapped shut, almost cutting the fish in half. Joseph had learned that the turtle was too big and slow to catch a fish, so he tricked the fish into coming to him.

He'd never used a woman as bait, but he'd allowed himself to be chased by the French in the war, and later by the bluecoats, into ambushes where his men laid in wait. He liked these kinds of operations, where his pursuers, like the fish who thought they'd caught the worm, bite and find out they were the ones trapped. Though the thought of using the woman as the worm this time bothered Joseph, she should have chosen a man who wasn't a rebel and traitor.

He made up his mind to go in at night when most of the soldiers slept. Joseph stayed up all night and the next, studying the cabin and bluecoats intently. He slept during the day, tying himself to the tree limb as to not be seen by any patrols in the area.

The woman hadn't come out of the cabin either night. Not even to go to the latrine. He realized he'd have to get past the soldiers, through the circles of tents, and into the guarded cabin, to get her.

On the third night after he'd located the woman, Joseph set out to capture her. The night was dark with only a quarter moon of light, and what light there was hid behind some clouds. He'd left his horse tied up in the tree line. Taking only his knife, hatchet, and warclub, he set out towards the camp. When he was close, he crouched and crawled through the high grass. During his two nights of watching, Joseph had found a blind spot the sentries couldn't see. Even so, he took no chances and stayed low.

Washington's cabin was situated on the north side of the camp. This was the side where Joseph made his approach. The camp was several miles wide, and to come from any other direction meant walking through a mile or more of enemy soldiers. The north side was harder but faster and safer.

The Schuylkill River was on the north side of the camp, providing a natural protection from any attacking army. The river was six or seven hundred feet wide, but the water didn't run too fast for Joseph to swim. He crawled to the river, and like a water snake moving towards its victim, he slithered into the water. The river was too wide for Joseph to cross the entire width, swimming underneath in one breath. He came up several times for a fresh breath of air, swam on top of the water using the breaststroke for a bit, then went back under.

When he emerged from underneath the water, it was dark above the water as it was below. Joseph crawled out of the river the same way he slid into it. Even in the open field, he was hidden by the night. He said a silent prayer the clouds held out and blocked what little moon light there was for a few more minutes. Torches flickered in the camp, so he would have to maneuver around the occasional circles of dancing orange light. He was dripping wet, and mud and grass stuck to his shirt and pants. Once close enough, he moved between the tents, head tilted, listening for any movement. Knife in hand, hatchet in his belt and mohawk club tied behind his back, he ran from one shadowy spot to another, keeping low.

One soldier popped out of his tent next to Joseph. The man was more surprised to see Joseph than Joseph was to see him. With one quick, silent slash at the man's throat, blood sprayed into the night and onto Joseph's chest. The man was dead before Joseph could grab him and lower him to the ground. Joseph dragged the man's body into the shadows before he moved closer to the cabin. He knelt next to a tree, watching his next targets. One bluecoat stood at the front of the cabin while another walked around it.

Preparing for his next attack, he sheathed his knife and pulled his club from behind his back and into his left hand while switching his hatchet into his right.

Joseph crept up to the guard as close as he dared, then waited for the soldier walking around the cabin to come into sight again. The bluecoat came around, and as he turned the corner away from the front, Joseph shot up, took two quick steps, and threw his hatchet.

The hatchet flew in a straight line while spinning steel head over wooden handle. With a loud smack, the thick steel blade embedded itself into the man's skull. He fell back and slid down the log wall. Joseph was at a full run by the time the walking sentry came around the corner. Joseph leaped into the air, coming down on the man with his warclub. Between the force of Joseph's swing downward, the added velocity of coming down from his leap, and the hardened round ball at the end of the club, the man's head caved in before he had time to react. A war cry surged in Joseph's throat, ready to declare him the victor, but he swallowed it back, staying quiet and in control.

Moving quickly, he dragged both bodies to the darkened side of the cabin. Using his foot for leverage, and with a sound of cracking skull and wet suction, Joseph pulled his hatchet free. The cabin was dim, so he hoped no one was awake on the other side of the door. With his warclub on his back and hatchet in his hands, Joseph worked the handle and opened the door. He stepped in and silently shut the door behind him, then spun around to study the cabin. He had no idea what room the woman and her family were in.

At the first door he came to, he put his ear against the cool wood, listening. Loud snoring emanated from this room, like a bear's cave. He surmised there had to be at least three grown men in that room and moved to the next room. At least one person snored in this room. He cracked the door open an inch to find a single lit candle on the dresser that provided a little light. The outline of an old man slept in the closer bed, while the woman and two daughters slept in the farther bed.

His leather shoes were silent as he stepped into the room. He crept up to the bed with the woman and girls. With his hatchet in his right hand, he slapped his left over the woman's mouth. Her eye flashed open wide in pure terror. To her credit, she didn't scream or make any noise behind his hand.

"Unless you want them and you to die, do what I say," he whispered. "Do you understand me?"

She nodded her head as best she could. In the other bed, the old man woke and sat up, rubbing his eyes. Joseph turned and threw the hatchet in one fluid movement. They heard a whack, and Ben fell back onto the bed, unmoving. She tried to scream, but he pushed down harder on her mouth.

"Think of the girls," he said in a harsh tone.

He was bluffing, but she didn't know. She'd seen him kill the old man, so she'd take the warning seriously. She nodded again, tears shining in her eyes.

"Wake them, but keep them quiet," he ordered, still whispering, and nodded his head toward the girls.

The woman did as she was told, waking the two girls and telling them not to make any noise. When the girls saw Joseph, they cuddled together and started crying. Their mother shushed them, putting a finger against her lips. All the girls could do was clamp their own hands against their mouths as tears ran down their cheeks and over their fingers.

"You're coming with me," he told her.

The woman shook her head in a panic.

"Don't fight or argue, and I'll leave the two girls here," Joseph told her.

Magic words. She glanced at the girls and, deciding quickly, she nodded her head.

"Get dressed," Joseph said in a hard tone.

Annie only wore her shift, but quickly got up, grabbed the calico dress hanging over the chair and pulled it over her head. Then she shoved her feet into a pair of sturdy shoes. Joseph reached into his shirt and withdrew the map. He'd already circled the spot on the map where he told his men to set up the ambush.

He set the map on the bed in front of the girls, tapping a finger on the spot he marked.

"This is where I'm taking your mother," Joseph said. "Hide the map. Show it to no one except the scarred one."

"The scarred one?" the older girl asked in a wavering voice, not understanding.

"Thomas," Annie said, knowing who he meant.

"Thomas," Joseph repeated, hearing the man's real name for the first time. "Yes, show the map to Thomas. Show no one else. Tell Thomas that this is where your mother will be. He's to come alone. If he brings any soldiers with him, I'll kill your mother. Do you understand?"

Both girls nodded their heads, lips quivering, unable to speak.

"Good," Joseph said. "One last thing. Your mother and I are leaving. If you scream or wake the soldiers, I'll be forced to kill your mother right now. Do you know how to count to a hundred?"

The older girl nodded her head.

"Good," Joseph said again. "Count to a hundred ten times, then scream for help, but don't show the map to anyone."

He didn't want them sitting in the room all night with the dead old man. Pulling out two pieces of rope he'd brought with him, he first tied Annie's hands in front of her. With the other, longer piece of rope, he tied it around her waist and held onto the end. Unsheathing his knife, he looked her in the eyes.

"If you give me away, I'll kill you. Then I'll come back for the girls." Joseph's tone left no room for argument.

Annie nodded her understanding. She would do nothing as long as her girls were in danger.

Joseph had the girls start counting but said they were counting too fast. They slowed their count, and he slipped out of the room, dragging Annie behind him. Joseph was counting himself to keep track of how much time he had left.

They walked out of the cabin and through the tents. No one had discovered any of the bodies yet. When they reached the last few outer tents, Joseph made Annie crawl in front of him. They slipped back into the water, and he untied her hands. He kept the longer rope tied to her in case she had thoughts about trying to escape. After making it back to the far side, Joseph pushed her to crawl to the tree line. He tied her hands again, then walked her to his horse and lifted her up on the animal's back.

"What is your name?" Joseph asked her as she settled onto the beast's back.

"Annie," she answered.

"You're the scarred one's woman?"

"Yes," Annie said, seeing no reason to lie.

"I don't want to hurt you," Joseph said. "But I will if you give me any trouble. Do as you're told, and I'll let you go, after I kill your man."

"I won't give any trouble," she told him. "I want to be there when he comes for me."

She thought he was going to jump on the back of the horse behind her, but instead he took off at a run, pulling the reins.

Joseph didn't mind running next to the horse. He preferred to use his own legs and only used horses because of his men. The

Mohawks were good runners, much quieter in the woods and easier to hide, but the loyalists seemed to find running beneath them. The one time he needed them to run, they only made it a few miles before giving out. Horses, he knew, were the future of his people.

He made it a few steps before a man's voice carried across the open field. Stopping the horse, Joseph glanced back. General Washington stood at the front of the cabin, yelling for his men to wake up. He pulled out his pistol and fired it in the air, waking up the camp. Men rushed around in different directions. They would be searching for him now. Turning his back on them, Joseph started running again. He knew he would be running all night and into the morning.

Chapter Five Homecoming

Lafayette and I rode our horses at a steady gait as we entered into sight of Valley Forge. The rest of our voyage after leaving Europe had been quick and uneventful. With the bounty on my head being so high, Lafayette and I decided it would be best if Jones dropped us off before he took the ship into port. He had orders to meet up with his new ship, the USS Ranger. Two crewmen rowed us to shore in the Jolly, near a village known to support the colonists.

The villagers were helpful and sold us the two horses we now rode. Near Valley Forge, a group of soldiers patrolling the area approached us. After identifying ourselves, the Lieutenant gave me a look I couldn't classify, with a furrowed brow and pursed lips. They rode back to the camp to inform the General we were coming.

We rode into camp, and I was surprised not to find the General waiting for us on his horse. So much for a warm welcome. We dismounted and walked the horses through the camp. A strange vibe hung in the air. Tension I couldn't explain and didn't like. As we walked through the camp, soldiers took off their hats. Was it a sign of respect or sadness? Our mission had been a success, and a secret, so their behavior couldn't have anything to do with France or the assassination.

General Washington stood tall and broad in full uniform in the dirt in front of his cabin. He wore such a look of sadness on his face, with dark bags under his eyes. His mouth was closed, lips pursed together. His sword belt was fastened around his waist, but this time, he had a pistol tucked into the belt. And was that a tomahawk next to the pistol? Like the rest of the men, he held his hat in his right hand while his left hand was clinched into a fist. An officer I didn't recognize stood next to him. He looked to be the same age as Washington but wore a black and gold uniform. He also had a sword belt with a pistol tucked into the black leather. His hands were behind his back, clasped together. The tingling oddity of the situation bloomed into a plume of worry. A large group of men stood around him but kept their distance, the closest men being about twenty feet from him. They didn't want to miss whatever was going to happen, but also didn't really want to be a part of it.

"Thomas, Lafayette," the general greeted us in a somber tone. "May I introduce Major General Friedrich Wilhelm August Heinrich Ferdinand von Steuben. He's here to help train the troops."

"General," I replied to Washington, ignoring the Major General. "What happened? Where's Annie? The girls?"

The general shook his head. "I'm sorry, Thomas. Annie was taken two nights ago."

"Taken?" I asked, my whole body tightening.

"A man came into camp late at night," he explained. "He killed three of my men, and Old Ben. He took Annie with him."

I ground my jaw as I glared at him. He made no excuses, didn't try to deflect blame. We both knew he'd sworn to protect her while I was gone. We both knew he had failed. He had no way of knowing, but it was his job to know.

"The girls?" I asked, holding my breath.

"They're fine. They are inside."

I glanced at Lafayette and without a word, he took off at a run for the cabin.

"I sent a thousand men out in several directions as soon as we realized what had happened," the general explained. "We later found footprints and drag marks leading into and out of the river. We found matching footprints and horse tracks on the far side of the river. The strange thing was, we only found one set of horse tracks."

"So, he took her, and they are riding double on his horse," I answered tightly.

"No," General Friedrich whatever-his-last-name-was replied in what sounded like a German accent. "The trackers said there were footprints next to the horse tracks. They said he must have been running next to the horse."

My head was too fevered and distraught to try to solve that puzzle. "Ben?"

"We found him dead on his back in bed," Washington answered. "This was in his chest."

The General reached down and pulled the tomahawk out of his belt, handing it to me.

"This hatchet. My trackers say these are Mohawk markings on it."

Lafayette emerged from the cabin holding Regan in his arms and Molly's hand. I handed the hatchet back to Washington as I ran to the girls. Lafayette set Regan down and the girls ran to me. I fell on my knees, crying as they collided into me, arms around my neck as they sobbed into my shoulders. I needed to be strong for them, but I couldn't stop myself. I cried because they were safe; I cried because their mother wasn't, and I cried because their grandpa was dead. I didn't know what to say to them. Every time I opened my mouth, nothing came out.

Soldiers standing around us turned away, either giving us our private moment or embarrassed that none of them had been able to stop the abduction.

"Grandpa is dead," Regan sobbed.

"I know, sweetie," I said. "I'm sorry."

"The bad man has mother," Molly added.

"I know that too. I'll do everything I can to get her back."

"How will you get her back?" Molly asked, wiping her tiny hand across her eyes.

"I have no idea yet," I answered honestly. "I don't know where he took her."

"We know," Regan said excitedly.

"What? Where?"

Molly reached into her dress front pocket and pulled out a ruddy map drawn in detail. She pointed to a small circle on the map.

"He said to show this to you. That they would wait here for you," Molly said. "He said for you to come alone, or he'd kill mother."

I took the map and studied it. The circle was far north of Valley Forge. He'd have to rest his horse and wouldn't be there yet. Before I did anything, I needed to figure out why he picked this spot. It was in the middle of the forest, nowhere near a town or city. A handwritten fancy capital letter T was scrawled in the top corner of the map. It stood out but meant nothing to me.

"Marie," I called to Lafayette, who always insisted I skip formality and call him by his first name. "Take care of the girls until I bring their mother back."

"I'm going with you," Lafayette said.

"No. I've got to do this alone. And I need the girls kept safe. I trust only you right now." I had to force myself not to flick my gaze to any of the soldiers. Or the general.

Lafayette's body tightened up, and he stood straighter.

"With my life, Thomas," he vowed, one hand touching his sword, the other caressing his pistol. "With my life."

I hugged both girls and asked Lafayette to take them back inside the cabin. Standing up, I walked back to the two generals. Taking the tomahawk back from General Washington, I tested the balance. It was made for throwing. I tucked the weapon into my belt.

"I know where she is," I told him.

"I'll have five hundred men ready to march in thirty minutes," Washington said.

"No. He'll kill her if I don't go alone. I'm leaving now. Little Joe should be well rested and ready to run."

"He's been well taken care of," Washington reassured me.

"Have you ever heard of a man called the Monster?" I asked.

"Yes," he said. "I've heard many people refer to you as just that."

"No. Not a monster. *The* Monster?"

"Yes," he said again after thinking for a few seconds. "But he's in Canada. Why do you ask about him?"

"What do you know about him?"

"Oh my God, Thomas," Washington said in a hushed voice as he grabbed my arm and looked down at the hatchet in my belt. "He's Mohawk. Loyal to the king. Very good at tracking and killing. Well educated. He's the only Mohawk reputed to lead white men."

"Anything else?" I asked.

"He's a lot like you," Washington told me. "He's a loyalist but has honor. His own form of honor, I should say. Might be why he didn't take the children. He doesn't care what others think about him. Like you, he will do whatever it takes to get the job done. He was given the rank of captain, I think. His real name is Joseph Brant. His enemies call him Monster Brant. And for good reason. You can't reason with him. You can't scare him off. You'll have to kill him or he'll kill you."

"How do you know him?"

"I met him during the seven-year war."

"He has men but came here alone?" I asked, confused.

"No. Most likely he came into camp alone. He will have ten to twenty men with him, depending on if it was more important to him to move fast or to bring all the guns he could."

I paused to let all his information sink in. My eyes swept the camp. "Where did you bury Ben?"

The general pointed past me. "In the burial ground. With my fallen troops. I can show you if you like."

"When I get back," I said.

I had my weapons and gear either on my back or in my satchel, so I didn't need to get anything. I could stop and buy food on the way.

I had my older British sword on my hip and my newer French sword on my back. I took off the French sword and handed it to Washington.

"A gift from the King of France," I told him. "Hang onto it for me. If I don't make it back, give it to Marie."

He pulled the sword from its scabbard and looked it up and down with appreciation. I removed the British sword from my hip. I wasn't sure if I'd need it or not, but if I was going into the woods, it might get in the way.

"This was Captain Bonifield's." I handed the sword to him.

I never said what he should do with it if I didn't return. It meant something to me but not to anyone else.

"Oh yes, the mission," he said as if just now remembering. "Franklin had sent letters telling me what a success it was, and he was most pleased. I know you protected our young country's honor by taking on the deed in your own name. I wanted to ask you about it."

"The deed." I laughed. "You mean the assassination. You gentlemen of honor have a hard time saying such words."

"True. But still, I'd like to hear about it."

"You'll have to ask Marie. It's a long, bloody story, and I've got no time to tell it."

Leaving my real authentic French Musketeer and British cavalry swords with Washington, I headed for the stables.

I walked into the stables and found Little Joe. He started whinnying when he saw me. I patted his neck as he rested his head on my shoulder, pushing into me. Putting a blanket on his back, I opened his stall and led him out as he started prancing.

"Easy, boy. I know it's been a while. I missed you too, but we'll have to catch up with each other on the road."

I placed a saddle on him and cinched it tight. Picking up a horse blanket off the wall, I tied it to the back of the saddle. It stunk like horse, but I didn't want to waste time searching for a clean blanket.

This time I was not avoiding problems. My guns and knives were ready to go and in plain sight. I pulled my black vest out of my satchel and slipped it on. I had never thrown or even used a hatchet, so I slipped it into my satchel for now. I was either going to drop it or cut myself with it, anyway. From the markings on the map, the spot he wanted to meet was about a hundred and sixty miles north of Valley Forge. It would take me five or six days to get there.

I had my hands on the saddle to climb on Little Joe's back when Lafayette entered the barn holding a bundle of food wrapped in a towel. He grabbed a saddlebag and without a word placed the food in the saddlebag and then attached the bag onto Little Joe. Grabbing a second saddlebag, he placed a horse feeder in one pouch and filled the other pouch with grain. He then set that bag onto Little Joe but in front of the saddle.

"You need to slow down," Lafayette said, his voice tight. "Riding off without food for you or your horse will not help Annie."

He was right and I knew it. I gave him a short nod to acknowledge his sage advice. He squared off with me, and we both stepped forward in a hug.

"Are you sure you don't want me to go?" he asked.

"You've learned all I could teach you by now," I said. "It's time for you to lead men."

"Goodbye, my friend," he said.

"I'll be back. With Annie."

Climbing up onto Little Joe was nice, like coming home. I really missed the coward. We trotted out of the barn.

"Thomas," Lafayette yelled from behind me.

I whipped my head around. "Yes?"

He had a side smile on his face. "If you don't come back. Can I have the musketeer sword?"

"I already told Washington to give it to you if I don't return," I told him.

General George Washington stood with his hat in one hand and both swords in the other. He expected me to stop and receive some words of wisdom from him before I left, but I wasn't in the mood. I needed him to ensure the Americans won the war, so I'd do the dirty work and see to it that he stayed alive. But after everything I had done for him, he'd failed me in the one task I asked of him. He failed to protect the woman I loved. He failed to protect Ben. And he failed to protect the girls. The girls were unharmed only because this man called the Monster chose to leave them unharmed.

I knew it wasn't directly Washington's fault. No one here expected the Monster to come to Valley Forge. But logic didn't help the pain that riddled my chest. I rode past him without a word and without looking back.

Chapter Six A Long Ride

I kept Little Joe at a trot most of the day. This man had a three-day head start on me, but if I pushed Little Joe, I might be able to cut it down to two days. This man couldn't run the whole way back, and his horse eventually would have to carry two people. The horse would be slower and need more rest breaks.

I fell back into my old routine of running Little Joe for an hour, then dismounting and walking him for an hour. We traveled all day and through the night, sticking to the only trail drawn on the map. I considered leaving the trail and following one of the rivers north, but if I missed a bend or took the wrong one, I'd be lost.

Little Joe seemed to sense my urgency and never protested our pace. I did stop and let him drink every time we came to a stream. I hadn't brought my canteens, so I also drank my fill. My canteens were still in Annie's room in my backpack, assuming she hadn't burned my backpack like I asked her to.

Lafayette was right. I had rushed off too quickly. But I was bound to run into a settlement somewhere along the way and would buy waterbags and needed supplies. I had no idea what else I might need when I came across this Monster. In my head, I started to say Joseph Brant, but I needed to think of him as the *Monster*, to remember who I was up against. If, and that was a big if, I was reading the map correctly, I had made it to a place called Wyoming Valley by morning of the second day.

According to the map, the fastest route to Cherry Valley was straight north. The map showed the trail I was on, cutting east to the Delaware River, then north to Cherry Valley. I bristled at staying on the trail, but the map was limited with its details, and I had only basic navigation skills. This was the only trail drawn on the paper, and I wasn't familiar with the area, so sticking to the trail was my only option.

We pushed hard the whole second day and made it to a fast-running river, which had to be the Delaware River. I stopped at a small farm and gave them coin in exchange for two waterbags, some apples, and extra grain. The couple seemed nice, but I didn't want to stay long. I was a man with a price on his head and never knew whom to trust. Instead, I found a safe place to sleep in the forest. I had been pushing Little Joe too hard the last two days and owed him a long rest and a bag of grain, plus a few of the apples.

I worried about Annie and didn't think I'd get any sleep, but I was exhausted having gone the last thirty-six hours straight without rest. I slept hard and, surprisingly, with no dreams. I didn't allow myself to light a fire for heat, and my only source of warmth was the smelly horse blanket.

I woke up blinking against the first rays of morning light rising in the east. Little Joe was still dozing, and I'd have to walk him for a while to loosen him up. I urinated on a tree, then fed and watered Little Joe. As soon as he was done eating, I resaddled him and walked him back to the trail I had been following.

Three hours later, I was riding Little Joe at a gallop. The trail had widened to about eight feet. Thick tree limbs bowed, covering both sides of the trail with large leaves that blocked out most of the sun's direct light. Sunlight broke through cracks between the trees, branches, and leaves like laser beams shooting to the earth. It made for an almost hypnotic effect and reminded me of a disco-tech with the disco ball lit up but not spinning.

It turned out this effect most assuredly had saved my life by making me a harder target to hit. Two shots rang out in front of me, and puffs of smoke wafted up from behind trees on the left and right side of the trail. The distinct sound of two twin cracks echoed as lead balls zipped by me at a high rate of speed and way too close to my head. Well, not too close. Too close would be actually ripping through my flesh, skull, and brains.

My gaze caught on one of the bigger branches above the trail where a Native man stood, balancing himself with his back against the tree trunk, aiming a musket at me. He was smarter than the two on the ground who'd shot too early. I kicked Little Joe's sides, and my horse shot forward, increasing his speed. The change in speed caused the man in the tree to miss like his friends. The two men on the side of the trail were already reloading their muskets. The Native dropped his musket to the ground with a clatter and pulled out a long knife from the leather sheath on his belt. He leaned forward, and I realized he was going to try to leap down on me as I galloped by.

Drawing my Tec-9, I started firing at the warrior. I had the same problems my opponents had when they shot at me. Between riding Little Joe at a sprint and the light playing tricks on my eyes, I missed the first four shots, hitting him in the shoulder on my fifth, but missing again on my sixth and last.

With my pistol now empty, I holstered it and leaned low on Little Joe's back. Even after being shot in the shoulder, the warrior took one long step out on the limb and rocketed from the branch. He missed colliding with me, but somehow managed to reach out and grab my shoulder. He flew by me but ripped me from the saddle as he leapt. Luckily for me, I didn't hit the ground. I landed on the brave but crazy bastard who had tried to take me out, even at the cost of his own life.

Between my bullet hitting him, him hitting the ground, and me landing on top of him, the crazy man wasn't moving. He was either dead or unconscious. My shoulder throbbed, but I didn't think anything was broken. I rolled to my right and then onto my feet. The man to the right of the trail was still loading his musket as the man to the left charged me, holding his musket upside down by the barrel like a club. Pulling my Thompson, I shot him in the chest. He fell backwards, his feet flying up into the air and landing on his back.

Dropping my Thompson, I pulled my knife free from its sheath and immediately ran for the third and last man. He was only a boy really, eighteen or nineteen years old. He'd finished packing the musket with his ramrod, and seeing me running at him, he dropped the rod and lifted the musket in the air. As the musket rose up, the barrel came downward in my direction. I grabbed the wooden frame below the barrel with my left hand, letting my momentum carry me into the man as my knife thrusted into his left side. The blade slipped between his ribs and into his lung. The soldier stiffened like a board as pain shot through his body. His mouth opened, but no sound came out. I yanked the musket out of his hand, then ripped my knife free from his ribs. He screamed in pain as my knife was suddenly jerked from his flank, and blood poured in a blooming crimson stain on his shirt. He collapsed to the ground, landing on his back.

I stood over the kid as he laid on his side in the fetal position. Blood sprayed out of his mouth with a wet, sickening cough. He tried to say something but only made a gurgling noise. He was drowning as his lungs filled up with his own blood. There was nothing I could do to save him, even if I had chosen to.

I wanted to walk away and let him die alone, in peace. But I couldn't do it. I went down on one knee, leaning over him and rubbed at my sore left shoulder while I tried to think of something to say to him. Nothing came to mind, so I wiped my knife off on his left pants leg and sheathed it. Reaching down, I gripped his left arm. I didn't know if he could feel my touch, so I squeezed, adding pressure. I may have been the one who killed him, but I still wanted him to know he wasn't going to die alone. I knelt there for about five minutes, maybe a little longer, while his breathing became more ragged. He kept coughing up blood until suddenly, he was still.

I ran my fingers down his face to close his eyes, then slowly stood up and walked over to the middle of the trail. I paused to glance down at the man who had bravely but insanely leaped from the branch even after I'd shot him. I shook my head in amazement. He was like me, willing to do what was necessary even at the cost of his own life. He wore deerskin britches and a long white shirt, much like my own shirt. Beaded arm bracelets ringed both his biceps and a blue cloth was wrapped around his head in the style of a bandanna. The angle of his head was so unnatural I knew he must be dead. Yet, he still had his knife clenched firmly in his hand.

I picked up my Thompson and holstered it, then I checked on the last man on the ground who I had shot. His eyes were open, but I didn't need to check him to know he was dead. Maybe it was because he was old enough to pay the price for his actions, or because I hadn't knelt there and watched him die as I had the boy, or maybe it was because I was so tired, but I didn't bend over to close his eyes like I had the younger man's.

The trotting of horseshoes caught my attention, and I lifted my eyes, smiling when Little Joe came back in my direction. I walked towards him, meeting him in the middle of the trail. He stopped in front of me and pushed me with his nose. I patted his neck and did something I had never done before. I thanked him for coming back and kissed his nose. He whinnied and pulled away. I grabbed his reins to calm him down, but something had him spooked.

"Good day to you," a cheery voice called from behind me.

I jumped in surprise, spinning around. A man in his forties sat casually on a horse. He also had on buckskin britches, which matched his buckskin shirt. Unlike the brave man lying on the ground dead, he didn't appear to be Mohawk. The good news, if there was any good news, he also didn't look or sound British. He had the look of a scout or mountain man. Three dead men laid on the ground next to me, but he didn't seem too concerned. I couldn't help but notice he was also holding a musket aimed at my chest. His musket was longer than the standard musket and reminded me of a musket I had taken off a sniper one time.

"Hello there," I answered cautiously.

"Would you mind greatly dropping that musket?" he asked.

The way he asked it, I wasn't sure if it was a real question or a demand. Unlike the musket I held, the hammer on his was cocked back and ready to fire. My two pistols were empty, and I was holding the musket by the barrel. Not that I'd had much practice shooting a musket. He was calm, so I had no doubt he knew his business or at least how do use the weapon he was presently pointing at me. With no better plan in mind, I opened my fingers and let the musket drop to the ground.

He seemed to have an easiness about him. He wasn't nervous – on the contrary, he was completely comfortable pointing his musket at me. In a strange way, it was comforting. Nothing makes you more worried than a nervous person holding a gun on you. When someone is afraid of you, there is always the possibility of them pulling the trigger by accident.

"I was on my way back home," he said. "Heading to the Big Sandy when shots echoed in the valley. May I ask what's going on here? Who are you, and who are these men?"

Trying to think of a good story, I simply said my name was Thomas, and these men were highwaymen, who I assumed wanted to rob me.

"Thomas," he repeated. "Highwaymen?" He did not hide looking me up and down. "You can call me Daniel."

He climbed off his horse slowly, holding his musket with one hand and never lowering it, while holding onto the saddle horn with his free hand. He let go of the horse's reins, obviously having no doubt his horse would stay in place. Walking over to me, he studied the man lying on the trail.

"He's Mohawk," he stated with surprise in his voice. "What's he doing this far south? The mohawk tribes are part of the Six Nations so he may not be trespassing on their land, but still, they live closer to Quebec, or New York at best."

"I don't know," I said.

"Is that a fact?" The man raised a doubtful eyebrow at me.

"Yes. It's a fact."

He paused a minute, scanning the area, taking in the three dead men, and looking me up and down again.

"How's General Washington doing?" he asked out of nowhere.

Surprise must've shown on my face because he started laughing. He didn't lower the musket but continued to laugh. Was that a good sign or a bad sign?

"The black vest and scar gave you away, son," he explained as he got himself under control.

My body tensed up, and I tried to think of the best way to grab his musket without getting shot.

"Relax," he told me, reading my thoughts. "I'm with the militia. In fact, I'm coming from the Continental Congress. I had to deliver some messages to them. Rumors say you're in France."

I released some of the tension in my shoulders but kept a wary eye on the man. "Was. I'm back now."

"How about you tell me what's really going on? These other two might be highwaymen, but Mohawks would never join them in such an act. He might kill you for his honor or if you offended him, but not for money."

"Really?" I asked.

"Yes," he said flatly. "Now, should I call you Washington's Assassin or the Pale Rider?"

"Just Thomas, if you please."

"Very well, Thomas. You can call me Daniel, as I said. What's really going on here?"

Since he'd already figured out who I was, I had no reason to continue lying to the man.

"A Mohawk took my woman and is holding her hostage," I said. "He wants me to go to someplace called Cherry Valley and meet him there, alone."

"Alone?" he interrupted. "Do you think he's alone?"

85

"No," I answered. "I'm betting he has between a dozen and two dozen men with him."

"I would say closer to a dozen. If he had two dozen, he would've left more than three on the road. The question is, how did he know you were coming this way?"

I pulled out the map and showed him the trail to Cherry Valley.

"He left this map for me to follow."

Daniel kept his gaze on the map. "And you thought it would be a good idea to stay on the trail he marked for you to take?"

"No, not really," I answered. "I didn't have any choice. I can read a map fine as long as I've large land markers to go off of. But the trees are so thick here, I'll most likely get lost in these woods or have to move slow to make sure I don't."

"Why would a Mohawk warrior come this far south to kill you? Did you offend his honor?"

I shook my head and took the map back, tucking it into my inner vest pocket. "No. Never met the man."

"What's this warrior's name?" Daniel asked with suspicion in his voice.

"Joseph Brant," I said.

"Brant the Monster? He's supposed to be in Quebec. He's a loyalist. His men call themselves Brant's Volunteers."

"Yes, well, as you can imagine, King George isn't happy with me," I told him. "The king sent orders to put this Brant fellow on my trail. I guess Brant thought it'd be easier to make me come to him."

He stood deep in thought, his eyes bouncing from me to the dead Mohawk warrior at his feet. He thumbed his hammer down and placed the butt of his musket onto the ground. He had a causal way about him, leaning on his musket while he talked. He looked comfortable standing and leaning.

"I need to get home," he said. "The Shawnee haven't been happy with the colonists lately. If things don't improve, there'll be fighting soon. I was meeting with the Continental Congress, asking for their help. Reckon I can get you to Cherry Valley first. I'll help you get your woman back. But we're not staying on this trail. There's a farm about ten miles from here. We'll make it on horseback and spend the night there. In the morning, we'll leave the horses and go on foot through the woods."

I hadn't wanted Lafayette coming with me because I was going to have to stay on the trail, and this Brant fellow said he'd kill Annie if I didn't come alone. But if this Daniel knew the woods as well as he seemed to think he did, maybe a little help was called for.

"I'd appreciate that," I said. "But what's a Big Sandy?"

"It's a river," he answered, laughing again. "It takes me back home. Now let's gather up these muskets."

Chapter Seven Setting the Trap

Three days ago, Annie and this man who told her to call him Joseph walked out of the trees and into camp, right before sunset. He hadn't given her his last name, only his first. Joseph held onto the reins of his horse, pulling the animal behind him, and forced Annie to walk ahead of him. To her, it felt like they'd walked half the long, tiresome journey. They had only stopped a few times to rest. She and the horse would sleep four or maybe five hours, then he'd wake her up and they would be back on the move. She'd never seen him sleep. If she had, she would have tried to get away. It was possible he slept after she fell asleep. She wasn't sure about much as tired as she was.

Blisters sprouted on her feet, and several of them had popped while they walked. When she complained about them, he looked at her with a blank stare, not caring if her feet hurt as long as she didn't slow him down. Joseph would run along the horse, pulling the reins while she sat in the saddle. Then he would slow them down and walk. It was the same thing every time. He'd pull the horse behind him while making her walk in front of him.

Joseph was a complicated person, and Annie had a hard time trying to figure him out. He pushed her hard, making her walk at a fast pace, and had no patience for her if she slowed down. He never let her out of his sight, but had untied her hands, permitting her free movement. At the same time, he saw to it she wasn't thirsty, making her drink water whether she wanted to or not. He never complained when she needed to relieve herself. He never smiled but didn't abuse her in any way. Then there was the whole *he killed her father-in-law Ben* but hadn't harmed her daughters. As hard as he was on her, he seemed to be harder on himself. He didn't appear to care for horses but refused to ride double for fear of hurting the horse's back.

A wide dirt clearing opened to the camp, situated in front of a fast-running stream. Thick clumps of trees enclosed two sides of the camp, and a cliff sat at the back side. When they entered the camp, the men there gathered around Joseph. Annie was surprised to see so many white men follow Joseph. These men weren't British soldiers, so they'd have to be loyalists. The two Native men dressed like Joseph, but the loyalist seemed to like wearing colorful blue, red, and brown shirts, marking them as Canadian. She was surprised to see that besides their long knives, these men had hatchets in the belts like the Mohawks had.

After the men in camp greeted Joseph and slapped him on his back, Joseph ordered one of the men to make her comfortable. One of the Quebecois men pulled her over by the arm and sat her down on a thick fallen log. He wasn't unnecessarily rude or violent but made no attempt to make her feel at ease, either. She noticed she'd been placed in the center of the clearing. Not close to the center, but dead center. A round fire pit made up of large rocks was at her feet, and four bed rolls spread out with rocks and grass laid underneath blankets. From a distance, she knew it looked like men sleeping under the blankets. Joseph had designed a trap for Thomas, but why? Thomas was in France. She'd tried to tell Joseph several times, but he either didn't believe her or didn't care.

She needed to focus on staying alive and not giving Joseph or his men a reason to kill her. If Thomas returned from his mission, she knew he'd be coming for her as surely as she knew the sun would come up in the morning. God help anyone who got in his way. She needed to stay alive, not only for her children, but for Thomas's sake. He'd already lost one wife to the British. She couldn't bear it for him if he lost another.

Thomas was a good man, of that she was sure, but Thomas viewed himself as a villain of sorts. If Joseph did kill her, she didn't know what damage that might do to Thomas, how it would affect his view of himself. What might snap inside him? What kind of villain would Thomas turn into? He was capable of killing and good at it, when necessary, but if Joseph killed her, she feared Thomas might lose himself completely in anger and grief. He might turn dark and truly become the Pale Rider that he was rumored to be – the blood thirsty demon from hell that the British believed he was. The one that killed for the sake of killing and who death followed on a leash.

Joseph called one of the two Mohawk men and two of the Quebecois loyalists off to the side for a private conversation. He knelt and drew a map in the dirt with his knife, and she thought he was pointing to a spot between where they were and where they had come from. The three men gathered their belongings and mounted their horses, riding out of camp. Annie counted the men she saw and as best she could. Nine more men, not counting Joseph, were in the camp. Only one of them was a Mohawk warrior; the rest were loyalists.

Joseph ordered three of the men to climb to the top of an outcropping behind them which had plenty of places to hide within the rocks. The horses were picketed in the trees and out of sight. She watched two men cross over the river, disappearing into the foliage on the other side. Joseph had told his men they may be there as long as a month, waiting for the man named Thomas. She wondered why he hadn't called Thomas *the Pale Rider* like everyone else did. A few of the men's faces bore worry lines, and she realized Joseph was trying to keep their courage up. By calling him Thomas, he was making the man more human, an easy kill. Calling him Pale Rider would only incite the men's fears until it got the best of them. He trusted his men, but they were only men, and since heading south, they had heard outlandish stories about the Pale Rider.

If she got ahold of a knife, Annie would kill this man in an instant, but he was smart and seemed to either know his men well or understood human nature. She could tell he was educated by the way he talked. She'd never met a Mohawk before and was surprised by this. He'd never let her get her hands on a knife or lower his guard enough to use it.

One of his men brought her a plate of food. It wasn't much, but it was good. Cooked rabbit and some fresh berries. As she ate with her fingers, one of the men started a fire in the circle of rocks in front of her. Then, as the sun went down, Joseph came over to her. He handed her a blanket and sat on the far side of the fire, well out of reach.

"If you need to go relieve yourself or want to wash in the stream, do it now," he said to her. "Once you lay down, you're stuck there. If you get up anytime between now and sunrise, my men will shoot you. I gave them orders and I'll be asleep, so I won't be able to stop them."

"I'm fine," Annie said curtly. She spread out the blanket on the ground, rested her head on her hands, and closed her eyes. As she fell asleep, she wondered how long it would take Thomas to find her.

Over the last three days, they'd fallen into a routine. She was allowed to go to the bathroom and Joseph brought her food twice a day. Relieving herself in the trees was her sole allowed reason for being more than a few feet from the log. She could sit on the log, stand next to the log, or sleep in front of the log, but Joseph had made it clear to her, the log was now her world.

Joseph cooked their food and took their plates to the stream to wash them. He didn't need to watch her; his men surrounded them. After the first night, she never saw any of them again, but she knew they were nearby. Every few hours, Joseph made a bird whistle. She didn't recognize the call, so it must have been a northern bird. Every time he whistled, three return whistles answered in turn. A different bird whistle from each direction answered his call. The men on the cliff face didn't reply but stayed hidden and quiet.

How much food and water do they have with them?

Joseph never looked around or appeared worried about the chances of someone sneaking up on them. He seemed relaxed, as if he were safe and sound in his element. Every night, he kept a large fire going. The fire put out more light than a campfire should or needed to. It put out a lot of warmth for them, but she figured it was the light he wanted. The brilliance of the fire made her eyes ache to the point that it made the dark woods seem darker. She finally figured out that he wanted the camp well lit – he *wanted* Thomas to be able to find them. Unlike this man Brant, she wasn't worried about Thomas finding them. If Thomas was in the colonies, he'd find her, that she knew. If he was still in France, well, there was nothing he could do for her.

One night, a bird whistle rang from the trees. Joseph rose easily, walked over to the tree line where he disappeared.

"It won't be long now," Joseph told her in his gruff voice after he returned.

"What won't be long?" Annie asked.

"One of my men checked on the three men I'd assigned to the trail," Joseph told her. "He found them dead. I'm starting to believe that your Thomas is as good as they say he is."

Joseph didn't seem too bothered by the loss of his three men.

"He's not just *my* Thomas," Annie spat out in a hard tone. "He's the Pale Rider, Washington's assassin. Some call him the bringer of death, and you took what is his. Think about that when you close your eyes tonight."

For the first time since he'd taken her, a flare of worry showed on his face. He quickly recovered, his unconcerned expression returning to his face.

"Maybe you're right," he said. "I'm sorry for what I must do next."

Just to the south of the camp

We had a small fire going in a minor clearing. Daniel had said we'd be safe here, but I was sleeping outside of the clearing behind the brush, just in case. I hadn't lived this long by feeling safe and relaxed. I had finished cleaning and oiling my pistols, and I focused on sharpening my knives, putting a razor's edge on them with my sharpening stone and gun oil.

From where I was, I could easily see the fire and see anyone who might venture into the camp looking for us. According to Daniel, we were about two miles away from where this Joseph wanted me to meet him. We'd left our horses at a farm owned by a family Daniel didn't know very well, but they luckily remembered him. He was likeable and had a way of making people feel special. When he didn't remember the farmer's name, he simply referred to him as *friend*. He made a point of bragging about the family's hospitality in front of them.

Daniel had left me here several hours ago, saying he wanted to take a look around. I was the one used to making the plan or taking action. Sitting around waiting for him to do the heavy lifting was new to me. And I was putting a lot of trust in someone I'd just met. I wasn't sure why I was here by the fire, and he was out there. One minute I was telling him we should scout the area, the next minute he convinced me he could do it faster by himself.

An owl hooted in the night. Daniel had told me he would make that call when he returned to prevent any *accidents*. Even with the notice, he was almost on top of me before I saw or heard him.

"I found them," he said as he crouched next to me. "Right where he marked it on the map."

"Did you see her?" I asked.

"Aye," he answered. "They're in a clearing. Sitting in plain sight as bait. Joseph, too. He's not hiding. They were both sitting in front of a fire."

"Great," I said, hope flaring in my chest.

Daniel shook his head, his face closed off. "No, it's not."

"Why not?"

"I found their horses," he said. "Ten of them. He had at least nine men watching the camp, waiting for you to stroll on in."

"Did you see any of the men?" I asked.

"Aye," he answered. "Three of them. The camp is in front of a rock base cliff. They have three in the rocks, waiting. Good positions. No way of getting a shot on them at night. I know there are more men in the woods around the camp but didn't want to confront them yet. I'd guess there are also a few on the far side of the stream."

I marveled at the information he was able to glean from his scouting. "Any ideas?"

"Divide and conquer," he answered with a measure of surety. "I can get the ones on the ground to chase me, and you handle the three up high, plus Joseph."

"When?"

"Normally, I'd say tomorrow night. Best time for us to attack. But they are waiting for that. Joseph is smart. He makes a bird call every couple of hours. If his men don't return the whistle, he'll know we killed them. His men must be sleeping in the daytime, and staying up at night, watching and waiting. We should attack at first light."

"He's in the middle of the trap, out in the opening with Annie, three men up high, and most likely two to each of the three sides," I thought out loud. "There is no way to strike five points at once. Whichever side we attack first, we'll be flanked by the others. And I think there is more to it. Something you didn't see. He's got a hidden card in the game."

"How do you know?" he asked.

"General Washington said this Monster was a lot like me," I answered. "I never play fair. My father taught me if you're not cheating, you're not trying."

Daniel pursed his lips at this. "Then what do you have in mind?"

"Can you make the bird calls his men did?" I asked.

"Aye, they are simple enough."

"We need to do what he'll never expect," I said. "We don't attack during the day or the night. We attack during both."

"Both?" he asked. "I can tell you're an ambitious man, but how do the two of us attack in both the day and night?"

"Are you as good with that knife as you are at moving around in the dark?" I asked, pointing to the hunting knife on his belt.

He looked down at the knife, smiled to himself, and gave a subtle nod.

Daniel led the way towards the trap. He'd taken us far around the clearing, and we were moving south from the north. We were on the wrong side of the stream, but we decided this was the best course of action. Daniel moved slower and slower as we got closer. By the time we were almost on top of them, he moved at a snail's pace. It was pitch dark, and though he was only ten feet in front of me, I could barely see his outline. Every step he took was slow and methodical. Sometimes he would start to put a foot down, only to lift it again, finding a new spot to place it. It was as if he could feel a twig or dry leaves beneath his foot, and instead of putting weight onto it, he'd find a new perch. He willingly sacrificed speed for stealth. No wonder he could get right up on me before I ever knew he was there. The man was a master woodsman.

I had one of my knives out, but I also had attached the suppressor to my Tec-9 in case I needed it. My night vision goggles were on my head, and I pulled them down over my eyes. Daniel was too focused on every step to notice that I had them on. My night vision had been through a lot with me. Between getting wet repeatedly and the bouncing around on horseback, I was surprised they still worked at all. They lit up the world in a sour apple green lens. The lens was grainy and had some fuzzy spots, but they still worked, if just.

Daniel stopped turning his head one way, then the other. He wasn't looking for anything; he was listening. Daniel motioned for me, and I moved closer. He pointed to me, then off to his right, then pointed to himself and then to his left. I didn't move my feet, but stared off in the direction he'd pointed. Not seeing anything, I crept forward, trying like him to step over or around any trigs on the ground. Then I froze in place as someone coughed.

I had to look twice, but there he was. A man standing perfectly still next to a tree. I was coming at him from his right side. He held perfectly still and blended in as part of the tree. I could hear the tinkling stream now. He was staring across the river to a clearing, waiting for me to step into the light given out by the fire. I got within ten feet before the muscles in his shoulders visibly tightened. He didn't move his musket or the left hand holding it, and if I didn't have my night vision on, I would not have seen his right hand slowly pulling out the tomahawk from his belt.

I had planned on butt stroking him in the head and knocking him out; however, in pure reflex, I threw my knife. The knife handle extended from the right side of his neck as blood sprayed the ground. He dropped his musket with a soft *plop* and made a gurgling sound as he pawed at the handle. Then his hands dropped down, and he fell onto his side, leaves crunching under his weight.

Back-tracking after I retrieved my knife, I located Daniel waiting for me, standing over the man he'd killed. I opened my mouth to speak, but a whistle sounded from the other side of the stream. Maybe it was bad timing or maybe the Monster heard the musket fall. Either way, he'd know we were here when his man didn't respond. Off to our right, a different bird answered the first. Another bird twittered off to our left. I held my breath until Daniel let out a long, low whistle. After the exchange of whistles, the night fell quiet again. I let out my breath in a heavy rush and wiped at the sweat that had sprouted on my forehead.

Daniel found a spot that provided a panorama across the river to include the rocky wall behind the camp. It was too dark to see the men in the rocks, and what light the fire gave off only managed to throw off dancing shadows. Four shapes laid under blankets in front of the fire. I wasn't sure which one was Annie, but Daniel had seen her earlier, so I knew she was there. I took off the two muskets I had on my back and laid them down next to Daniel.

"You're not keeping a musket for yourself?" Daniel whispered.

"I'm fine," I answered.

"I heard you were better with a pistol than most men are with muskets. I assumed it was an exaggeration."

"It's not," I whispered as I walked away.

I moved off downstream, finding a place I could cross over without getting too wet. I wasn't afraid of getting wet as much as I didn't want to be sneaking around in the woods with mud on my boots, picking up leaves and such. I finally located a spot with large rocks, big enough for me to jump from one to another. The sound of running water covered any noise I might have made jumping across the stones. Once on the far side, I entered the tree line and copied Daniel's movements, going slow. My knife was back in my hand as I moved slowly and carefully from tree to tree. After every step I took, I stopped and looked around.

When I finally spotted the men, I found them clustered together and not apart. I slid my knife back into its sheath and pulled out my Tec-9. I was still too far to use the pistol at night with night vision. I moved closer at a painfully slow pace. One of the two men glanced around. He had a similar look and dress as the Mohawk I had killed on the trail. His hand moved to get the other man's attention. He must have heard me. As they started surveying the area, I leaned to my left, putting one of the trees between us in front of me.

I was still fifteen to eighteen feet away, and as dark as it was, there was no way they could see me yet. I didn't think I had made any noise, so how did this man know I was here? I peeked around the tree. The Mohawk man leaned his musket against a tree and pulled out a long knife with his right hand and a tomahawk with his left.

The Quebecois man next to him held onto his musket and lifted his flat beaver hat up for a better look around. He swung his head back and forth, trying to see in every direction at the same time. The Mohawk moved slowly but faster than I'd been moving. Even watching him move, I still couldn't hear his steps.

How did he know I was here?

I stepped forward and put myself right behind the next tree. Even without night vision, I was close enough for him to see my outline if I hadn't been standing behind the large pine.

I peeked around the left side of the tree and saw the Quebecois still in the same spot, musket stock pulled in tight to his shoulder, swinging the barrel back and forth. I didn't see the Mohawk warrior, so he had to be on the right side of the tree. I could hear him now, breathing. He was close, a few feet away. Then it hit me. He wasn't just breathing; he was inhaling air through his nose, inhaling deeply. Was he smelling me? My sweat? My stink? Maybe the horse blanket I had been using?

I took one step backwards and away from the tree. Extending my arms, I pointed my pistol at the center of the trunk. I practiced the next movement in my head several times, visualizing what I was going to do. Practicing it without actually moving. Then, as the Mohawk man inhaled again, I moved, leaning the upper half of my body to the right of the tree, arm extended in front of me. The Mohawk warrior filled my vision, his chest covered by the front sight of my pistol. He saw me as I squeezed the trigger. *Thunk.* Without waiting for him to fall, I leaned to the left and fired twice more at the Quebecois man, who was looking right at me but not seeing me, sheltered in the darkness. *Thunk thunk.*

With the night vision goggles on, I couldn't see colors, but two twin dark spots bloomed in the center of his chest. He dropped to his knees, and without a word, he fell over backward in a very unnatural position, knees high in the air.

Leaning back to the right, I saw the Mohawk was on his back, unmoving. I froze in place, looking for any additional threats. The night fell quiet again. I didn't see any movement or hear any bird whistle challenge. I stepped forward and dropped on a knee to check the Mohawk warrior. His eyes were open and tracking me. I couldn't tell exactly where I'd shot him, but his blood was soaked up by his cotton shirt and expanding to cover his whole chest.

"How?" I asked him.

"Gun oil," he said in two clipped words, before closing his eyes. His chest stopped moving.

I was in awe of this man who I'd killed. I knew where he was and had night vision to see in the dark. He had nothing, yet he came right at me because he was able to smell and identify the gun oil I had used a few hours ago. I cursed under my breath. These men were excellent, better than I'd anticipated. A shiver coursed down my back as the realization struck me. If I hadn't met Daniel, these men would have killed me before I knew they were there.

Rising quietly, I reloaded my pistol and moved to the edge of the tree line. The four forms still laid under their blankets. None of them moved or whistled, so that was good. I had paid attention to the whistles from men on this side of the camp, and I was sure I could copy them. Since we'd killed four of the nine men, we'd stay in place. I couldn't be in two places at once, so I couldn't kill the men on the far side of the trees yet. It was too dark to kill the men in the rocks, and I needed the others alive to reply with the whistle if another challenge was given. The only thing left for us to do was wait for enough light to see the men in the rocks.

If Daniel was right and two more men waited across the way, I'd have to kill the Monster and whoever else was in the bed rolls without killing Annie. Then I'd have to kill the two on the other side of the camp from here, while shooting over Annie. The plan was for Daniel to take out the three in the rocks. Daniel had three muskets now, so he would not need to reload unless he missed.

He better not miss.

Chapter Eight Bird Whistles

As the sun came up, waves of golden light filled the blue, early morning sky, but the encampment stayed dark as the cliffs blocked out the direct sunlight. Although the sky provided enough light to see by, the camp and the face of the cliff were still encased in shadows.

My Thompson was out and I was ready to go on Daniel's signal – firing his first of hopefully three shots, so it would be hard to miss. The Monster, Annie, and the two in front of the fire still hadn't stirred. I had expected this Joseph to be awake before sunrise. I was a little disappointed.

A musket shot rang out from across the river, followed by the crunching sound of a man tumbling down the rocks. The sound of the shot bounced off the rock wall and echoed over and over and must have carried for miles. I aimed at the fire, ready to shoot the first man who sat up. None of the figures moved. The two on the side of the camp moved forward to see who was attacking.

Daniel fired his second shot, and another man fell from the cliff side. I fired and one of the two men across the way dropped onto his face. The last man on the cliff side fired at Daniel as the last man across the way fired at me. Neither man, to my joy, hit his target. I reloaded and fired my second shot as Daniel picked up and fired his third musket. Unlike them, we did hit our targets, and the shootout ended as quickly as it had started.

Daniel was reloading his own musket as I reloaded my Thompson. We aimed our weapons back on the encampment, but none of the four forms had moved.

Something was wrong. They should have moved. Daniel rose and picked his way across the stream, musket held high and aimed in on the fire pit. I stood up and moved forward out of the trees. Daniel stopped about ten feet away and lowered his musket as if there was no threat. The forms were piles of rocks under blankets.

Fuck.

Without a word between us, we each spun around, back-to-back, facing the way we'd come, looking for threats that weren't there. We were met by only stillness and silence. Daniel lowered his musket and walked into the trees where he'd found the horses last night.

"Two of the horses are missing," Daniel said, walking out of the trees.

"They are gone? How? Why?" My head filled with disbelief. How had we messed this up?

"Something spooked him," Daniel answered. "He set a good trap for you, but I don't think he knew about me. He snuck out after I scouted the area. I bet he was here with the horses when we killed the first two. He heard us, and he whistled, testing us. Maybe I didn't get the whistle right. He's got at least a three-hour head start on us. You were right, he had extra cards in the deck."

"Can you follow them?" I asked, hoping I didn't sound as desperate as I felt.

"Two horses?" he asked back. "Are you joking? I can track a fish downstream in deep water."

I had to believe he was as confident in his skills as he sounded. "We can take two of these horses and set the rest free."

We saddled up on two of the horses and let the remaining six loose. Daniel set out at a slow pace at first as he leaned over his horse's neck, studying the ground, following the horseshoe divots in the dirt and leaves. He instructed me to ride next to him and keep my eyes focused ahead. While he did all this, he regaled me with a funny and unbelievable story about tracking an eagle and how he followed the trail right off a cliff. The story reeked of bullshit, but his point was well made. You couldn't follow the tracks on the ground and keep an eye out for a trap up ahead.

The tracks headed south for a while, then turned east. I could follow the trail myself most of the time, but he turned east while walking the horses over hard, clear rock. Daniel pointed out a few scratches on the hard rock. I never would have seen them.

"They are heading into Oneida territory," Daniel said.

"Is that good or bad?" I asked.

"Mohawks and Oneida are both tribes of the Six Nations," Daniel explained. "It's bad if they come across any Oneida and ask for protection. I know this territory better than he does, so it's good if they don't find any aid to assist them. As soon as I figure out where they're going, we should be able to catch up to them."

We followed the horse tracks for several hours. The tracks turned again and led down a mountain. If they continued east, they could turn south back to Pennsylvania or north to Quebec. I was betting they were heading to Quebec, to Joseph's stomping grounds, but Joseph had managed to stay ahead of us, so he might head south to confuse and lose us.

"There's no forks on this trail," he explained. "It's a long switchback trail leading to the bottom. I've taken it before. It's about five miles long. There's nowhere along the way for them to abandon the trail. I don't know a faster way down. We don't have to follow their tracks, and if we ride hard, we might catch them at the bottom."

"If they go off the trail, and you don't find them again, we might lose them forever," I said. "She's only good to him as a hostage. If he loses us, her life is worth nothing to him."

"I won't let that happen," Daniel promised. "We can go slow and stay on their tracks, staying behind them, or you can trust me, and we can catch up to them."

I was never one for playing it safe, but it wasn't my life we were talking about.

It was Annie's.

Joseph woke Annie up with the toe of his boot against her shoulder. She looked up to see fading stars, and the moon was no longer in sight after dropping below the trees. It must have been early in the morning, not long before sunrise, close to four or five in the morning. He helped her up and walked her over to the tree. He motioned for her to sit down next to the horses with her back against the tree.

Joseph stood among the horses, soothing them with his touch as he whispered in their ears. After calming them down, he stood next to one of the trees, his brow furrowed in deep concentration. He seemed to have the ability to transform himself into a statue, holding perfectly still, not moving. The only movement she saw was the whites of his eyes, moving from left to right.

Suddenly he cocked his head, listening to something Annie couldn't hear. He whistled one of his bird challenges. Three more whistles followed Joseph's initial bird call. Joseph didn't say a word but closed his deep-set eyes and tilted his head pensively. He opened his eyes and nodded to himself as if he'd made a decision. With a hand, he motioned for her to stand. He kept quiet and pointed to the saddle of one of the horses. She stood up and mounted the horse he pointed at. He grabbed the reins of her horse plus the reins of another horse and walked them through the trees away from camp. He kept looking back at the horse tracks on the ground they left in their wake, as if they'd be his doom.

"Horses leave tracks a child could follow," Joseph commented in a low voice.

"If you're worried about the horses, we could leave them behind and walk," Annie offered.

"I would if I were alone, but you're too slow. If I took you off the horse, I think you might slow me down on purpose."

"Why are we leaving your men behind?" Annie asked, glancing back the way they'd come.

"Some of them are dead already," Joseph answered. "The rest will be, come first morning's light."

Annie swiveled in her saddle. "I don't understand."

"You were right about your Thomas," Joseph said. "He's already here and has already killed two of my men."

Annie's heart leapt in her chest but narrowed her gaze at her kidnapper. "I thought you wanted him to come to you?"

"I wanted him to walk into my trap," Joseph bit out, "not turn my own trap against me. I may have made the same mistake the British Captain made when he took your daughters. I thought my men were too good to be spotted, and I underestimated him. I'm starting to believe maybe the scarred one really was raised by a shaman."

"You're leaving your men to face his wrath alone?" she asked.

"They'll buy us time," he said, as if to justify their deaths.

Joseph climbed onto his horse's back and laid his heels into the animal's sides. They didn't ride fast but at a steady gallop. As the sun crested the horizon, the boom of muskets echoed in the valley. Joseph yanked the horses to a stop and looked back the way we had come.

"Where are we going?" Annie asked.

"They'll catch up to us before we can make it to Canada," Joseph said. "We'll ride for the six nations. I'll be welcomed there. If I can find one of the six tribes, I'll be safe."

They turned and started riding down a narrow trail, and as far as Annie could see, extended down the side of the mountain, heading southeast. She knew Quebec was north, so he must be telling the truth. The trail wasn't steep, but a gradual decline down the side of the mountain. It looked like it extended a mile, then backed in on itself, still going down at a slight decline. Looking down the mountain, she could see several trails. The trail switched back several times, so horses didn't kill themselves and their riders falling down too steep of an angle.

After the second switchback and last leg of the trail, Joseph stopped, again pulled on the reins of his horse, stopping the animal. He studied the top of the mountain. Annie realized what he was looking at. High above them on the first leg of the trail was a man on horseback staring down at them. He was too far away to make out, but he wore a black vest. Everything inside Annie exploded.

"Thomas!" Annie screamed, her voice echoing up the mountain.

The man high above, only five hundred yards away by way a crow flies, yet miles behind by way of the horse trail, kicked his horse into a run. Joseph slapped the hindquarters of Annie's horse and kicked his own horse. The wind rushed through Annie's hair as her horse broke into a run. They were on the last leg of the switchback and a field opened before them.

Twenty minutes later, they reached the bottom of the mountain. Annie panted, trying to catch her breath from the rough run. Joseph slowed them to a walk, and they turned around to look back the way they'd come. There was no sign of the Pale Rider, but just as neither expected him to ride down this path yet, they were at the same time surprised he wasn't right behind them.

They sat on their horses in an open field fifty or sixty yards wide. Joseph twisted his head back and forth as if he was searching for something in particular. Spotting something on one side of the field, he looked to the opposite side and again kicked his horse and pulled on her reins. They crossed the open field quickly, and Joseph jumped off his horse before it had stopped. He reached up and yanked her off her horse and onto the ground. She was too shocked to fight back before she was face down in the grass. His face was tight with anger, yet he moved quickly, letting desperation dictate his actions.

She'd never seen this side of him in the week since he'd kidnapped her. He was a hard man, but had never treated her rudely or handled her roughly. The contrary was true – he'd always exhibited a level of patience with her. When she tried to slow him down, he pretended not to notice and pushed her to move faster. He almost appeared to regret forcing her involvement in this matter.

But now, he was a different person as he dragged her to a young but sturdy tree, sharply pushing her back up against the trunk. She kicked and punched at him, but he grabbed her hand and tied a thin strip of leather around her wrist. Then he stepped behind the tree and grabbed her other hand, pulling her wrist together. She stopped resisting when he tied her hands together. Nor did she fight when he ripped the sleeve off her dress. He tied the sleeve around her head, forcing the cloth into her mouth with his grimy finger. She realized he was preventing her from giving any warning. When he was sure she could not free herself or scream a warning, he slapped her horse on the rear, making it break into a run. He lifted his musket from his own horse and slapped its hindquarters as well. The horse raced through the trees as Joseph turned his back on her and ran across the field.

Joseph found a nice spot in a tight grouping of trees. He'd have liked to have done this at night, but it didn't matter. This Thomas seemed as good at fighting at night as Joseph was, so they may as well do this in the daylight.

From his position next to the tree, he had a clear field of sight of the trail leading into the field and of the bait he'd tied to the tree. This time, he was certain this killer's better judgement would be overwhelmed by the sight of his woman bound in plain sight. He'd be an easy shot from this distance. The tree Joseph had picked out was thick enough to shield his body when he stood behind it and had a low branch where he could rest his musket for a steady shot when the time came.

Joseph only had to wait fifteen minutes before his opportunity to finish his mission rode towards him. The man in the black vest trotted down the trail to the open field. Joseph hunkered down low, waiting for the man to ride fully into the clearing. Thomas pulled his horse up short and, scanning the field over, he quickly dismounted from his horse. He turned the horse's body to shield his own while he peered over the saddle, surveying the field. Joseph wouldn't be able to get a good shot off from this distance. He'd have to wait for the man to get closer. When Thomas went to his lady, he'd only be fifty yards away. Even if this Thomas used the horse as a shield, Joseph would get a shot off. If Thomas peeked over the saddle, his head alone would be a big enough target for Joseph to hit. If he didn't, then Joseph would shoot one of the man's legs from under the horse.

Thomas lingered at the end of the trail, no doubt searching for Joseph. Joseph moved back an inch, completely out of sight. He had to wait until he heard the horse steps before bringing his musket up and firing. He'd only get off one shot, so he needed to make it matter.

The horse's hooves started moving. Joseph gave the man a few seconds before exposing himself to take the shot. As Thomas closed in on his woman, Joseph drew back from the tree and raised his musket. Exhaling calmly, he slowly thumbed the hammer back on the musket with three loud, distinct clicks. Moving to the side, he eased the barrel downward, setting the wooden stock on top of the low branch, then he brought the brass plate musket butt into his shoulder. Joseph took careful aim at the horse's saddle, waiting for the scarred one's head to pop up. The scarred one, however, kept his head low. He knew the field was a trap and was keeping his head down to remain protected by the horse. The Pale Rider closed in on his woman, and Joseph knew he needed to do something quick.

Why was he now thinking of him as the Pale Rider and not as the scarred one? That consideration made Joseph grimace.

Shaking the thought from his head, Joseph shifted and aimed for the man's legs. He could take out the legs, then run over as the man tried to stand and kill him with his war club. Joseph's finger caressed the trigger, and for the first time in his life, Joseph felt dread. He knew he shouldn't kill the man with the war club. Instead, he'd reload his musket and kill the man as he continued to hide behind the tree.

Final Chance

Chapter Nine Two Monsters Meet

"Is there any faster way down the mountain?" I asked.

"Just one," Daniel said as he pointed straight down the mountain. "But you're more likely to kill your horse and break your own neck."

I looked down the mountain and knew he was right. There was no way to make it down the mountainside on horseback. After thinking for a moment, I pulled off my vest and handed it to Daniel.

"Put this on," I said. "He'll think you're me. If I don't make it, get Annie back to Valley Forge."

Without question, he took the vest from me and nodded his understanding as he slipped it on over his tawny-brown buckskin shirt. Then I tied my horse to a nearby tree and hoped I'd live to untie him later. Turning my attention to the trail, I studied it to make the best plan possible, given the limitations. The reason the trail switched back several times was that going straight down the hill was too steep. Not a straight drop down, but not too far from it, either. With a deep breath, I leaped off the edge, landing on some loose dirt far below. As soon as my feet hit the dirt, I skidded, then ran non-stop straight down the mountain.

It would've been impossible for a horse to make it down the mountain, but not impossible for a man. Extremely difficult, I knew that now, but not impossible. I ran down as fast as I could manage, letting gravity do the work. My legs moved as rapidly as they could, but they were trying to prevent me from falling on my face more than they were focused on moving me forward. I crashed to the ground several times and rolled more of the distance than I cared to admit. I came to a crashing, dusty stop on the second leg of the trail, but not knowing if they had already passed this point or not, I forced myself to my feet. Brushing clumps of dirt off my legs and chest, I raced forward like a crazed bull down the hill again.

This time, I managed to go a little slower – the incline was not quite as steep – and only fell twice, still rolling head over heels more of the distance than was good for me. My head was spinning by this point from all the rolling. Stopping at the third leg, I stayed low and looked both ways down the trail, but again, didn't see them in either direction.

Taking a deep breath, I pushed off and again charged down the last portion of the mountain. I crashed into a tree on my way down, hitting my head, and my whole body ached from the stones and sticks that battered and bruised me as I went down. I tried to stop myself and gain my composure, but I slipped on a rock and tumbled again. Air rushed from my lungs as my knee collided with a large rock. I pushed my arms out to my sides, trying to stop myself as I slid on my stomach down to the bottom of the mountain, like an airplane landing without its wheels.

Holy fuck. That was a ride. Did I break anything?

I rolled to my back, catching my breath and assessing my bruised body. I didn't think anything was broken, yet. I gazed up at the way I had come. When I launched myself from the top, I thought it was a crazy idea, but now, lying on my back, looking up the way I had come, I realized it wasn't crazy; it was pure stupidity. No wonder Daniel had looked at me cockeyed when I leapt from the edge.

The end of the trail was several hundred yards to my right. With an achy groan, I stood up, and almost dropped back down to my knees. I felt around the skin under my torn pants. Nothing felt broken, but my right knee hurt badly. Lifting up my pants leg for a better look, I counted bruises, cuts, and a deep gash on the side of my knee. Blood seeped from the injury, but it wasn't life-threatening. I moved slowly, testing my leg. Once I realized my leg was going to hold up, I increased my pace to a run, but it was more like a fast, painful limp.

My right leg throbbed with every step, wet with sweat and blood, and the dirt covering me turned into a light covering of mud as I sweat through it. I could see a clearing up ahead where the trail leveled out and entered a valley. Annie was there or would be there soon, depending on if I'd beat them down the mountain or not. After that harrowing run-fall I'd had, I really hoped this half-assed plan worked.

I had to force myself to slow down. Moving away from the mountain and deeper into the woods, I slowly crept from tree to tree. I paused and looked around before I moved to the next tree. A sudden thought struck me, and I pulled out my Thompson pistol to check that it wasn't damaged. It seemed fine. Better than I was, at least.

As I got close to the edge of the tree line, I laid down and crawled to the last tree, grimacing as I moved on my knee. My breath caught in my chest when I saw her. Annie was tied to a tree off to my right. A movement caught my eye – Joseph was running across the field. He was so close, I thought he was running at me at first. He moved right past my view, stopping in the tree line not fifteen yards from me. I couldn't see him but knew where he was.

I want to get closer, but he'd either hear or smell me. Hell, I was surprised he hadn't already magically sensed my presence. Truth was, this guy was too good. I still had no idea how he knew we had been at the last ambush spot. I froze where I hid, afraid of moving now that I was in place. Annie's face was tight, lined and pale with worry. I couldn't imagine what hell she'd been going through this past week. I wanted to run to her. I felt like a piece of crap lying there when I was so close to her.

I had been laying in the brush behind the tree for over fifteen minutes when Daniel came riding down the trail. I pursed my lips – surely, he was going to ride right into Joseph's line of fire. Then he pulled his horse up short. He slid off his horse and put the animal's body between himself and the open field. The top of Daniel's head popped up over the saddle, then disappeared. Daniel was clever, and I didn't think he noticed Annie tied to the tree yet, but he recognized an ambush spot when he saw one.

I focused on the group of trees Joseph was in but had not seen any movement from there yet. Joseph was using Annie as bait to kill me and I was now using Daniel as bait to kill Joseph. Washington was right, Joseph and I were alike. The world did think of us both as monsters, and perhaps the world was right. Daniel's horse moved forward towards Annie, so he must have seen her. He didn't rush to her and remained behind his horse, so he was careful not to give Joseph a clear shot.

A musket slowly stuck out horizontally from behind one of the tree trunks. The red wooden stock and black steel barrel pointed right at Daniel. Aiming my Thompson at the trees, I waited for a chance to kill Joseph. The seconds ticked down painfully slow in my head. I wanted a shot at him but couldn't wait for him to shoot Daniel. I realized I was out of time when the barrel of Joseph's musket tipped downward a few inches. He was going to shoot the only target he'd seen. Daniel's legs.

I could hear my range coach and sniper instructor from years ago standing behind me talking. His voice was powerful and demanding, but also calming.

Breathe, he said in my head.

I took two more deep breaths, holding them in for a two count, then releasing them slowly.

Focus on your sights, the voice said.

I focused on my front and rear sights. I aimed for the wooden stock of the musket. My sights were clear in my view.

Sight alignment, sight picture.

The musket was blurry, but that meant my eyes were focused on the pistol sights. The top of the front sight was parallel with the top of the rear sights. There was equal distance between the front sight and the left and right portion of the rear sight. I was shooting at a two-inch-long target from fifteen yards away.

Now, let the shot surprise you.

I'd been squeezing the trigger with the center of the first pad of my first finger. I pulled slowly. I knew the gun was going to fire at any moment. I kept squeezing oh so slowly and smoothly. Then, as my instructor had ordered, the pistol surprised me when it bucked in my hand.

The barrel of my pistol lifted up and then went back down. Joseph's musket laid on the ground a few yards away, but Joseph himself rose and broke from his hiding spot. He ran through the bushes and between the trees, and he was fast, so fast. I jumped up, holstering my Thompson, and gave chase. He ran hard, and although there were plenty of trees between us, they were spread out enough for me not to lose sight of him. My knee throbbed as my legs pumped, but it was holding up.

I pulled my Tec-9 out and fired twice at his back. The first shot splintered a tree, the next hit nothing. He spun around and pointed a flintlock pistol at me. I rolled to the ground as he fired and came up, firing my pistol. We each somehow missed the other. He ducked back behind a tree and out of sight. I kept moving forward, only not straight at the tree. I shifted to the left as I moved forward. I was only ten yards from the tree when I realized he was no longer there.

I spun around in a full circle, pistol out in front of me, but didn't see him anywhere. Where was he? He had to be here, hiding and waiting. As if he read my mind, he stepped out from behind a larger tree, and with a high-pitched scream of anger and effort, he swung his Mohawk war hammer. The blow was powerful, like a lumberjack trying to down a tree with one swing of his axe.

The round ball of his club chopped at my left side, jarring me as it hit. It was a crippling blow, or would have been, if he hadn't struck my leather satchel hanging at my side. His own hatchet still rested in my satchel, and by the bell-like sound that rang out, I knew his club had struck the steel head of the hatchet, preventing the club from crushing my kidneys. He did knock me back a few feet, and catching my balance, I swung my pistol around, intending on putting three rounds into his chest and ending the fight quickly. He stepped forward, and before I could react, kicked out with his left foot, knocking the pistol out of my hand. Gripping his club with both hands again, he stepped forward and bringing the club over his head and straight down, intending to club in my head. I jumped back and avoided the life-ending swing. His club smacked into the earth, tearing up grass and dirt as I drew my two knives.

The sight of my twin twelve-inch blades in my hands was enough to halt him from advancing on me. He repositioned his club in his left hand, holding it out in front of himself. Then he pulled out his own large, leather-bound knife with his right hand.

His knees were slightly bent, and he started circling me to my right. I countered, circling to my left, ready for him to charge. From his stance and movements, I could tell this wasn't the first knife fight this man had been in. He knew what he was doing and was operating on reflex. Action and reaction without thought. He held his knife in the more traditional blade-up style but appeared a little confused by my boxer stance, holding both blades point down. He had the longer reach with the war club, but the club could also impede his vision if he kept it in front of him like he was. My knives were set for slashing and blocking, but not as effective at stabbing.

He attacked first, launching fast. Stepping in, he poked at my face with the club. I pulled back to avoid the club, and he came in with a knife thrust for the easy target of my stomach. I deflected his knife with the blade in my right hand, then followed up with a slash for his throat with my left. His club collided with my left wrist. He didn't break my wrist, but he knocked the knife out of my hand and rattled my joints.

I only had one knife now, and he came at me in full attack mode, swinging the club with his right hand and the knife with his left. I was forced to block his knife with mine as I kept treading back to dodge the club. On my third step back, I found myself against a small tree. I slipped behind it as his club smacked into the tree with a loud whack. Then I leaped forward, surprising him and slashing his forearm with the knife. My blade bit deep in a rush of blood, and his blade fell from his hand.

Now we were on more equal footing, each of us with only one weapon, his club and my knife. We began circling each other again, with the tree between us this time. My knife was the better weapon for up close fighting, but his club had the longer reach. And *damn,* he was good with that club. Dangerously good. His arm bled freely, but he acted as if he didn't notice. He must have seen me favoring my right knee because he kicked out for it. My knee buckled, and I crumpled, catching myself on the tree between us. His club came down as I was on the ground, and I dived into a roll, coming up on my left leg, knife out front. His club came back in an upward arc, knocking the knife out of my right hand.

As my knife flew into the air and away from me, I did the only thing I had left. I pushed forward and punched him in the face. It wasn't a devastating blow but enough to knock him back a few steps. He shook his head to recover, and I stepped up with a quick one-two jab-punch combo. He spiraled back and started falling onto his ass, but managed to bring his club up at the last minute, crashing into my chin.

My teeth cracked together enough to break one. The sound of him hitting the ground and rolling filled my ears as stars clouded my vision. I stumbled back, creating distance between us. Tears filled my eyes and blood poured down my chin. My vision blurred, but I made out the shape of him rolling backwards and to his feet. He regained himself before I did.

I turned to run, and the predator in him took over, and he gave chase. I knew I couldn't outrun him with my bum knee, so I stopped and spun around, throwing the hatchet I had grabbed from my satchel. The weapon flew through the air, head over shaft, and the steel blade sunk deep into his chest, throwing his upper body backwards as his feet came up in front of him. With a lock of complete shock on his face, he landed hard on his back.

I stood unmoving for a few seconds, waiting for this unbelievable warrior to get back up as he'd done before. My brain couldn't quite reason that I might have actually injured him enough to defeat him.

Straightening my aching body, I limped over to stand above him, looking down. His eyes were open, and he was alive. Still alive! His hands dropped the club and grabbed at the hatchet imbedded more into his side and he was bleeding. He tried to pull the instrument of his death out of his own body, but it was too deep, and he was too weak. His eyes grew wide as recognition showed on his face – he'd been struck with his own hatchet.

"For Ben," I said, panting and holding my side.

"The old man?" he guessed.

"Damn right."

"They were right about you," he whispered.

"And you," I conceded with a nod.

"Will you do a dying man a last request?"

I stared at him for several moments.

"No," I said at last, as I turned my back on him and walked away.

Hobbling back to where most of our fighting had taken place, I found my pistol and two knives. I left Joseph where he laid and headed to Annie. I checked my satchel and found that his war club had not only found the hatchet blade in my man-purse but had also destroyed my smart phone. I bit at my lips – a whole library of information lost to me. Pulling the mangled, broken plastic phone out of the satchel, I quickly buried it in some loose dirt.

As I entered the field, I found Annie standing next to Daniel behind his horse. Daniel rested his musket over the saddle, ready to kill Joseph if he happened walk out of the trees instead of me. Annie broke away and ran towards me. I would have run to her, meeting her in the middle, but I was doing my best not to fall on my face.

She collided into my arms, almost knocking me over. I grimaced and would have fallen over if she'd not also wrapped her arms around me, holding me up. She was crying, and I wasn't surprised to realize I was crying, too.

"Thomas! You're hurt. You're bleeding again."

One of her sleeves had been ripped off her dress and hung around her neck like a necklace. She pulled it over her head and pressed it against my bruised and aching chin. I winced but let her hold it in place. God knew I didn't need to lose more blood than I had. I don't think I had much left.

"Hold this," she instructed.

I grabbed the rag and held it in place. Daniel joined us, pulling his horse.

"Joseph?" Daniel asked with one raised eyebrow, not needing to finish the question.

"Dead," I said. "But he didn't die easy."

Daniel nodded his head as if it's what he expected me to say. I'm sure my appearance was a testament to the battle I'd just fought.

"You realize the loyalists will find someone else just like him to take over and continue his atrocities on the colonists? "

I shrugged. "That sounds like a problem for the loyalists."

Daniel leveled his gaze at me. "I'll let you two talk while I go round up the horses Joseph scared off."

"I see you two have met," I said.

"Not formally," Annie responded, holding onto me. "But he untied me, so I knew he was with you."

"Daniel," I said. "May I introduce Mrs. Annie O'Neil. Annie, may I introduce Mr. Daniel …"

121

I realized I never gave Daniel my last name and he never offered his.

"Daniel Boone, ma'am," Daniel said with a smile on his face and a polite bow. "With the Kentucky militia. A sure pleasure to meet you."

Then Daniel rode off, searching for the two horses while Annie took out my first aid kit. Using my curved needle and medical thread, she stitched up my chin.

"I'm afraid you'll have yet another scar, Thomas," Annie chided me. "I'll keep the stitches tight. It'll be about two inches long, but thin."

She asked after her daughters, and I told her they were safe, though worried about her. "Marie is watching them back at Valley Forge."

Once she set the needle back in the kit, she exhaled, then buried her face into my chest and cried about Old Ben. Annie told me she hadn't had a chance to cry about him since she'd been attacked.

"I love you, Annie," I said, surprising her.

"I love you, too, Thomas," she answered into my shirt.

"Marry me?" I asked.

The words came out of my mouth before I knew what I was saying.

She lifted her face from my chest. "Are you sure?"

"I've never been surer," I told her.

"Yes," she answered. "Yes, yes, yes. When?"

"As soon as we get back to Valley Forge."

We held each other tight, afraid of letting each other go. Neither of us spoke another word for quite some time.

"Where did you meet Mr. Boone?" she asked me when she finally pulled away. "And is he the same Daniel Boone who founded Boonesborough?"

"Who?"

I didn't know what Annie was talking about, where this Boonesborough was, or how she knew of Daniel. I didn't remember ever reading anything about him in history, so he couldn't be anyone famous.

Daniel came back with one of the two horses. We would have to ride double back up the mountain. There was no way I was walking back up.

"I need to get back home," Daniel told me, handing over the reins. "I have a lot of Oneida country to go through to get there. Can you two make it back to Valley Forge without me?"

"Yes," I said. "I think we can manage. But we plan on being married as soon as we get back to Valley Forge, and we'd like for you to be there. You're the reason I was able to find her, after all. Will you come back with us?"

Daniel grinned. "I was never one for missing a party."

Final Chance

Chapter Ten The Wedding

Six days later, it was May 24, 1778. We stood on a hill in the middle of Valley Forge. It was a beautiful day, and the sun was still up but had started to crest over the hills. Golden rays of light slanted across the sky, contrasting with the long purple shadows of the trees. Birds flew overhead, twittering as they called to each other. General George Washington himself agreed to marry us and stood in his full-dress uniform. Lieutenant Colonel Hamilton was behind Washington and to his right, ready to help in any way needed. Annie and I leaned close together, holding hands and facing the general as the girls giggled behind us.

Annie wore a creamy, borrowed dress and had spring flowers in her hair. Washington had kept his promise and promoted me to Lieutenant Colonel. Not that it mattered much to me. I had Annie and the girls now and planned on getting out of this arrangement as soon as I could. I wanted to be the one deciding how I risked my life.

Hamilton had let me borrow one of his uniforms. Though I'd said I would never wear one of the uncomfortable stiff uniforms, Annie had requested it, and I couldn't say no to such a simple request from my new bride. I wore my musketeer sword and both my pistols. Lafayette insisted I not wear the pistols, but I wanted to make sure Annie knew who she was marrying, so I wore them.

Annie's two daughters stood behind us, excitably holding the rings. Lafayette was to my right, looking refined in his fancy blue French uniform as my best man. Lafayette, being the romantic Frenchman he was, let a single tear roll down his cheek. General Washington's wife Martha Washington had arrived in Valley Forge while I was gone. She and Annie became close friends in minutes. Martha stood at Annie's left, holding a silk handkerchief that she openly cried into. With Old Ben now dead, Annie had asked Daniel to give her away. He was honored to do so and told her as much. He had brushed out his buckskin shirt and pants for the event and looked all the wild mountain man he was.

Lafayette and Daniel seemed to get along nicely. Daniel loved to tell stories about himself and his adventures in the wilderness. Lafayette, for his part, loved to listen to them. I really liked Daniel but wasn't sure if I believed his grandiose, larger-than-life and very descriptive tales. Mostly because they were about how fast, strong, smart, or brave he was. Tall tales indeed.

A crowd of about a thousand soldiers witnessed the ceremony. They wanted to say they watched the great General Washington officiate the wedding of the infamous Pale Rider. The fact I'd ridden with Daniel Boone, and we had rescued Annie from the notorious Monster Brant, seemed to only make my legend grow more. Even with the man standing right next to us, I didn't understand why or how Daniel was so popular. Maybe the enigma of Daniel made me like him more.

The camp's blacksmith had melted down some gold coins I had given him and made two simple gold rings. He had carved the moldings into a piece of wood and poured the liquid gold into them. Nothing fancy at all, but he polished them to a smooth shine.

Many people in the world wanted Thomas Nelson dead. Before the wedding, I confided to Annie my real name, and we were married as Mr. and Mrs. Cain. I'd stick to the name Nelson until my

126

part of this war was over, but later, to protect the family, we would go by the last name of Cain. If I was going to spend the rest of my life here, I wanted to do it under my real name. Especially since, after the death of my first wife, I never imagined I'd be getting married ever again.

After the wedding, the entire camp hosted a reception. Food was no longer in short supply – spring had been bountiful – and Washington had paid for several barrels of whisky and beer to be delivered. The General told me the wedding party wasn't solely for us but for his men as well. After a cold, hard winter, they needed something to lift their spirits. He'd been looking for a good reason to reward them and let them blow off some steam, and my wedding served that exact purpose.

Some soldiers played the banjo, guitar, and the fiddle. Dancing broke out in the camp. Men who had not smiled in a year were now laughing, singing, and dancing with one another. Daniel danced wildly, his legs kicking up as he spun in circles and hooted. Annie found herself dancing with Washington, Hamilton, Lafayette, and Daniel. The men were nice enough to let me have the first dance with her, but after that, she took turns dancing with the officers.

Annie was a little hurt when none of the enlisted men asked her to dance until Lafayette laughed and pointed out her new husband was *the* Pale Rider. How could she expect them to take the chance of offending the bringer of death by asking his wife to dance?

A few fights broke out as well, but the General let the men sort those issues out among themselves, so long as none of the men were hurt too badly that they couldn't fight the British. Fighting was a good way to blow off steam.

The girls stayed with Lafayette that night, and Daniel bedded down in Hamilton's room. Annie and I had her room to ourselves. After we consummated our marriage, we remained under the covers, naked, nestled together, and discussed our future. Not the two of us, but the four of us with the girls. Five of us, if we counted Little Joe. We talked about where we would settle down and build our new home together.

Annie wanted to go back and take over Old Ben's farm, and I knew that was what Ben would have wanted. However, I didn't know much about farming and wished I still had my smart phone. I didn't know what kind of farming information was lost when Joseph destroyed it with his war club, but whatever was on there was better than what was in my head. I could and would learn what I needed to know to grow corn, apples, and maybe raise some pigs. With my knowledge of the future, I had no doubt I could find a way to survive. I could breed horses or invent something. Sure, it was cheating when I knew the future, but so what? I had already messed with the future in significant ways, so a few small tweaks couldn't hurt.

One thing my mind kept returning to was how I had learned to make matches in one of my survival classes years ago. Matches weren't invented until the 1820s, so there was a chance I wouldn't mess up the future too much if I produced and sold them forty years early. For the first couple of years, matches would be worth more than their weight in gold, until someone tried to copy them. But it would take years to figure out the process. With my connections through General Washington and Benjamin Franklin, I could obtain a government contract with the colonial army. As I cuddled with Annie, I realized I was going to have to put more thought into this plan. Aden had always been the businessman; I was the muscle. Now I needed to learn how to be both.

Those thoughts would have to wait until the war was over, but we could find a place to settle down temporarily for now. The war wouldn't last forever, and if I survived it, I needed to make plans for my new life. I was forever stuck in this century, which was the deal I had made with Aden when I entered that blue, time-traveling alien ship.

My left thumb reached inside my hand and turned my new wedding ring on my ring finger, causing me to realize my future was here. I hadn't worn a wedding ring in a long time, and the feel of it on my finger was comforting. For the first time in years, life seemed good to me. I knew it wouldn't last, but I held onto Annie, trying to force time to slow down, so I might enjoy this moment as long as possible.

The next morning, I woke up alone in bed. Annie had already snuck out, letting me sleep in. I needed it. Even sitting up in bed made every part of me ache, and my head swam a bit. Twisting and turning to assess the damage, I noted too many cuts and bruises to count, including a large, melon-sized blackish bruise across my ribs. *Were they broken and I hadn't noticed?* I touched them gingerly – only a nasty bruise, not broken. It must have been when I fell down the side of the hill. I was lucky it wasn't worse.

I forced my tired body out of bed and dressed. Not in the uniform Hamilton had lent me but in some new clothes I had bought while in France – a white shirt with only the suggestion of a ruffle and black pants that narrowed at the ankle.

As I walked, or rather limped, through the cabin, I heard Washington was in his office, speaking with someone else. They talked in low voices and the person with him was hiding under a brown cloak. The mysterious person's face was tucked under a hood, seemingly hiding their identity. I could tell the person was male, tall, and skinny, but not much more. One of Washington's spies, no doubt. I headed outside and caught Daniel climbing on his horse.

"You're leaving?" I asked.

"Aye," he answered. He looked shockingly refreshed for a man who'd spent the previous night drinking and dancing. "Past time for me to head back home. Family and friends will be worried about me. They'll be thinking the Oneida had captured me, or worse."

"Thank you for everything you've done for us. I never would have gotten Annie back alive without you."

He reached down. and we clasped forearms in a firm shake. We let go after a few seconds, and he turned his horse and rode off.

I stood there as he rode into the horizon until General Washington's voice called out behind me.

"Thomas, a word, if you please."

I swiveled around to face General Washington, who was standing in front of the cabin alone. Without waiting for an answer, the General walked back inside. I paused, trying to decide what to do. Something inside my head told me this wasn't going to be good for me, but avoiding a problem never made it go away. I followed him into the cabin and then into the library-turned-office. With an open hand, he motioned for me to take a seat across from him at the table. I had expected something like this, but was hoping he would have given me a few days before we talked. Before he had the chance to say a word, I reached into my shirt pocket and removed a piece of paper I had written on last night. I set the paper on the table and with the first two fingers of my right hand, I slid the paper over to him.

"What's this?" he asked with some suspicion in his voice.

"I resign my commission as an officer in the Continental army."

"What's this about?" he asked. "Why?"

"General, I've done everything you've asked of me, including taking the full blame for the assassination of the Prime Minister of England," I told him. "That's after I saved your life and turned the tide of the battle at Saratoga."

"This is true," he said slowly.

"Before I sailed for France, you promised me that when I returned, I could bury the vest and pistols, letting the Pale Rider disappear forever," I reminded him. "I'm now married and have a wife and two stepdaughters I'm responsible for."

"This is true," he repeated. "Your point is well taken, Thomas. However, I believe the war effort still needs you. History is not done with you, Thomas."

I found it strange he chose those words; history was *not* done with me. If he only knew the half of it.

"Maybe not, sir," I said. "But maybe it's time for me to be done with history."

"I need you, Thomas," Washington said in quick words as if they hurt to say. "This country needs you."

"Why me? You have other, competent men."

He raised a hand in supplication. "The Pale Rider. The name breeds fear and doubt in the enemy and inspires courage in our troops. Since your trip to France, your name has grown even larger, if that's possible. Stories of you have spread through the thirteen colonies. The killer of men, thief of ships, and the man who walked into the king's castle, killed his Prime Minister, and managed to escape. Many new young men have joined our cause because of you. Because of your legend. You've proven what one man can do against the British. The young men of this country see themselves as the next possible Pale Rider. They want to be you. Your name is worth a hundred cannons to the war effort, five hundred, a thousand, for God's sake."

I coldly recalled his promise that I was done once I'd killed the Prime Minister. Now he was trying to convince me to stay. "And your promise? What is your promise worth?"

"Quite a bit," he said defensively. "Release me from my promise. Name your price."

I laughed out loud. The general mistook my laughter and turned red in the face. I held up a hand to calm him.

"Forgive me, sir," I said. "I'm not laughing at you. I was thinking about the king of France. Something he told me the day I left Paris. The last thing he told me, in fact."

"What did he say?" Washington asked cautiously, one eyebrow raising higher than the other.

"He said, 'don't be too hard on the General when he pushes for the Pale Rider to kill again.' He said you wouldn't let me bury my guns. At the time, I didn't believe him. I took you as a man of your word."

"I'm sorry, Thomas," Washington said as his downcast eyes studied his hands that rested on the table. "You know what my men have gone through this winter. You know we've lost more battles in this war than we've won. My army is like glass, ready to shatter at the next blow. I'm holding this army together with sheer will power."

I nodded my head, conceding to what he said but did not voice agreement.

"Friedrich Von Steuben has been training the men hard," he said, looking me in the eyes again. "They are starting to act like a proper army. They are almost ready to go against the British and win."

"If that is so," I said in a noncommittal tone, "then go out and kill the British. That's how you win wars. You find, fight, and kill the enemy. You can't win a war sitting here while your food runs out and your men grow old."

"May I remind you, Thomas, coming here to train was *your* idea," he said, not yelling but on the verge of losing his temper. "And a good idea it was. Leaving Philadelphia and coming here is the only reason we're still alive and haven't lost the war already. Besides, I thought this war meant as much to you as it does to me."

I rubbed my hands down over my face. "It does."

"Then why resign?" he asked.

"What is it you want from me now? I'm not a soldier who stands in line, firing shot for shot with the British. That's why I want to resign my commission. I'd rather pick my own battles and decide how to fight them. I work better alone."

"Give me thirty days," Washington said as he stood and leaned on his fist planted against the table. "Name your price for thirty days."

"Thirty days?" I asked. "What can I do in thirty days?"

"As you say, we can't win a war sitting here as my men grow old. I plan on marching from here and taking back Philadelphia. We need a victory, Thomas. We need a victory soon, or people will lose faith. We need to show our men, France, and the British that we can win."

"How?" I asked, leveling my gaze at him.

"General Von Steuben assures me the men can fight and will win if I give him another month to train them. I wish to attack Philadelphia in mid-June. But if we lose, our backs will be broken, and we'll have lost the war. I want a guaranteed victory. Let the men think they won the battle on their own if they wish, but I want an advantage."

I leaned back in my chair and crossed my arms across my chest. "An advantage? What kind of advantage?"

"Fear and suspicion," he argued. "You once told me I could win this war with luck and surprise. I think we've used up all our luck and surprise to get us this far. I want you to go into Philadelphia and cause havoc. Destroy any supplies that you find and kill any officers you can. Let them know the Pale Rider is among them, and they may turn on one another in fear and suspicion. I want them ready to run from Philadelphia before we leave Valley Forge. My men need this victory, Thomas, and I need the battle to be half-won before we march, so we can give them their much-needed conquest."

"You seem to expect a lot from one wanted man running around a city with over ten thousand enemy troops," I said.

"There's your advantage," he said. "Ten thousand of them, plus thousands of civilians. You'll be a needle in a haystack."

I bit at my scabbed lip. He had a point. A group of men would be easy to find, but a single man, even one with a bounty on his head, among thousands, would be harder to locate.

"Ben's farm rebuilt," I told him.

"What?" He pulled his head back in surprise.

"My price," I answered. "You'll inform Congress as soon as Philadelphia is yours that Congress will pay to rebuild Ben's farm. A two-story house, made of brick, not wood, plus a large barn for the horses and a second barn for me, also made of brick and twice as long and twice as wide as a normal sized barn."

"What do you need with a barn that large?" Washington asked.

"Workspace," I answered. "I have plans for after the war."

Washington nodded. "I'll send a letter to congress the first night I'm in Philadelphia."

"Annie and the girls? They'll travel with Martha to my estate until this is done and their new house is built." Then I stood and looked him straight in the eyes. "Thirty days."

Even as we shook hands, I wondered what excuse he'd have next month for wanting me to stay on.

"Martha leaves for home in four days," Washington said. "Spend time with your new wife. You leave for Philadelphia the same day the ladies leave Valley Forge."

"We'll need to pick a date for your attack before I leave so I can prepare for it," I said. "And I'll need a British uniform. I'm not walking around Philadelphia with my vest showing."

Washington squinted at me. "It's the scar you need to worry about."

There wasn't much I could do about that. The vest I could hide, but not the scar on my forehead. Perhaps all my other recent scars would distract from it.

I spent my time over the next few days enjoying my time with Annie and her girls. I told Annie about the deal I'd made with Washington. To say she wasn't happy with it was an understatement. Her eyes jumped from one bruise and scab to the next. The thought of me going into Philadelphia by myself sounded as crazy to her as it did to me. Still, she agreed to take the girls and stay with Martha Washington until it was safe for her to return to the farm. With any luck, that would be soon. I made a note to find out who among the loyalists had informed the British about the farm in the first place. I wasn't going to kill a bunch of civilians, but a face-to-face talk couldn't hurt.

We held a funeral ceremony for Ben so Annie and the girls could say goodbye. Washington buried Ben next to Jonas's grave. The two men never met, but both had helped me when I needed their help. Most of the gravesites had no markers, merely mounds of dirt or a stick in the ground, if they were lucky.

When we had buried Jonas, Lafayette and I had placed a large rock at the head of the grave so we could always find it. We had chiseled Jonas's name into the rock so his parents would know which grave was his.

While I had been chasing after Annie, Lafayette had picked out and carried another large rock over to Ben's grave, matching the one we place over Jonas's. Lafayette had chiseled the name *Ben* into the large rock for us. Molly and Regan then planted blue wildflowers around the rock. Both Jonas and Ben deserved more, but this was the best I could do.

On my last night at Valley Forge, Annie and I reclined in front of the fire, more for light than heat. I had my back to the wall off to the side, and she sat between my legs with my arms around her. We were wrapped under a blanket, our shield against the real world, and I didn't want to let her go.

"How will you do it?" she asked me as she linked her fingers through mine.

I didn't see any reason to keep secrets from her. "The first two attacks will be easy."

"Why the first two?" she asked, glancing back at me. Her hair tickled my nose, and I blew at it gently.

"They have no reason to think I'm back," I said. "They won't be looking for me. The first attack will be a big one. I don't know what I'll do, but I'll make it big."

"Then what? What about the second attack?"

"Every time I've gone to Philadelphia, something bad has happened, and I'd get away, or run away, depending on how you looked at it. The thought that I might stay this time and do something else the next night probably won't occur to them."

"They won't think you're still there the next night?"

"Correct," I answered, nodding. "After the second attack, I think they'll catch on and start looking for me. Maybe go door to door, searching for me."

"How will you hide?" she asked.

"Don't worry," I told her. "I have a plan."

Then I kissed her soundly, ending the conversation.

Hamilton located a captured British uniform for me. He'd acquired several, actually, but only two looked to fit me. One was a common soldier's uniform, and the other was a Lieutenant's. I chose the Lieutenant's uniform – less chance of someone wanting to talk to me if I looked the part of an officer. It was big enough for me to wear my vest under the thick white shirt. A black leather sword belt went over the head and laid across my body, sitting on my hip at an angle. I kept the belt but gave back the sword. I wanted to use my own sword. Since it was a British Cavalry sword, it would fit in with my disguise nicely.

I kept my satchel and placed one of my knives in it, not wanting to walk around with two knives showing. Its twin was tucked at the small of my back. My Thompson still sat in its shoulder holster under the thick red coat. My Tec-9 sat in the black leather belt with a leather loop I'd used before. Originally, it had belonged to the first captain of the HMS Ariel. My cowboy-styled holster would draw attention to me. My boots had been through a lot over the past six months, so I traded them for the finely made black leather boots that came with this uniform. After I made sure the whole uniform fit, I took it off and placed it in a sack. I didn't want to put it on until I got close to Philadelphia. Remembering the most important part of the disguise, I placed the officer's hat and wig into the sack. I then included the black shirt and pants I had asked Hamilton to provide for me. They weren't new, but they didn't have any holes in them, either.

The next morning, after I shaved and dressed, I walked Annie and the girls out to the horses. Martha sat up high on a wagon while General Washington stood on the ground next to her. He was tall enough that he wasn't noticeably lower than she. Several trunks were tucked in the bed of the wagon. Annie and I embraced while the girls climbed up next to Martha. Molly had already tied Little Joe to the back of the wagon and promised to take good care of him for me. I didn't like not taking him with me, but the Pale Rider was known for having a horse with a white stripe on its nose, so he couldn't come with me.

After the ladies rode out from the fortified encampment, General Washington turned to walk into his cabin.

"Gentlemen, with me, if you please," Washington said as he walked away.

Generals Washington, Lee, Steuben, Hamilton, Lafayette, and I sat around the long oak table in Washington's office. This was the first time I had met General Lee. He wore the pinched face of disapproval and didn't seem happy about what we were planning. A pitcher of water and six empty glasses sat on the far end of the table next to an untouched plate of bread and cheese. Washington and Steuben had papers in front of them. Hamilton brought in pen and paper, but Washington gave a slight shake of his head, and Hamilton set them aside. Lafayette had been promoted to Major General since returning from France and now proudly wore his new American uniform. It looked uncomfortable and itchy to me. I needed to remember to include him in the list of Generals from now on. He outranked me now, but I would not let it go to his head.

Washington stood up and took a sip of water. Setting the glass back down on the table, he started the meeting off with a brief vision of his plan.

"Gentlemen, as you already know, General Howe has been relieved. He was replaced by General Clinton, who is now in command of Philadelphia."

He took another sip of water while letting those words set in.

"I've been informed General Clinton may be more inclined to pull out of Philadelphia than General Howe was," Washington added. "I've been persuaded that Clinton needs a hard push.

Thomas will push him off balance for us, then Lee and I will push hard with the army."

The room was quiet as Washington stood at the head of the table, looking down at us. He made a point of looking each of us in the eyes, one at a time.

"Mark my words, gentlemen," he continued. "We'll be taking Philadelphia back. There will be plenty of time for fighting and killing the British after we drive them from the city. The first real battle will be about the city. Today, we need a victory more than we need to kill the British. This is the reason why Thomas will be going in first. To soften them up, as it were. If we can get them to leave the city and head north towards New York, we'll have them on the run. General Lee will ride ahead and attack the enemy's rear while I come from behind with the rest of the men."

"You were informed by whom, sir?" I asked. "And persuaded by whom?"

"It's not important," the general answered.

"It's important to me," I said, staring the general in his eyes. "With all due respect, General, if you want me to risk my ass yet again for you, I'll have an answer."

"Spies, Thomas," Washington said, raising his right hand and then slapping it on the table. "I have spies in General Clinton's camp."

Steuben took the pause between us to stand and attempted to get the briefing back on track. Washington noted the gesture and sat down, turning the conversation over to Steuben.

"The army will be ready for a hard, bloody battle," Steuben explained. "We're working on speed now. If the men move well in line together, they'll move faster as a group. They know what's expected of them, but now we need to work on speed. The maneuvers are simple enough, and the men are getting better at them. If we can move the army fast enough, come time for battle, it will at worse cut down on our losses, and at best, overwhelm the enemy, forcing a retreat."

Lafayette was next to talk, and when Steuben sat down, Lafayette rose, standing proudly in his uniform. He stated that he was going to lead a small force of a thousand men and move closer to Philadelphia. He'd then wait for Steuben to train the rest of the men, but would be ready to attack if there was any change. I think he wanted to act as a blocking force in case I came out, riding with half the British army chasing me. The army was broken into two main forces. The first was under the command of General Lee, and the second was led by General Washington. Washington would be joined by Lafayette, if everything went according to plan.

General Lee didn't bother to stand, only voiced his opinion from his seat. Lee stated the attack was foolish. He promised to do his part but thought we'd lose in an open fight against the British. I flicked my eyes at the complaining man. Something in my gut didn't like him much.

"Gentlemen, please give General Lee and I the room," Washington intoned with heat in his voice and his head bowed, not wanting his anger to show in front of everyone.

The rest of us walked out of the room and out of the cabin. I wondered why Washington was giving command to Lee when Lee didn't believe in the plan. Washington must have had his own reasons for not telling us.

Hamilton had an old wagon with two of the old horses hitched to it, waiting for me just outside of Valley Forge. General Washington had placed spies in Philadelphia, and thus he worried about the British having spies in *his* camp. Lafayette and I rode out of camp on horses, my British uniform stashed in the gunny sack tied to the back of my horse. I think we both rode a little slower than we needed to.

I had faced the British so many times since I had come to this century. I preferred to charge into them, knowing that attacking was better than defending. Also, I had known that my life didn't matter as long as I got the job done. But now, I wanted to live. For the first time since my first wife's murder, I had a *reason* to live. A reason besides killing those that would one day contribute to my first wife's death. And now I was going to ride into a city with at least ten thousand British soldiers. Every one of them knew the price on my head was more than they could earn in a dozen lifetimes.

I shook my head and focused on the trail before us. I had to stop thinking this way and get my head on straight if I was going to survive this.

Chapter Eleven Spies

When Lafayette and I reached the wagon outside Valley Forge, we discovered that, as promised, it was an old wagon with two older horses pulling it. The most beautiful black stallion was also tied to the back of the wagon, a fine animal to be sure. Probably not as smart as Little Joe, but worth a lot more money. A small circle of rocks rested on the ground, surrounding a modest flickering fire. But the fire wasn't big enough to warm us or to cook with. So, what was it for?

"What's with the horse?" I asked Lafayette.

"He's our way in," a man who emerged from the other side of the wagon said, surprising me. My hand went to my Tec-9.

He wore a brown cloak and stood beside the wagon. He hadn't moved, and I hadn't noticed him. He was the same man I'd seen talking to General Washington the morning after my wedding.

I narrowed my eyes at him. "Our way? Who are you?"

"Major Benjamin Tallmadge," the man answered. "And yes, our way. The General has asked me to get you into the city unnoticed."

"I can get myself into Philadelphia fine on my own. I've done it many times," I told him.

"Yes, but there are guards at every entrance now," the man said. "It seems a Captain Brant came through the city three weeks ago. He showed a letter to General Clinton. I spoke to this captain myself. He was an intelligent man to be sure, although I think he hid it intentionally. The General later told me the letter was from George Germain himself. If you didn't know, Germain is the Secretary of State for the American Department. I don't know what the letter said, but the General also told me this Captain Brant said he was there to kill you. Captain Brant never returned. General Clinton is now worried you may return instead of this Brant. As it turns out, he was right. The guards check everyone entering or leaving the city. I'm sure you knew this and have a plan to get by the guards who're looking for you."

"I don't know you," I said in a hard voice. "I'll take the wagon, and you keep the stallion. We part ways from here. I don't want to see you following me. It would be most unpleasant for you."

"I don't know this man, Thomas," Lafayette interjected. "But I've seen him talking to *Monsieur* Washington a few times."

"So have I. But I told you before, Marie, you're the only one I trust. I'll go it alone."

The man reached into his cloak, and my pistol was out and pointed at his chest before his hand could grab whatever was in there.

"Easy, sir," the stranger said. "I have a letter for you in my cloak."

I kept my pistol on him but nodded my head for him to continue pulling out his hand. When his hand appeared from under his cloak, he indeed held a letter. A folded piece of paper, really. With my pistol, I motioned for him to step closer to us. Raising his hands, he walked around the wagon and stallion, stopping about five feet short of us.

"Marie," I said with meaning.

142

Lafayette pulled out his own pistol and thumbed the hammer back as he leveled it at the man.

"*Monsieur,* I believe you are who you say you are," Lafayette told the man. "However, if you move, I'll be forced to shoot you dead."

The man nodded his head and with an amiable smile said, "I believe you, sir. Major General Lafayette, are you not?"

"*Oui,*" Lafayette answered.

Taking two steps forward, I snatched the piece of paper from his hand and took two steps back and out of reach. Opening the letter, I recognized Washington's handwriting.

Thomas, I knew you wouldn't want help and would have refused any offered. The man handing you this letter is Major Benjamin Tallmadge. He's my chief of spies and will get you into the city safely. I know you only trust yourself and Lafayette, but now I ask you to trust the Major and to trust me.

The letter was signed *General George Washington.*

Trust him? That didn't work out so well last time. Washington and his little secrets. Lafayette was fond of Washington, so I kept the thought to myself. The historian from my century who'd told me about General Washington, Dr. Rock, never talked about Washington being involved so deeply with spies. Maybe because in her history books Washington was hung in the streets of Philadelphia in 1777, and he hadn't yet had the chance to use them so readily.

"Fine," I grumbled, lowering my pistol.

The man reached out in a silent request for the letter back. I handed it to him, and he touched it to the fire. He watched it burn, and when it was nothing more than black and gray ash, he kicked dirt on the fire, putting it out.

I gave Lafayette a final hug and whispered in his ear, "If I don't return, kill this man next time you see him."

"*Oui,*" Lafayette whispered back, then smiled at Tallmadge as we pulled away from each other.

I climbed onboard the wagon with my sack, and Tallmadge climbed up next to me, grabbing the reins.

"You'll need to change into the uniform before we get there," Tallmadge said, pointing to my sack.

The fact he knew about the uniform made me uneasy. Since his job revolved around information, I would have to say he was good at his job.

"Let's get going, Tallmadge," I told him.

"Call me, Benjamin," the spy said, holding out a hand.

"Let's get going, Benjamin," I answered, ignoring his hand.

"What do I call you?" Tallmadge asked, letting his hand drop back down as if he hadn't noticed me ignoring it. "I mean, what's your name?"

The spy was collecting information. I guess Washington didn't trust his spy master with all his secrets. Nor did I. He had to know my first name. Half the camp had heard the General or Annie call me Thomas. I figured he was hoping I would give him my last name. What would my last name be worth to a spy master?

I had watched a lot of spy shows as a kid. I knew exactly what this guy was doing. He would act all buddy-buddy with me and try to collect any information he could.

"Call me Lieutenant," I said. "That's the rank of the uniform you already seem to know about."

"You don't trust me?" Tallmadge asked, looking hurt.

I turned away from him to look straight ahead. "Not even a little."

"Maybe I can earn your trust with some information," he said, smiling.

"Like?" I asked, shifting towards him again.

This guy used information like it was currency to spend or trade with.

"You should know that after Captain Brant left the city, General Clinton sent a rider out with a message," Tallmadge said. "I was there when he handed the dispatch to a rider. I don't know what was written or who it went to, but he told me it was added assurance in case you returned."

That's odd, I thought.

"And?" I asked.

"And," he continued, "just a few days ago, he had a meeting with a man, someone I had never seen before. He held himself and acted like a soldier but didn't dress like one. General Clinton told me that this man was his added protection against you."

I rubbed at my chin. "Did he give a name?"

"I'm afraid not," he answered. "I didn't want to ask and bring suspicion to myself, but I thought you should know."

"Have you ever heard the name Testa?" I asked.

"No," he said. "Is that who you think this man was?"

"Maybe," I said more to myself. "Or someone that Mr. Testa sent to kill me. What did he look like?"

"English," he said. "Your age, more like a hunter."

"If you see this man again, point him out to me," I instructed.

Great. Maybe Testa is importing hunters to America to kill me. I let the topic drop but kept thinking about it as we continued down the road.

Tallmadge stopped the wagon about a mile out of Philadelphia, and I changed into the British uniform Hamilton had given me. Tallmadge didn't like the wig. He was afraid the guards would ask me to remove it. He walked over to the rear wheel of the wagon. Reaching under the wagon, he scraped some axle grease from the wheel axle. He held out his hand as if offering me a gift. Tallmadge told me to put it in my hair and to part my hair on the left side instead of the right. He smeared the grease into my hand and then produced an ivory comb from his cloak. With my hair parted to the right, my scar was covered. Why had I not thought of that? How many times had I been forced to wear a wig for no reason?

When I handed the comb back to him, he held up a hand and told me to keep it. He was right; I might need it again.

We rode right up to the guards in front of the city, behind a line of people on foot, on horses, or in wagons, waiting to enter. The soldiers searched every one of the men and recorded the names of the men in the twenty-five to forty age group. Tallmadge drove the wagon around them to the head of the line. The guards stopped what they were doing and focused their attention on us.

"Why are you drawing attention to us?" I asked under my breath.

My hand started to move towards my pistol.

"I'm doing what they'd expect me to do," he answered in a tight whisper. "Stay your hand or you'll get us killed."

My hand froze halfway to my pistol as five soldiers walked up to us.

"What's all this about, Benjamin?" one of the soldiers asked, lifting his arm and pointing the way we had just come. "Get to the back of the line."

"I have the general's new horse," Tallmadge said, jerking his thumb at the black prized stallion. "Isn't he beautiful? General Clinton won't want to wait for him. Best you let me and the Lieutenant pass so we can deliver him."

The soldiers saw my rank and saluted me. I returned their salute with a bored look on my face. The soldier talking was a sergeant.

"Forgive me, sir," the sergeant said. "I don't know you and have my orders."

"Carry on, Sergeant," I ordered.

"The general ordered Lieutenant Smith here to pick up the horse with me," Tallmadge said, clapping me on the back. "I guess he didn't trust me with that much money."

The sergeant motioned towards his hat with his right hand. I looked at him until he made a coughing noise. I realized what he meant and removed my hat. He was looking for a scar, but it was well hidden under my combed-over hair. He might have noticed if he was really looking. But he gave me a cursory once-over and saw what he expected to see, or in my case, he didn't see what he didn't expect to see.

"Begging your pardon, sir, but could you please step down from the wagon," the sergeant said, intending to search me. "Like I said, we have our orders."

I started to climb down when Tallmadge quickly but surreptitiously grabbed my arm, stopping me.

"Right so, Sergeant," Tallmadge said to the redcoat. "Right so. Orders and all. But the general is waiting. Could you please send one of your men to General Clinton and let him know we'll be along with his new prize stallion as soon as you're done molesting me and the Lieutenant?"

The sergeant thought about that for a heartbeat before stepping back and looking hard at the black stallion. He stepped back again and waved us through.

"Hurry up, Benjamin," the sergeant said, waving his hand for us to pass by him. "Don't keep the general waiting."

Tallmadge slapped the reins, and the horses pulled the wagon forward. We rode through the busy streets of Philadelphia, packed with people and wagons. The two- and three-story red and brown brick buildings crammed tightly together, fighting for space in the ever-growing city.

"The general will be at his headquarters," Tallmadge said. "He really is expecting the horse, so I'll go straight there. Where will you be?"

"I don't know yet," I lied as I jumped down from the wagon with my sack.

"One last piece of advice, Thomas," Tallmadge said as he leaned over the wagon seat, confirming he did, in fact, know my first name. "I didn't suggest this to Washington because I knew how he'd react, but don't kill General Clinton. Kill anyone else, but not him."

"Why not?" I asked.

"If you kill him, who will order the British to leave the city?" Tallmadge asked.

I nodded my head in understanding. I didn't like or trust this man, but I had to admit between the axle grease idea, getting me in the city past the soldiers, and now pointing out what I should have already planned on, he was useful. In truth, I *had* planned on killing Clinton first. But Tallmadge had made a good point.

I turned and walked back the way we came as Tallmadge smacked the reins on the horses. When the wagon was out of sight, I turned around and headed towards the harbor. I didn't want Tallmadge to know which way I was really heading. As I headed down to the harbor, I took notice of the city and where the officers and soldiers were staying. The soldiers were housed everywhere. According to a nice older lady at one bakery, Clinton's command staff resided at one of the biggest and nicest inns that Philadelphia had to offer. She gave me the name and told me how to get there. I was getting hungry, so I bought a couple loaves of bread from her and placed them in my sack. I stopped at a smaller inn and ordered food. After two bowls of a fish stew, I continued towards the harbor.

The entire harbor was ringed by soldiers, two soldiers every hundred yards. They were ensuring I didn't get into the very ring I was now in. On the beach and away from the piers, I found what I was hoping to find. The HMS Sandwich. She was or had been used as a floating battery in the middle of the harbor – a huge ship with three decks of cannons. She looked like she'd gone through hell, which I knew for a fact she had. I expected her to have been stripped clean of her ninety guns, but I could still see cannons in some of the cannon ports.

The Sandwich had tried to sink us when we stole the HMS Ariel. Forty-five of those guns had fired at me and the Ariel. Six of those cannons had hit our ship and killed a dozen of my men. If a couple more of those cannons had hit our ship, the floating battery would still be in the middle of the river, and it would have been us that had been sunk.

Her crew was forced to beach her or sink to the bottom of the river after I had exploded several barrels of gunpowder at the waterline. The barrels had been placed in a rowboat and tied to the anchor's thick hemp rope. The explosion had ripped an enormous hole in the front of the ship. I was amazed that the captain and crew kept her floating long enough to run her onto shore.

She now sat like a gigantic beached whale. Her ass sat wet in the water and her bow was beached dry in the sand. Being half in and half out of the water, the British had no way of stripping her of everything. She sat on the shore, canting to the left, with her port side leaning down and her starboard side tilted up. It was only a ten-degree angle, but enough to notice. In the end, they'd left her here to rot like a bloated carcass. The hole I had blown into her was more than wide enough for me to walk through. The back end of the bottom deck was still flooded, but the front end was dry enough for me to walk without getting more than my boots wet.

The hull was empty of its cargo. Only water sat in it now. Either the British had taken everything from it, or the ocean claimed it when the ship started flooding. I had learned the hard way that the ocean, like a vengeful God, had a way of taking what it thought it was owed. The ship was dark, but several holes in the sides let in enough light to see. It gave the dead ship a haunted and eerie look, which explained why no curious kids were playing in it.

I ascended the first set of stairs and searched the ship. The British had not bothered to pick the ship completely clean. The magazine was still filled with the large barrels of gunpowder, but someone had come back to take the pistols, muskets, and swords. It was apparent that the British had reclaimed everything light enough to carry. What food I found was rotten and reeked of decay. Rats and seagulls were now the ship's only crew members.

On the top three decks, I found the cannons still in their slots. A few had been knocked over, either by the explosion or the beaching of the ship. Cannons could be lifted off the ship with pulleys, but with the ship half in the water and half beached, they couldn't load them onto shore or another ship. Most of the cannon balls had been taken, but I also saw a few tucked into the corners where some of them had rolled.

I entered the captain's quarters and found two moldy hammocks hanging from the rafters. The captain's desk was empty, so he must have returned to remove his property. Several seagulls had built nests in the rafters.

I decided this would do nicely as a place to hide and sleep. I also had a few plans for those cannons. Plenty a gun powder and enough cannonballs laid around, but I needed to get my hands on some fuse. What fuse I had located sat in seawater, soaked, and of no use to me. A cannon ball was nothing more than a big bullet without the fuse. Cigar shaped fuses were stuck into the cannonballs and ignited when they were fired, turning them into bombs.

I returned to the first set of stairs I'd climbed and pulled one of my two remaining grenades out of my satchel. I had brought some string with me this time and tied the grenade to the banister at the top of the steps. Taking another string, I tied one end to the pin in the grenade and strung the string across the stairs, knee level, securing the string to the railing. This would give me plenty of warning if anyone came up the steps.

I took some time going through the ship's three decks and inspected the cannons on the starboard side. Two or three on each level laid on their sides. Weighing about sixteen hundred pounds each, I wasn't turning them back over by myself. Of the remaining thirty-eight cannons on the starboard side, only a few were loaded and pushed forward into the ports, locked into place. I had seen the cannons loaded many times during my voyage to and from France, so I knew how to do that part. I spent the rest of the day using the gunpowder that I'd found to load thirty-eight cannons. I set a cannonball next to each cannon as I went. I'd load the cannonballs after I got my hands on some fuses.

Pushing them forward and aiming them was going to be the hard part. They were tied to ropes that went through two pulleys so men could pull them back into place, but that was a two-man job, and I was by myself. I could run the ropes to the pulleys leading to the opposite cannon across the ship, and that might help. Four pulleys were better than two and would make the work half as hard, but I was still pulling them up at a ten-degree upward angle. Gravity was not going to be my friend in this endeavor.

I didn't have a target yet, but I did have a basic understanding on how to aim a cannon. After all, they shot in a straight line. It was the elevation to distance that I was unsure of and worried about. The way the ship was beached, cannons on the starboard side pointed north and a little west, basically, along the beach line. The only actual targets were the piers and ships docked to them. I already knew from personal experience that different ships would be tied to the pier for loading or offloading every day. Using my range finder, I determined the pier was nine hundred and sixty yards from the ship, well within range of the cannons.

If I still had my smart phone, I could have looked up how to determine the elevation of a cannon for any known distance. Joseph destroyed that option for me with his war club, not to mention he almost destroyed my kidneys. I had seen it done, but had never aimed one of the cannons myself. Wheels fastened under the cannons to raise or lower the elevation. I didn't know how high to raise it for any given distance. Plus, when I did have a target, the cannons would already be at a ten-degree upward angle to begin with, due to the tilt of the ship.

By the time I finished loading the cannons, the sun had mostly set and the sky was dark gray. And I was tired. I went back to the captain's quarters. Setting my sack on the floor and taking off my coat, boots, and sword belt, I climbed into one of the mildewy hammocks. No one was going to look for me on this dead abandoned ship. I set the alarm on my watch to wake me at seven in the morning. I wasn't sleepy, but I was tired and knew sleep would take me soon.

General Washington wanted me to run around killing officers as soon as I got here, but that was not going to happen. I had at least two weeks before my planned attack and getting myself caught was not going to help anyone.

The next morning, I dressed in loose-fitting clothing and worked on the cannons again. One by one, I used four sets of pulleys to pull the cannons into place, chalking the wheels so that the cannons didn't roll back. By midday, I had pulled the cannons on the top deck forward and into place. I had also drunk the water in my two waterbags and ate my bread.

That afternoon, I needed a break and wanted to scout around the city anyway, so I changed into my British uniform again and headed into the city. The streets were busy this time of day, with soldiers and civilians. I stopped a young soldier who looked to be seventeen or eighteen years old. He about crapped himself when he noticed I was a lieutenant.

"Where will I find General Clinton?" I asked the young man.

"There, sir," he answered, pointing behind me.

I turn to see he was pointing at Independence Hall, the birthplace of the United States. I should have guessed that since it was the largest building in the city, the state building for the colonists and the former headquarters of General Washington. I walked over to the large, red brick building and its towering clock with confidence, like I belonged there.

Checking the clock made me think of the first time I had met General Washington. We had used that clock to time my distraction and his retreat from the city. A group of officers walked up to the front door, and I fell in behind them as if I were one of them. The front door was an ordinary, single wooden door held open by a soldier. The group of officers strolled through the door without so much as acknowledging the soldier holding it open for them.

Walking into the hall was like walking into chaos.

This was the second time I had been here in this building. The first time was right after a British attack to kill General Washington. That time, injured and suffering men were scattered everywhere. Yet even that scene, with those mutilated men laying on the hard wooden floors where they'd fallen or sitting with their back to the wall waiting to be attended to, seemed to have more order and purpose than what was going on here and now. Men marched with purpose from one office to another, like salmon swimming upstream. Messengers ran around, delivering messages from one department to another. Names were etched onto different doors for the higher-ranking officers. I had to push my way through a tight throng of men, a single boat going against the current in a sea of red coats. I grabbed a few documents off one of the desks with an empty seat behind it. The documents themselves appeared unimportant. A quick look showed they were requests from different inns wanting to be reimbursed for rooms and food eaten by the British troops.

At the end of the long, busy room was the assembly hall, which held a large desk on a podium facing outward and a skinny British officer standing behind it. He had an uncomfortable look to him, with his long neck, protruding Adam's apple, and sharp nose. His uniform was so baggy on him he looked like an awkward child wearing his father's uniform. His thin, bony wrist poked out of the oversize sheeves of his coat as he held a paper in his abnormally long, thin hands and fingers.

I had no doubt I could have broken the man's wrist just by squeezing it hard. He held a piece of yellowish paper in his hand and was reading it aloud to the room. His voice was high-pitched and irritating. A dozen desks faced him in two rows of six and formed in a half circle around him. At each of the desks sat two more men who seemed to be writing down what he was reading. The man standing in front of the larger desk read orders and directed they be sent out to the commanding officers in the area.

At least no one notices me.

Turning and walking to my left, I walked up the steps to the next floor. Less commotion disturbed the second floor, but I didn't see anything that might have been General Clinton's office. I continued around the landing and went up to the next floor. On the third floor, I found what I was looking for. A line of officers sat in rickety wooden chairs, waiting to be seen by General Clinton. As one officer would walk out of the office, a voice from inside would yell for the next officer to enter. As the next officer smartly stood up and walked into the office like he had a stick up his ass, the remaining officers would also sharply stand up, just to sit back down one chair closer to the door. It was mind-numbing to watch them.

I walked past the office and noted a major sitting at a desk. He was tall but not large, and his coat hung from a peg on the wall. Behind him was an open door that led to a larger office. The officer I had seen walk into the office now stood tall in front of a man sitting at his neat, oversized desk. The man behind the desk spoke while reading a report in his hand, but never bothered to look up at the man he was talking to. That had to be General Clinton. The major had to be his personal assistant, or one of them at least.

Turning back the way I had come, I headed back down to the first floor and out the same wooden door I had entered. I made it about five steps before I was stopped in my tracks. Tallmadge stood in the courtyard, off to the side, talking to several officers. We locked eyes for a heartbeat, but it was so quick the three British officers never noticed his diverted attention. I walked to the side of the building, keeping Tallmadge in my view. I was leaning my back against the brick wall, pretending to read the documents I had swiped from the empty desk.

Tallmadge laughed, flashing uneven teeth, and slapped one of the officers on the back as they walked away from him. He worked his way over to me with that broad smile on his face. The same smile he wore a minute ago talking to the real British officers.

"Lieutenant," he called out, raising a hand to me in greeting. "How did you know I'd be here?"

"What I know might surprise you," I lied, pushing off the wall to stand straight.

I wasn't going to admit that I didn't know he was going to be here, and I wasn't going to tell him why I was at Independence Hall.

"I'd expected the bodies to start piling up by now," he said through his smiling teeth as he watched me roll up the papers in my hand. "You've been here almost twenty-four hours and, as far as I can tell, you haven't killed anyone yet."

If he was trying to compliment me, he'd failed. "You worry about your job, and I'll worry about mine." I tapped the now rolled up papers against his chest.

"General Washington will be disappointed if you don't start doing your part."

I wanted to tell him to shut the fuck up and mind his own damn business, but I needed him. "I need you to get something for me."

"Very well," Tallmadge responded with a subtle sigh. "What do you require?"

"Fuse," I told him. "Cannonball fuse."

He nodded his head. "That's easy enough. How many?"

"I don't know yet. Forty should be more than enough."

"Very well," he said again. "Anything else?"

"I also need cannon fuse for the cannons," I said.

He raised an eyebrow. "How much fuse exactly?"

"A thousand feet would be grand. Uncut rolls. The longer the better. They come in hundred-foot strips if you can manage to get them before they're cut smaller."

"A thousand feet?" he asked, eyes wide, smile gone as he forgot himself and let his true expression show. "My God, man! Do you really need that much?"

"Can you get it or not?" I asked, ignoring his question. "You said you wanted to earn my trust. This is your chance."

"I can get you fuse," Tallmadge said, regaining his composure and restoring his fake smile. "Yes. But not that much."

"How much can you get?" I looked around to make sure no one was close enough to overhear us.

"Two hundred feet," he said, lowering his voice. "Maybe three hundred. But that's pushing it. The more I take, the sooner the quartermaster will notice it missing."

"Fine. Get me as much as you can. The more the better."

"Anything else you require?" he asked sarcastically, taking off his hat to keep his hands busy.

"Yes," I answered. "Now that you mentioned it. I have a riddle I need you to answer. Three riddles, actually."

His face twisted up. "Riddles? What kind of riddles?"

"If I wanted to fire a twelve-pound cannon nine hundred and sixty yards, how much elevation would I need to raise the cannon?"

He gave me a flat look. "And the other two riddles?"

"Same question, but for eighteen- and thirty-two-pound cannons."

"Where are you going to find cannons to fire?" he asked.

"I'm going to capture another ship from the pier," I lied, still not fully trusting him. "I'm going to open fire on one of the ships in the harbor."

He grabbed my arm with his left hand, his hat still in his right. "That's madness."

"Can you get me what I need or not?" I asked. I reached over, grabbed his hand, and removed it from my arm.

"Thomas, you don't need fuse to set off a cannon," he informed me. "You can use black powder and just ignite the powder. I don't think the navy even uses fuse for cannons on ships. I think you only use them for cannons on land."

"I'm aware of all that," I told him. "I'll be using the fuse as a delay."

He shoved his hat back onto his head. "Meet me at the intersection where I dropped you off. In three days. Noon. No way for me to get that much fuse before then. But your riddles will be easy enough to answer."

"Fine," I said. "In three days. How do I contact you if I need something else?"

"I'm here almost every day," he said, gesturing to the courtyard. "You can always find me here around this time of day."

He turned and walked away from me, heading into Independence Hall. I went to a nearby inn and ordered some lamb stew with corn and bread. I also refilled my waterbags at a city water pump. The pump was in the center of town for everyone to use, but the water looked clean enough and tasted good.

On my way back to the ship, I stopped at a general store of sorts. The large, painted wood sign in the front window read, *Gibbe's Store*. Opening the door, I entered and saw the gentleman who I assumed owned the place speaking to two customers. He wore a full-length brown leather apron. He paused long enough to look up at me with a smile.

"Good day to you, sir," he called out to me, with a friendly wave of his hand, before continuing his conversation.

I nodded my head and as I walked past them, I overheard the owner saying he intended to move his store and family out farther west. One of his customers, a younger man, seemed to agree with him, while the other customer, the younger man's wife, was shaking her head. Her refined brown dress clung perfectly to her curves, so I think she preferred the creature comforts of the city life.

Walking through the store, I started picking out a few items that I might need. A solid plan hadn't fully formed in my mind yet, but I knew one of my first targets was going to be the warehouses filled with supplies. Burning them down appealed to me, as long as I didn't get caught.

I picked out three coils of rope, several clay jugs of lamp oil, and a small metal tub that I thought might be used for washing clothes. Business must have been slow, because the owner appeared excited to see me come back to the counter with the items. Some dried beef jerky sat in a glass container on the counter, and I told him I'd buy all the beef jerky he had. Not the best diet, but it would last and was a good source of protein. He tallied the price for my items and placed everything into the metal wash basin.

I pulled out my coin to pay when I noticed a section of knives on the counter. Looking them over, I selected the largest one. It was as long as my two knives, but not as finely made. The cherry wood handle had been sanded down to a smooth finish. It looked sharp enough and had a fine point to it, so it would do for what I wanted it for. The owner smiled when I asked him to include the knife in the tally. I soon realized why when he gave me the new amount. The knife alone cost more than everything else in the wash basin. He noted the look on my face and explained that the knives were hand made here in the city by a local blacksmith. I replaced my wide-eyed look with a smile, then paid the man and left the store, heading back to the docks.

When I returned to the ship, I first checked on my grenade to make sure it was still in place, trip wire and all. I moved to the captain's quarters, where I set down my groceries and changed out of the uncomfortable British uniform. A few hours of daylight remained, so I changed into my soft cotton garments, the kind of lightweight garments a fisherman or sailor might wear. Now that I was more comfortable, I went to work on the cannons. I had moved half of the cannons on the second deck into place by the time the sun started to descend into the cityscape horizon.

Putting my British uniform back on and making sure my hair was combed in place, I headed back to Independence Hall. My Tec-9 was still in the leather loop on my sword belt, and I screwed my suppressor onto the end of the barrel.

I didn't want the sentries at the doors seeing me go into the Hall, so I skulked around to the back side of the building. A window to an empty office was open a few inches, and after looking around and making sure no one was watching, I pushed it open and climbed through it. I landed quietly in a small office with only one desk. Opening the door and walking out of the office, I only saw a few people milling about, getting ready to leave for the night. No one paid any attention to me.

I went up the stairs to the third floor. The door to General Clinton's assistant's office was still open and flickering yellow lamp light shone through the open doorway and danced on the worn floorboards. I figured that the general's assistant had to be the kind of man who was first to arrive every morning and last to leave every night, and it seemed I was right. I stepped into the office and saw him leaning over his desk, busy writing. The door behind him was closed, so the General was most likely at home in bed by now.

The major looked up at me and opened his mouth to speak when I shot him in the chest. His whole body jerked back, then his head fell forward, landing on the desk. He knocked over the ink bottle and black ink spilled onto the floor. His hand opened, and the pen dropped onto his desk. I watched the pen roll across the desk and off the edge as the back of his shirt soaked up blood from the exit wound.

Tallmadge had advised me not to kill the general. He didn't say I shouldn't kill the general's right-hand man.

I wanted to be out of here as quickly as possible, so I opened the door behind the dead major and headed into the general's office. I didn't bother looking for plans, maps, or orders. I strode up to the desk, and drawing my newly bought, locally made knife from behind my back, I slammed it down, point first and into the center of the general's desk. A dead major who was the general's assistant and a knife in the center of the general's desk would get my message across. I'd let his own imagination do the work for me.

Blowing out the lamp that the major had been using, I left the office, closing the doors behind me. I stopped before the doors fully closed – something in the office had caught my eye. Going back in, I returned to the desk and picked up a white candle that was stuck in a flat brass candle holder. The holder was the size of a saucer for a teacup and had a small handle for carrying. A spark of inspiration lit inside me. Candles were sometimes used as a long fuse. I could use it to burn down the warehouses and, at the same time, make sure I was well away before the fire was noticed. I slipped the candle in one pocket and the small brass holder in the other.

On the far side of the desk was a flint and iron. Reaching over the desk and avoiding the sticky blood and the black ink, I grabbed the flint and iron. I tucked them in a pocket as well. Finally, I left, walking back down to the first floor and right out the front door. The soldiers might see me leave but only my backside and not my face. I wore my stupid looking hat, so they'd just see another officer leaving the building for the night.

I figured this would cause a big enough shit storm when the general found his dead major and my knife in the morning, so my work for now was done. I headed back to the ship to get some sleep. As I walked in the sand down the beach, a torch near the HMS Sandwich came into view. I slowed my pace, trying to see who it was and what they were doing. The torch wasn't bouncing up and down in the air, so whoever was holding it wasn't walking. I didn't bother with my night vision; the torch would have made them useless.

What are they doing?

I moved closer silently in the sand with no branches or dead leaves to step on and give me away. Two men stood at the bow of the ship, peering into the massive hole. They kept sticking their heads in the hole with the torch but seemed unable to step into the ship.

"I'm telling you its haunted," one scared voice said.

"Don't be a child," a deeper, older voice answered.

"The souls of those that died are stuck here," the first voice said. "That's what happens when the Pale Rider kills you. Your soul is tied to where he killed you."

Were these guys idiots or children? The stories that were spread about me seemed to get worse and worse, like a bad game of telephone.

Wait, I'm the one who started that rumor, nine months ago. I guess it spread.

I was right behind them now, inside the circle of light the torch put out. They were oblivious.

"Let's look around and see if anything valuable was left behind," the deeper voice said.

"It was stripped clean," I answered.

They jumped in the air and spun around at my voice. The scared one landed holding the torch in front of himself like a sword.

The older one with the deeper voice pulled his bayonet from his belt and held it like a knife. Seeing I was in a lieutenant's uniform, they came to attention and saluted me. The one with the torch brought it back up high, and the older one put his bayonet back into its sheath.

"Relax, lads," I said, returning their salutes. "What are you men doing out here?"

"We are off duty, sir," the scared one spat out as fast as he could.

"Some of the lads back at the inn were saying that the ship was haunted," the braver one of the two said. "They say that ghosts guard the treasure that the crew left behind."

I threw my head back, laughing loudly, trying to make it sound as real and natural as I could.

"Lads, have you ever in your life known the Empire to leave gold, money, or any type of treasure behind?"

They looked abashedly at one another with "oh yeah," expressions on their faces. I needed to get them away from the ship, and I hoped to get them to leave without killing the two morons.

"This ship *is* haunted," I told them. "I've heard the ghosts myself. But they aren't guarding treasure. They attack anyone who goes on board their ship. That's why the admiral chose to leave her here, discarded, rather than repair her."

"Truly, sir?" the scared one asked.

"Truly." I nodded.

"I heard they left it here like this because it wasn't salvageable," the braver one said.

"I'm sure its sea-worthiness, or lack thereof, had some part in the decision," I said.

"Begging your pardon, sir," the braver one continued, pointing at me. "What are you doing out here, so close to the perimeter, this late at night?"

Well, shit. I didn't have a good answer to that. I'm sure I could have thought of a suitable answer if I wasn't under pressure and given a minute to think about it. As it was, the braver, and evidently smarter, of the two was now looking suspiciously at me.

He then started glancing around the beach when he noticed I was alone.

"You caught me," I said. "I'm the Pale Rider."

They laughed together until they noticed I wasn't joining them. Their laughing slowed and then tapered off as they realized the situation had shifted and something bad was now happening.

Awareness dawned on them, and they understood I wasn't joking. The three of us staring at each other, bodies tensed to move, like we were in an old western gun fight. The only sounds were the low waves breaking against the ship's decimated hull, and the surf lapping into shore. Gentle waves rushed at our boots near the boat. The braver soldier moved first, grabbing his bayonet again. The younger one dropped the torch on to the sand and brought his hands up as if we were going to box.

Poor, naïve fools.

I had been in enough knife fights in the last six months to last me a lifetime and was in no mood to box anyone. I unceremoniously drew my Tec-9 and in a very unjust and inequitable manner shot them. They both died without any real chance of ever winning or surviving this encounter. There was no honor to be earned in this act or glory to be found. They laid before me, face down in the wet sand, boots in the cold water, with only me there to see them die or hear the quiet *thunks* of my Tec-9. It was a shitty ending to a long night in the middle of a bloody war. Fairness wasn't a word that I could afford to have in my vocabulary, and I wasn't sure how I felt about that.

No, that wasn't true. If I was being honest with myself, I knew I was fine with it.

I dragged their bodies, one after another, into the ship and stowed them out of sight. It took time, but I managed to get them to the very back of the ship. I hoped they hadn't told their friends that they were coming to pilfer the ship, looking for valuables. Shooting them left me with a pit in my stomach, and I didn't relish dealing with anyone else who might come snooping.

Setting my satchel on the floor next to my gunny sack, I emptied my pockets of my ill-gotten booty onto the captain's abandoned desk. I slipped off my coat, boots, and sword belt. When I climbed into one of the hammocks, my thoughts ran wild with what tomorrow would hold. I was sure no one was going to look for me here, at least not tonight. I set the alarm on my watch to wake me at seven in the morning, in case I was more tired than I realized. Then I fell asleep.

Final Chance

Chapter Twelve   Fear and Suspicion

I woke up the next morning to the sound of water slapping against the ship and seagulls crying. Sunlight burst through the open windows along with a slight breeze and the smell of briny water. The smells and sounds of the river assailed my senses as if I was outside. I had opened the windows in the back of the captain's quarters the night before in case I needed to make a quick getaway. If the bottom of the ship was sitting on the sand, the water would still be plenty deep enough that I could jump out and survive the fall.

Taking a few minutes to stretch my muscles, I realized they were sore from the work the two days before. Non-stop hard labor that I hadn't done in a long time. I grabbed my Tec-9 and did a security sweep of the ship. When I was sure the ship was secured and I was still the only person on her, I began working on the cannons again. It was long, hard work. My back, legs and arm muscles burned with lactic acid, the deep ache from the previous day's work building until my back screamed each time I bent over.

Three days of pulling ropes and moving cannons was harder than I'd first thought it was going to be.

I finished with the second level of cannons by midday drenched in sweat and didn't think I was going to be able to do anymore work until my muscles had time to rest and recover. I also wanted to head back into the city and see what kind of fruit was borne from last night's efforts.

I looked a mess with dirt, sweat, and grease caking on my hands, face, and clothes. I made sure my hair was combed over my scar but didn't clean up or change clothes. My shirt was plastered to my skin, thanks to the sweat that poured out of me and the rising humidity. I had drunk through my water bags again and needed to refill them. I'd been dressing as a British officer the last three days and had to remind myself not to get cocky. With the practice of dressing like one of them, I knew the British would learn many of my habits. Tallmadge knew my British disguise, and I still didn't trust him. With only my Tec-9 tucked behind my sweaty back and under my grimy shirt and a hand full of coins in my pocket, I left the ship dressed as a common sailor.

As I walked along the beach, I didn't see anything out of the ordinary, and no evidence of my encounter the night before. Three small fishing boats and two canoes were tied to anchors on the beach between the HMS Sandwich and the docks. I had seen some fur traders in the city and assumed the canoes must have belonged to them. A pack of dogs ran past me and down to the harbor, hoping for a handout of scraps from some generous person.

Unaccustomed to walking bare-footed, I relished the warm sand under my feet. I didn't own any common cheap shoes, and my boots would have given me away at worst and caused me to be accused of stealing at best.

The soldiers on guard around the cargo ships were still present, but the guards surrounding the warehouse had been doubled. An entire platoon of soldiers now camped out in front of the large wooden structures.

I turned away from them and headed into the city, the stony
dirt paths and rough wooden walkways abrading the soles of my
feet. Nothing seemed different at first, but the deeper into the city I
went, the more the colonists and the soldiers were acting nervous.
Skittish. Whole platoons of soldiers marched through the city, with
people scrambling out of the way for fear of being knocked down
and stepped on.

Not a single soldier walked by themselves. I rushed to the
far end of the city where soldiers banged on doors, demanding to
search people's homes. Anyone who objected or argued was butt-
stroked with a musket or struck in the head with a cudgel.

I turned again and headed in the direction of Independence
Hall. When I got there, Benjamin Tallmadge was pacing in the
courtyard. I stood across the street and watched him for a few
minutes. His hands were clasped behind his back and his head
bowed. Several officers stopped to talk to him, and he put on that
wide, fake smile and laughed as he patted them on their backs like
he had personal friendships with them. The officers moved on, and
Tallmadge started pacing again. After twenty minutes, he finally
looked over my way and noticed me watching him.

Tallmadge stormed across the street my way. He came
alongside of me, and motioned with his head for me to walk beside
him.

"What in the bloody hell did you do?" he asked in a whisper
as we walked.

"You advised me yesterday to start killing people," I
answered. "So, I started."

"I also told you to leave the general alone," he spat out.

"No, you didn't," I retorted. "You advised me not to kill
him." I put emphasis on the word *advised*, as opposed to the word
told. "I didn't kill the general."

He turned the corner and walked towards several of the
larger inns.

"No," he said. "You didn't kill the general. You killed the
major. Slight difference. He was the general's personal assistant.

Now the general is on the warpath. He somehow knows it was you. I don't know how he knows, but he knows."

"Might be the knife I stuck in his desk," I said as if I was unsure. Might as well feed the rumors, as extravagant as they were.

"What?" He whirled around to face me and grabbed my shirt. "Are you mad? He's lost control of himself. He's ordered the guards doubled on every post. He's forbidden any British officer from wearing wigs. No officer or soldier is to walk in groups of less than three. Any soldier seen walking by themself is to be taken and brought before him."

"Anyone brought before him yet?" I asked, shoving his hand away from my shirt.

"Several," he answered. "They hadn't been told of his orders yet, but that makes no difference. After he determined they weren't you, he ordered them whipped in public for their misstep. To prevent the rest of the soldiers from making the same ... error."

"He may be scared, but he still has his wits," I observed. "Prevents me from dressing as one of them."

Tallmadge resumed walking, and I fell in next to him.

"Two soldiers are missing," he hissed under his breath. "The general is blaming you for that as well."

It was a statement with the unasked question left hanging in the air like a thick cloud.

"Soldiers desert all the time," I finally said. "Nothing unusual there."

"The general has also ordered every house in the city searched," he said, stopping to face me again. "Door by door, house by house."

"They already searched the house where I'm staying," I lied, still not knowing if I trusted him. "That's why I'm out and about. By tonight, it'll be safe for me to go back."

"Where are you staying?" he asked.

There was no way I was answering that question. I decided to change the subject. "My fuses?"

"Tomorrow," he said curtly and turned along the walkway again. "I've kept them in my room at the Inn where I'm staying. I didn't think it'd be a good idea to walk around with them, hoping to see you. I can bring them to you tomorrow."

"And my riddle?" I asked.

"The answer to your riddle is eighteen degrees upward. Turns out that it's eighteen degrees for all of them. The gunpowder should be half the weight of the cannonball. The bigger the ball, the more gunpowder used."

"Yes," I said. "I know how to load a cannon. I didn't know they were all the same as far as elevation. Thank you for the information."

"What's next for the Pale Rider?" he asked, lowering his voice to a whisper again.

"Nothing for tonight," I said. "I'll wait until the bees return to the hive and calm down."

"That's probably wise," he told me as he stopped again. This time, he turned his whole body to face me. "But I have a problem that I was hoping you would help me with."

"Washington used almost those exact words with me the first time I met him," I commented. "His small problem almost got me killed. In fact, every small *problem* since that first one has almost been the death of me."

"This particular problem is more likely to kill me, not you," he said.

"What's the nature of this problem?"

"General Clinton has been rounding up some colonists. Questioning them."

"Which colonists?" I asked.

"Did you notice the day we arrived that the soldiers were writing down the names of the men who entered the city?" he asked.

"Aye," I answered.

"They're collecting those who are on those lists," he explained. "They started with the list from the day after we arrived here. The day you killed the major."

"And?"

"One of the men they collected came to see me that day," he answered. "He came to the city to deliver a message to me from General Washington. The messenger's name was on that list. They're questioning about twenty men right now, and he's one of them. If he breaks, I'll be the next person they collect."

"Then you should leave the city," I told him. "The sooner, the better."

"General Clinton has locked down the entire city. No one can leave until you're found."

I rubbed my forehead with my finger and thumb. I knew what he was asking of me. "Where are they being held?"

"In the inn directly across the street," he answered, keeping his gaze down.

At least I knew why he brought me in this direction and why he stopped here. Without turning my head, I tried seeing what I could of the inn. Like most buildings in this area, it was a three-story, red brick building. Two soldiers guarded the front door. A three-foot-wide alley separated the inn from the buildings on either side.

"In the basement?" I asked.

"No," he answered. "I'm told they're being questioned on the second floor."

"How would I know your man?"

"His name is Samuel," he said. "Late twenties, scar on his right hand where he was bitten by a wolf as a boy."

"You want him back or dead?" I asked.

No matter what he said, I would not kill the young man, but I wanted to know what his answer would be.

"I want him out of their hands," he said indirectly, not really answering my question. I didn't like that.

"Ok. I'll see if I can find a way in tonight."

"They'll have broken him by then," he said, heatedly.

"Fine," I answered, shifting my eyes to the buildings next to the inn.

A lot of soldiers had to be milling about in that building. To do this in daylight hours was crazy, bordering on suicidal. On the other hand, it'd invoke more fear and rumors if I got away with it.

"I'll be wanting my cannon fuses tomorrow at noon," I told him, bargaining. "And this better not interfere with my other plans. I want to start burning warehouses right away."

"It won't," he promised. "Get this done today, and you're free to cause all the havoc you want."

I turned away from him and walked towards the city water pump and fountain to refill my water bags.

When I made it back to the ship, I grabbed my gunny sack with everything I thought I might need in it. Staying barefoot and in my same cotton garbs, I headed back out to the inn taken over by the British for their questioning. Instead of going up to the inn with the prisoners, I entered the inn next door.

I entered the inn and was met by a very unpleasant lady in her sixties who didn't seem too fond of sailors. I sat down at one of the large common tables with several men who I assumed were staying at the inn because she didn't give them the stink eye like she was giving me. I ordered a bowl of beef stew with a glass of what she called her famous lemonade, for which she made me pay in advance. My stomach growled when the food arrived, beef jerky not being the most filling meal, so I ate the stew and drank the lemonade.

A young boy entered the inn. He looked to be about ten years old and as barefooted as I. Two large rabbits tied to a thin rope by their feet hung easily over his shoulder. The lady saw him and smiled. She didn't say anything and pointed the boy to the kitchen.

"Beef stew, my ass," the man next to me muttered to himself.

Looking up at the man who had just spoke, I noticed a man in a fur coat at the far end of the table. He was a little older than me, his face covered with a thick beard. He was staring at me, but when he caught me looking at him, his eyes flicked away.

Could this be the hunter that Tallmadge warned me about?
He fit the description. I wasn't the best at guessing people's
occupation in this century, but he looked more like a furrier. Then
again, furriers did hunt, so perhaps there was little difference.

I ordered a second helping of the stew, and after dropping
another coin in her open hand, I asked her about relieving myself.

"There is a public outhouse behind the inn," she said,
pointing down the hall. "You can use the back door. Your stew will
be waiting for you when you get back."

The hallway was next to the stairs that led upward. I picked
up my sack and walked down the hall. After waiting a few seconds,
I headed back towards the main room and hooked around, going up
the steps leading to the second floor. I stopped on the second floor
and waited to see if the man in the fur coat was going to follow.

He didn't follow, so I continued up to the third floor. I was
getting jumpy, thinking everyone was out to get me. Then again, in
this city, they really were. I was also starting to believe that
Tallmadge was full of shit. That whole story about someone in the
city here to hunt me down might have been designed to scare me
and gain my favor. Perhaps it was designed to slow me down and
prevent my work in Philadelphia by keeping me looking over my
shoulder. Washington trusted the man, but I didn't.

I crept down the hall, studying the walls and ceiling. In the
center of the hallway, I found what I was hoping for – a trapdoor in
the ceiling that gave access to the flat roof. There was no ladder I
could see, but someone had nailed mismatched scrap wooden
boards horizontally to the wall, every two feet from the floor to the
ceiling as a makeshift ladder.

I placed a toe on the first nailed stud when the room door
next to me opened. An open-mouthed British officer stood in the
doorway, staring at me. He jerked when I dropped my sack and
stepped forward, punching him in the throat with a quick left jab.
He gurgled and stumbled back into his room, holding his throat. His
eyes bulged, but I didn't give him a chance to recover. He turned his
back on me to run further into the room, when I grabbed the back of

his coat with my left hand and my Tec-9 from behind my back with my right. He staggered in place, fighting to pull away, when the butt of my pistol grip struck the back of his head. A crack broke the air, and he went limp, crumpling to the floor.

I realized I may have hit him harder than I'd intended. I checked the butt of my pistol grip and found it to be undamaged. I hadn't intended on killing him – I wanted to knock him out, but given the choice of the cracking sound being my pistol grip breaking or his skull, I had hoped it was his skull. I rolled him over onto his back. He was breathing, but I couldn't guarantee he'd ever wake up after that blow to his head. The man would be lucky to live through that assault on his skull. I had planned on heading up on the roof of the inn, but now that I had a room to use, I wasn't going to let it go to waste. Stepping out into the hallway, I grabbed my sack and closed the door behind me as I slipped back into the room.

I dug out my British uniform again and put it on. I'd been walking around barefooted so much that it felt nice having the stiff boots on. Then I pulled on my black bullet-proof vest. My shoulder holster and Thompson Contender came next, followed by my black leather belt and my two knives. My oversized red coat covered everything up. I shoved my stupid looking three-point hat on my head. Last but not least, my sword belt with the additional leather loop for my Tec-9 went over my head and across my body.

After listening at the door for several seconds and not hearing any movement, I cracked the door open an inch to peek out. The hallway was still empty, so I made my way to the makeshift ladder again. This time, I made it up the ladder without being discovered. The hatch in the ceiling pushed up and opened easily enough on two hinges. Climbing up and through the hole, I found myself on the roof of the inn under the blistering sun.

The roof of the building I wanted to be in was only three feet away, an easy jump. The two roofs looked very similar, so I searched for an access hatch like the building I had jumped from. I found one that was a twin to the one I had climbed up through.

Cracking the hatch open a few inches, I didn't see anyone in the hallway but heard movement and voices muffled from either downstairs on the second floor or inside one of the rooms on this floor. I grabbed the lip of the open hatch and dropped through the square hole and swung down, landing to the floor with little noise. Well, I did make some noise. My sword scabbard caught on the lip and the handle thrust downward as the blade pointed upward, and my sword slid out of my scabbard, landing on the floor with a clang.

I drew my Tec-9 and froze in place, ready to shoot anyone who decided to investigate the hallway. None of the doors opened, and no one came out to see what had fallen. Feeling stupid but at the same time pleased that Lafayette hadn't seen me let my sword fall out and hit the floor, I picked up my sword and slid it back into my scabbard.

Tallmadge had said that the British soldiers were stopping anyone in uniform walking around the city by themselves, but I figured I was safe at the inn. I hurried down the steps to the second floor. Six rooms were on this floor, and every door was opened. British soldiers marched up from the first floor while others passed in and out of the rooms. The soldiers nodded their heads to me in greeting as they walked past.

I grabbed the arm of a hard-looking sergeant who was walking by and stopped him.

"Sergeant," I said. "I'm looking for one of the prisoners."

I took a second and tilted my head to the side as if I was trying to think of the name. Then, letting go of his arm, I snapped my fingers as if I had remembered it.

"Samuel."

"Aye, sir," the sergeant responded. "Last room on the right."

"Thank you, Sergeant," I said.

"So, I take it you heard?" he asked as I started to walk toward the room.

No, I hadn't heard. What did he mean? "Heard?"

"That we broke him, sir," the sergeant continued. "He gave up the name of his contact in the city. Benjamin Tallmadge."

"Oh that," I said, nodding slightly to cover my shock. "Yes, Sergeant. We were informed about that. General Clinton wants me to question him about it personally."

"Very good, sir. I was going to send word to the general. We have two platoons out looking for the spy Tallmadge as we speak. He has no way of knowing that we know about him yet, so he should be easy enough to find."

"Yes, yes, Sergeant," I told the sergeant. *Did* Tallmadge not know yet? The man seemed to know everything. "I'll deliver that message to the general next I see him. For now, I need to speak to this prisoner alone. I'll take him upstairs to the third floor. I'll need one of the rooms."

The sergeant stared at me for a minute with a quizzical look on his face, but I was taking the prisoner upstairs and not out of the building, so he must have decided that there was no harm.

He looked over at a young soldier in his late teens and pointed to the room. "Jeffery, take the prisoner Samuel and the Lieutenant here upstairs to one of the empty rooms and wait outside in the hall so they can speak in private."

The young soldier doubled-timed it to the room and came out a minute later with a beat-down young man who had trouble standing on his own. His right eye was swollen shut and his pants were not much more than rags. He didn't have a shirt, and his entire body was covered with dark purple bruises the size of a man's fist. He was barefooted and rubbed at deep red indents on his wrist as if he'd been shackled to a wall or chair. The soldier held him upright with one arm, more to offer support than to prevent him from running.

With an expressionless face, I let them walk past me, and painfully for the prisoner, they made their way up to the third floor.

No wonder he'd given up Tallmadge's name. They'd beaten him so badly that he still might die, even if I was able to get him out of here. By the way he held his arm against his side, I guessed a few of his ribs had to be broken.

I thanked the sergeant and followed the two up the stairs. When they reached the top and started down the hallway, the young soldier stopped and looked up at the open hatch to the roof that I hadn't closed.

Fuck. How had I forgotten that?

"Sir, look at this," the soldier said to me, pointing up to the open hatch. "If you will watch the prisoner, sir, I need to report this."

I moved forward as soon as he let go of Samuel's arm. I drew my pistol with my right hand and grabbed the back of the soldier's coat with my left. I pushed him forward into the wall and brought the butt of my pistol down on his head, much like I had done to the last soldier. His body went limp, and I held him up, pinned against the wall. Reaching over and grabbing the doorknob next to us, I opened the door we were next to and dragged him into the room as a bewildered Samuel stared at me. I laid the young man down on the floor, trying not to cause him any more injury than I already had. I moved back into the hallway, shutting the door quietly behind me.

"I'm here to get you out," I told Samuel. "Can you walk?"

"At least two of my ribs are broken, but I'll run to get out of here." His pasty face brightened as he spoke. That was as good a sign as any.

"Good lad," I said, pointing up to the hatch. "Up you go."

Samuel painstakingly worked his way up the nailed-in ladder and through the hatch, with me behind him pushing him up the whole way. Once we were on the roof, I closed the hatch and helped Samuel move forward to the ledge.

"Can you make the jump?" I asked as we both looked straight down to the alley below.

He groaned. "Yes, but I'll need your help."

I jumped over first and then reached out a hand over the short distance for him. We locked wrists, and as he jumped, I pulled back as hard as I could. He made it across but screamed as his broken ribs moved and tore into his flesh. The poor kid turned even paler, pure white, and was sweating buckets. I thought he was going to throw up, but he managed to hold down whatever might have been in his stomach.

I was needed to wrap his ribs tightly as soon as I could so he could keep moving. By the time we had made it through the hatch and into the soldier's room whom I had knocked out, Samuel was spent. He couldn't walk. I laid him on the cot, and he passed out from the pain. Not wanting to make the same mistake twice, I ducked back out into the empty hallway and shut the hatch leading to the roof.

Glancing out the window, I studied the street below. Men were running out of the inn next door. They must have discovered that their prisoner was gone. No one would think that we had stopped and were staying in a room in the inn next door, so hopefully we'd be safe for a while.

I stripped, gagged, and tied up the still unconscious soldier on the floor and shoved his body into the tall, standalone wardrobe. I had to fold him over to get him in and even then, had to force the double doors closed.

Samuel, for his part, had passed out on the cot. I took advantage of his inert form and wrapped a sheet that I'd cut up tightly around his broken ribs. I didn't think he was going to be able to dress himself when he woke, so I went ahead and put the soldier's uniform on him as best I could. The uniform was loose on his frail body, but better too loose than too tight. I gave him a shot of morphine to help with the pain when he finally woke. It'd also relax him a bit.

I sat in a chair, pistol in hand, letting the kid sleep. Outside, soldiers scrambled around like ants whose nest had been kicked. General Clinton was going to shit himself when he learned about the rescue of his prisoner. His men wouldn't need to describe me – he'd know I was the one responsible. He'd also have to know that if I could walk in and take a prisoner from his men right under their noses, that I might be able to come for him next. At least, I hoped that would be his concern. Between the rescue of Samuel and the burning of the warehouses that I had planned, he'd start seeing threats in every shadow. I needed to warn Tallmadge before I started on the warehouses. He might have to hide or get himself out of the city.

After a while, the activity slowed down and appeared to return to normal. They were looking for us, but they had no idea *where* to look. Samuel finally woke up after three hours and his dazed eyes danced around.

"How are you feeling?" I asked as I handed him one of my filled canteens.

"Better," he answered in a hoarse voice. "The ribs don't hurt as bad as they did. What'd you give me?"

He tilted the canteen back, drinking deeply from it.

"Don't worry about that," I told him. "What'd you tell the British?"

The kid brought the canteen down from his lips to answer. He caught himself and glared at me with a healthy dose of cautious suspicion. *Fricking spies.* I whipped off my hat and showed him the scar running along my head from front to back. His eyes widened, and his mouth dropped open even more with recognition for someone he'd never seen but apparently knew of. You would have thought the kid saw Elvis or something.

"It's you," he said with awe. "The Pale Rider."

"It's really me, kid. But right now, I need to know what you told them."

I must have had a hard edge in my voice because it scared him. He started to take another long drink but stopped and sat up on the cot. He parted his lips, a panicked look shadowing his face as if he was ready to explain. I lifted one hand up, signaling for him to stop, and I gently placed the other on his chest and pushed him back down on the bed.

"Don't worry," I said, softening my tone, trying to calm him. "I know you didn't have any choice. You were beaten half to death. But I do need to know, and I need to know now, so I can decide what must be done next."

"Benjamin," he said, then continued after taking another drink of water. "I told them everything about Benjamin. It might take time for them to discover where he stays. But they will discover it and they'll send men to arrest him."

"Where would they take Benjamin?" I asked.

"I don't know," he answered. "But they took some others to a ship. They talked about taking me to the ship in the morning. The inn was just where they questioned us to find out who had information they wanted. This is where they broke us. Maybe they'd take him to the ship."

"What ship?"

"They didn't say. And I didn't care enough to ask."

Well, this was going to be a problem. I needed to find out if Tallmadge had been captured or not, and if he was, where they had taken him. I knew for sure that they weren't going to bring him to the inn. Not after what I had done there today.

"I need to get you out of here," I told Samuel, "then find Tallmadge. I don't care for the bastard myself, but he knows too much about Washington to let him fall into British hands." I eyed him up and down. "You'll have to walk to where I've been hiding."

The last part was more of a question than a statement. Samuel caught that and nodded his head, sitting up again. He was slower and more careful about sitting up this time. He bit his lip and sucked in air as I helped him stand.

Now that he was upright, we pulled, tucked, and tightened the British uniform I had put on him when he was unconscious. It was still too large but passible. Heading down the stairs, Samuel clung onto the railing to help him stay standing. We moved straight to the front door and outside before anyone got a good look at us. Outside, I held on to him, and he acted as if he was drunk. British soldiers were supposed to walk in groups of three and we were only two, but the bottom line was that they were really looking for soldiers walking alone.

We worked our way towards the inn that Tallmadge had been staying at. It turned out that it was not a real inn but a large house that rented out spare rooms. We made it to the street, about half a block away from the house, when a platoon of soldiers paused outside the house. We slowed our walk and kept a wary eye on them.

Suddenly, the front door to the house burst outward with a flood of soldiers dragging a half-beaten but still kicking Tallmadge. An older couple tried to protest the soldier's treatment of Tallmadge but knew better to interfere too much. Their protest was loud but made from a distance. One of the soldiers had enough of Tallmadge's resisting and slammed the butt of his musket into Tallmadge's stomach. The spy master doubled over with an agonizing grunt. He was still conscious, but his body was limp. Two soldiers held him up under his armpits and dragged him to a waiting wagon. His leather boots dragged in the dirt, leaving twin snake marks on the ground. The two soldiers threw the spy master into the back of the wagon, not like a prisoner but more like a sack of potatoes.

With a loud slap of the reins, the horses moved forward, and the wagon lurched down the street. A sergeant in front of the soldiers yelled for them to move double time, and the soldiers ran along both sides of the wagon. I had intended on getting Samuel to safety, but if I lost Tallmadge now, I might not be able to find him later. Samuel was going to have to suffer the pain a little longer.

"Sorry kid," I said. "But we need to follow them."

Samuel nodded his head. He was either in too much pain to talk or the morphine was still affecting him. We weren't able to keep up, but we did follow as best we could. They headed towards the docks, so there was no rush.

By the time we made it to the docks, Samuel was leaning most of his weight on me. The British already had Tallmadge face down in a rowboat, about twenty feet from shore, heading out to one of the warships. Four soldiers in the rowboat guarded Tallmadge, plus two sailors at the oars. I could tell which ship they were heading to, but from this distance, I couldn't read the name. She had three decks of guns, like the Sandwich, and appeared to be charged with blocking the river and stopping ships from entering or exiting without her captain's permission. This was the ship that had replaced the Sandwich after I'd damaged her. Since she was sitting in the middle of the river, she made for a good makeshift brig to hold and question potential spies. The ship that had been tied to the docks offloading cargo was gone, but another had taken its place and was starting to offload its cargo.

The wind was picking up and clouds moved across the sky at a fast pace. The sun would be going down in about two hours, so whatever I was going to do, I'd at least have the cover of darkness to hide me. The rest of the platoon of soldiers that had escorted the wagon to the docks were marching back to the city and headed straight for us. They moved noticeably slower, not looking as cocky as they had when they left the house. The run to the river in full gear had taken a lot of the wind out of their sails and haughtiness out of their attitudes. Just the same, I didn't feel like crossing paths with them or trying to answer any questions. We were also dressed as British soldiers, after all.

Now that I knew where Tallmadge would be, I turned Samuel north-west, doubling back into the city and away from the harbor. I led Samuel down the cobblestone streets to the only place where I knew he'd be safe.

Jonas's parents, seeing us standing in their doorway in British uniforms, were at first surprised and scared of us, until I took off my hat and they recognized me. After laying Samuel in Jonas's old bed, I spoke to them quietly in the parlor. They agreed to watch and take care of Samuel until I got back. Samuel, the poor lad, faded in and out of consciousness, but I was proud of him. He hadn't complained once while we were trailing Tallmadge.

I gave the boy some more pain killers and then left him in the very capable and motherly hands of Jonas's mother. Then I glanced down at my sweat-stained officer's uniform. If I walked around the city in this uniform by myself, I'd be stopped and

181

arrested for certain. Jonas's father lent me some modest but clean clothes, and I changed before I left.

Chapter Thirteen   Change of Plans

The house that Tallmadge rented was fortunately close to
Jonas's parents' house. I left the uniform behind and made my way
to the house, refilling my two canteens at a public pump along the
way. The owners of the house, Mr. and Ms. Woodberry, were very
kind. They were quick to point out that they had no room for any
more guests and that I'd have to seek rooms elsewhere. I explained I
was a friend of Tallmadge and needed to retrieve something from
his room. They refused to let me into his room until I convinced
them that I was here to help the man. I lied and said that I was his
lawyer and needed his belongings to prove his innocence. Mr.
Woodberry finally nodded his head and led me to Tallmadge's
room. The stifling hot room had been torn apart and searched. An
open trunk sat at the foot of the overturned bed, now emptied.
Papers covered the floor, and the dresser drawers had been removed,
their contents unceremoniously dumped out onto the floor.

The British had searched the room and taken anything of
value from it. There was no sign of any cannon fuses. I let out a
long-frustrated lung full of air, blowing it out of my mouth in an

unusual show of emotion for me. I moved to raise my right hand but forced my hand down so I didn't run my fingers through my hair and reveal my scar. Mr. Woodberry saw the disappointing look on my face and knew that I wasn't finding what I was looking for.

"If Mr. Tallmadge possessed anything of value," Mr. Woodberry said, tilting his head, "it would be under the floorboards."

I spun on the toes of my boots. "I'm sorry. What?"

"The floorboards," he answered, pointing to the corner of the room.

I knelt next to the large brown rug that covered most of the floor and pulled back the corner. I had to look hard, but there was a square cut out in the floorboards. Not a large one, maybe one foot by one foot. I stuck my finger into a small hole in the middle of the cutout and pulled the boards up. I looked into the hole to find a white pillowcase, which I grabbed and pulled out. A rush of relief breathed out of my lungs. At least thirty cannonball fuses and what looked like several thin coils of rope but were really coils of cannon fuses. As I'd requested, the coils had not been cut into smaller pieces.

I replaced the floorboards and rug and stood up with the pillowcase in hand. I thanked Mr. Woodberry for his help and left the house with the pillowcase. The wind was still picking up as the suffocating humidity rose, and it looked like a storm was blowing in. I needed to hurry. I headed towards the HMS Sandwich unmolested by any soldiers, and I was surprised to have something finally go my way.

The sun had nearly settled on the horizon by the time I made it back to the Sandwich. The final golden rays of light let me see what I was doing, but I would lose that soon enough. I didn't have time to push the last of the cannons back into place. Twelve cannons sat on the main deck and thirteen cannons on the second deck to work with. I had planned on using the cannons on all three decks the day Washington attacked, but now I was having to use what cannons I could for this rescue.

Tallmadge had better be worth it.

Pulling out the fuses, I found Tallmadge had obtained what looked like four, one hundred-feet-long coils of fuse. It was more than he'd promised and not less. I cut twenty strips of fuse, each fuse twenty feet long, which would take a little over twenty minutes to burn from end to end. The tradeoff to giving myself twenty-minute-long fuses was I'd only be using twenty of the twenty-five loaded cannons, and the thirty-eight total cannons that I could have used if I had more time. This plan was not going as well as I imagined when I came up with the idea.

I loaded the cannonball fuses into twenty of the cannonballs and then loaded the twenty cannons with the cannonballs. The sun had completely sunk before I was able to finish, and dark clouds obscured most of the moonlight. I had to put the last of the fuses in the cannons in the dark. When that was done, I went around and raised the ten cannons from the main deck and ten cannons from the second deck to the right elevation. I was only guessing, but I was confident they were eighteen degrees upward, give or take a few degrees.

Close enough for horseshoes and hand grenades.

I didn't like using any light for fear that someone might see it, but when I thought I was finished, I lit the lantern and double-checked my work, satisfied that I did an adequate job.

I then changed back into my dirty white sailor's pants and shirt, leaving the rest of my clothes behind. After some thought, I decided to put on my vest and boots. If the British saw me coming, they'd shoot me, vest or no vest. Might as well let them know who I was. In my satchel, I placed my weapons, medical supplies, and ammo. The lamp oil and supplies I'd purchased or stolen sat in the corner of the captain's quarters. I had planned on using them to burn down some of the warehouses, but I was forced to abandon them as well.

I started to remove the grenade that I had set up on the stairs but decided to leave it where it was. When this show started, the British were going to board this ship, and this would serve as one last surprise for them. Once I was ready, I lit the torch that I had taken from the soldiers I'd killed on the beach and stood on the top main deck. I set a twenty-minute timer on my watch so I'd know when the cannons would go off.

With my sword and two canteens in my left hand and a torch in my right, I walked down the length of the ten cannons. I lit each of the fuses as I passed by and ran down the steps to the next level. I lit the ten cannon fuses on the second level, then raced down to the hull of the ship. Throwing my torch into the water in the hull, I ran out of the ship and down the beach. Three minutes had gone by when I untied and pushed one of the canoes I had seen earlier into the water. Setting down my sword and canteens, I picked up one of the two oars that rested in the center of the canoe and rowed towards the gigantic war ship where Tallmadge was being held.

Lamp and torchlight lit up the whole main deck of that ship. Men moved around on deck doing who knows what. A bright bubble of light circled the ship. The ship was so tall and stood so far out of the water that the light didn't reach the black surface of the river. The cannon ports were open, and I could see that the lower levels were dark, allowing sailors to sleep.

The lookouts focused on the distance and were on guard for any warships trying to enter or exit the harbor. They weren't looking down or watching for tiny canoes coming at them quick and quiet.

I made it to the ship without being seen by any of the lookouts. The humidity broke while I was rowing, and as I set the oar in the canoe, fat raindrops started to fall. I tied my canoe to the thick hemp rope attached to the ship's anchor, and then I removed my satchel and took out my night vision goggles, putting them on. My grenade and two of my four remaining pistol magazines went into my pocket, one of my knives behind my back, and my pistol slipped into my belt. My watch said fifteen minutes, so I had about five minutes before the first cannon fired.

I was feeling good about my plan when lightning lit up the night sky in a bright flash of momentary light. Thunder broke the silence four seconds later in a boom that echoed the night. The main body of the storm was still far off but heading this way. Would the storm wreck my plans? Hell, I hoped not.

I climbed up the thick hemp rope to the closest open cannon port. The whole third deck was dark, but I misjudged the port and struck my head against the opening. I grimaced and forced myself to focus through the pain. In the green haze of my night vision, a few men slept on benches. Ducking low, I pulled myself through the port and squeezed in around the cannon. Going in headfirst, I used my hands on the floor and walked myself forward until my whole body was inside. I knelt and peered over the side of the cannon, searching for any movement.

I had three minutes before the cannons on the Sandwich started firing. I knew the captain wouldn't keep prisoners in the living quarters where he or his men slept, and they weren't going to give up the two lower decks where the cannons were mounted. The prisoners must be kept in the hull deep in the belly of the ship, far under the water line. Footsteps pounded on the deck above me – back and forth along the ship. When I was satisfied that I was the only person on this level awake, I stood up and made my way to the steps going down.

The next level was for cargo, mirroring the layout of the sandwich. The deck was quiet and dark but also overloaded with cargo, as if they'd moved the entire ship's supplies to this one deck.

Voices drifted up from the next deck down. As I made my way toward the stairs, my night vision slowly turned solid white, and I slipped them down below my chin. Yellow lamp light reflected off the walls at the bottom of the stairs. A lot of light. Shadows danced from the mix of people walking around and the lamps being moved.

I laid down on the deck and lowered my head into the stairwell to see what was awaiting me. The entire deck had been transformed into a . . . well, I don't know what it had been transformed into. Something between a prison and a torture chamber. Lanterns hung on wall pegs every twenty feet or so. The entire deck was well lit.

I counted five British soldiers plus two more British officers. They were soldiers, not sailors. Four of the soldiers sat in wooden chairs at a round table. Though cups littered the table in front of them, they drank from a shared bottle, staying out of the way of the officers. They were about ten feet from the stairs to my right. The fifth soldier stood behind the two officers, about fifteen feet to my left. He appeared to be some kind of sick torture butler in case they needed anything.

Three men were chained standing up against the bulkhead, and Benjamin Tallmadge was one of those men. The other two seemed to be young men in their late teens. The two teens weren't moving, and their heads hung down, knees bent with their own weight pulling on their arms. They didn't appear conscious. The three had been pounded on brutally, and from the looks of them, they'd been beaten more than once. Although they were bare-chested and bore their fair share of bruises, it looked like the questioners had spent most of their time beating on the prisoners' faces, which were a mess of blood and bruises and even exposed bone.

The stairs extended between the two groups. A huge black iron pot in the middle of the deck was filled with glowing, red-hot coals. Branding irons poked into the coals, their long handles hanging over the side of the pot. A second table stood behind the pot, topped with what looked like maps and official papers.

The officers stood in front of Tallmadge, screaming questions at him. Tallmadge, for his part, shook his head in the negative. This earned him a solid punch in the ribs. Tallmadge violently coughed out blood. From the looks of his beaten body, he was keeping his mouth shut.

An hour ago, I was mad about having to come rescue Tallmadge, but now I was glad to be doing it. This bloody, inhuman scene before me was beyond belief. I'd seen interrogations before, but these officers took it to the next level. Blood and vomit dripped down from Tallmadge's chin. My cold, calculating personality was crackling, ready to jump in, as anger filled me.

Maybe I had read Tallmadge wrong. I didn't trust or like the man, but he seemed to be holding up under a vicious beating. That's when things took a turn for the worse. The second officer barked out orders over his shoulder, and the soldier standing behind him moved to the iron pot. He picked up one of the branding irons and held it out for the officer. The officer took it and held it up to Tallmadge's face.

My watch said that the cannons were going to fire in less than a minute, so I had good timing for once. I'd go as soon as the cannons on the Sandwich started firing. But that would be a long minute for Tallmadge's searing skin.

I reached into my pocket and pulled out my last grenade with my left hand and yanked the pin as I held the spoon in place. Then, with my right hand, I pulled out my pistol with the suppressor and readied myself to move. As soon as the cannons fired, they'd go one at a time, and all hell would break loose. I'd throw the grenade to the right, kill the men at the table, and then finish off the three with my pistol. I readied myself for action, repeating my mental checklist – throw the grenade, wait for the explosion, run down the steps.

Nothing happened. No cannon fire. No ship's bell ringing. No men running around in a panic. Nothing. I waited but was disheartened when still nothing happened.

A loud, painful scream cried from below. I stuck my head into the stairwell again. The officer had slapped the glowing red iron against the right side of Tallmadge's chest. Smoke poured from where the iron touched the skin and made a sick sizzling sound. I could smell his acrid, burning flesh from where I was. The officers placed handkerchiefs over their noses.

The officer pulled the iron away from Tallmadge's chest, taking a chunk of skin with it. A deep red brand now suppurated on Tallmadge's chest. Tallmadge faltered, ready to pass out until one of the officers slapped him and screamed in his face, asking about

Washington's plans to attack the city. Tallmadge, or one of the two teens, must have broken earlier and said something about Washington's planned attack.

I needed to move before he told them anything else. I listened but still didn't hear any cannon fire. If I couldn't hear the cannons themselves from where I was, I would have heard the ship's crew running around. Something had gone terribly wrong. Someone may have seen me leave and stopped the fuses from burning down. Maybe the rainfall killed the fuses and had ruined my plans, or maybe I'd loaded the cannons wrong. I cursed under my breath.

Most of my fights seemed like a battle of wits between the twenty-first century way of thinking and the eighteenth-century way of doing things. I won most of those battles because the people in this time period weren't capable of thinking like me. There was a chance I wasn't as smart as I thought I was. Maybe this time, I had put myself into a kill box that I wasn't going to be able to get out of.

Another slap of the iron against flesh and Tallmadge screamed as the same sickening, searing sound penetrated my ears. This time, the officer had placed the glowing red iron on the left side of Tallmadge's chest. The screaming stopped and Tallmadge stood with his back arched, mouth wide opened with no sound coming out, as if he was in too much pain to scream. His senses were overwhelmed and overloaded.

Tallmadge's head fell forward, and his body became dead weight, pulling against the chains that were holding him up. He had mercifully passed out with the iron still against his flesh. The officer removed the iron, pulling off more flesh still stuck to the hot iron from Tallmadge's spindly looking body.

Lifting my head, I thought I heard cannon fire, but no, it was another thunderclap. I had to do something, fast.

"Here," the officer with the iron said to the soldier behind him as he handed him back the iron. "Fetch a bucket of water so we can wake him for another round of questioning."

The soldier took the iron and placed it back into the fire. *And these men called me a monster.* The soldier then walked over to the table where the soldiers sat and picked up a bucket of water from the floor by its rope handle. A dozen buckets rested against the wall. Most of the buckets looked emptied, but three of them contained water. They were going to wake Tallmadge and start over. I needed to move soon, with or without my distraction, or Tallmadge wasn't going to survive. I backed away from the stairs, trying to think of a Plan B.

Thunder struck again in the distance. The storm was much closer now. Or was it? The ship's bell rang out, calling the crew to their stations. Running feet above told me that the entire crew of several hundred men was now awake and running. Not thunder. My cannons had worked. I calculated the timing wrong.

"Go see what's going on up there," a voice yelled from below.

It was too late to throw the grenade as men were already running up the steps. Three came into view, and I shifted to shoot them in the back, but I was hidden in the shadows, and none looked my way but continued up to the next deck. I let them go up to the next deck as I placed the pin back into my grenade. I ran down the steps toward the torture room below.

A fourth soldier was halfway up the stairs when he saw me coming down. He must have thought I was one of the crew and opened his mouth to say something to me. I put a round in the center of his chest. He fell backwards and rolled down the steps to the deck below. The last soldier ran to his side, kneeling to check on his friend. I put a bullet in the center of his back as I leaped to the deck, skipping the last three steps. The two officers stood in disbelief, mouths hanging open, trying to process what they were seeing. They had to know who I was.

I walked forward and shot them in their faces before they were able to give warning, or even move for a weapon. They each did a matching spin and crashed face first onto the deck.

I woke Tallmadge, but the two teens chained next to him weren't passed out. They were already dead. Tallmadge's eyes were swollen, but he could still see out of the thin slits.

"What are you doing here?" Tallmadge moaned when he could finally focus on my face.

"Saving your ass," I said.

"How?"

"Still working on that part of the plan."

"Oh good," Tallmadge mumbled around his swollen lips, "there's a plan."

"Not a plan, as such. More of an evolving idea."

I located the key to the manacles around Tallmadge's wrists on the table and freed him. He collapsed into my arms. He was having trouble talking but pointed to the two young men still chained to the bulkhead.

"Sorry," I said, in an apologetic voice. "They're already dead."

Our side of the ship jerked upward, almost knocking us off our feet, as cannons from above on our side fired. They were firing at the Sandwich, I assumed. We moved towards the stairs with Tallmadge leaning on my left side, his arm draped around my neck. He kept his feet under him and moved forward, but his head hung down and we left a thin trail of blood as we walked.

When we reached the bottom of the stairs, the three soldiers who had been down here a minute ago returned to report what they'd found above deck. The first one halfway down tried to stop in mid step, when the two behind him kept going, crashing the first one forward. He flew face first down the stairs and hit the deck, landing on his face, not moving. I raised my arm, shooting the two behind him, who also careened face down on top of the first one. I reloaded my pistol, and we started up the stairs again.

We made it to the next deck and could hear men yelling orders, running in a fury, and the sounds of cannons rolling forward, ready to fire again.

"We need to move while they're distracted," I said.

"Distracted by what?" Tallmadge asked.

"By the attack on the cargo ship that is offloading supplies."

"Who's attacking the ships?" he asked.

"Me," I told him. "I'll explain later."

We made it up to the third deck, which was also the first deck above the water and the lowest cannon deck. Men were busy aiming cannons on the side facing shore. I pushed Tallmadge to the front of the ship towards the cannon port where I had entered the ship. Men noticed us – the bruised Tallmadge and his limping were difficult to miss – and a few started walking our way. I might have passed as a sailor, but Tallmadge looked like a man who had been beaten half to death.

"Climb out that port and drop in the water," I directed him. "There is a canoe tied to the anchor rope. Climb in and wait for me. Untie the canoe if you can manage it."

I let go of Tallmadge and pulled my grenade out of my pocket again. Several of the sailors moved faster, coming right at us. I pulled out the pin and threw the grenade down the length of the ship. The men heading towards me had no idea what I had thrown past them, but increased their speed, one of them yelling for others to stop us. I shot the two closest men to me, watching them fall onto the deck.

I scrambled backwards to the cannon port as Tallmadge's feet disappeared into the dark, followed by a splash in the water. I shot two more men and holstered my pistol right before the grenade went off with an eardrum-destroying blast. A dozen men laid on the deck, and a dozen more stumbled around concussed. Several fires burned, and the deck was filling up with black smoke. Men who hadn't been injured by the grenade screamed about getting the black powder away from the fire.

On the upside of things, no one was paying attention to me anymore. I rocketed out the cannon port and dropped straight down headfirst into the bone-jarringly cold water. I dropped like a torpedo in the water, going deep. The water was pitch black, and in my disorientation, I had to think about which way was up. I blew out some air and followed the bubbles. I swam upward, and when I broke the surface, Tallmadge was climbing into the canoe, ten feet away. I sunk back down into the dark river as my vest and boots weighed me down. I kicked as hard as I could, in order to break the surface again, stealing a lung full of air. I struggled to keep my head above water when something bumped against my leg.

Shark? The memory of sharks feeding on dead men while I ordered my would-be killer suspended by a rope over them to get the answers I needed popped into my head. Was this karma? Was the great and frightening Pale Rider to be eaten by sharks? The thought made me double my efforts, and my head broke the surface again, barely. I was going to drown tonight, and I knew it. I couldn't keep this up with my vest and boots pulling me down, like the devil himself had a grip on my ankle. I fought back the panic that filled me and told myself to keep calm.

Something hit my head just as a flash of lightning lit up the rainy night. As I started to go under the dark water again for what I thought would be the last time, I reached out to find that I had been struck by a rope. I tugged on the rope, pulling myself towards the surface and the canoe. Tallmadge had not only untied the canoe rope from the thick anchor rope, but he'd thrown the canoe rope to me.

I grabbed and held onto the side of the canoe until I was able to regain enough strength back into my arms to pull myself in. Rain pounded down on my head as the storm reached full force. The sudden thought of whatever had bumped my leg in the dark water helped my strength return enough to haul my wet waterlogged body back into the canoe and to moderate safety. I tumbled into the canoe when a secondary explosion blew a hole out of the side of the ship and lit up the night.

One of the smaller fires reached the black powder.

The ship didn't look to be in danger of sinking yet, but flames licked through the enormous gaping hole that poured out black acrid smoke. The cannons of the third deck had gone silent, but the cannons on the second level and main deck fired again. I grabbed an ore from the bottom of the canoe as Tallmadge laid back and passed out. Though I was worn out, I dug into the water hard with my ore and drew away from the large burning warship. The slender canoe shot through the water with little resistance.

We cleared the bow of the now damaged warship, and I wiped rainwater from my face to see that the HMS Sandwich was still in one piece but was breaking apart from the cannon fire it had endured. Cannonballs were still tearing into the side of the Sandwich. The good thing about her being beached was that her hull was already sitting in the sand, and she couldn't sink.

As we glided farther away from the warship, soldiers with torches ran along the beach, attacking the unmanned Sandwich. Musket fire roared over the storm's wind as the soldiers shot at the empty and crewless ship. The smaller cargo ship tied at the harbor was sinking fast, so at least a few of my cannons had been aimed correctly. It was a truly uplifting and horrific sight, depending on whose side you were on. The sheer violence and destruction of the conflict was only amplified by the lightning and thunder breaking the night and increasing the confusion.

The bell from the ship continued to ring out as the cannon fire stopped, and men yelled about the fires below deck. A second explosion tore from the ship, spraying wood in all directions, wood chip rain mixed with the storm rain. The fire must have reached more of the black powder. If the crew didn't get the fire under control, soon the entire ship would ignite.

The dancing torch light on shore told me that as the warship was no longer firing at the Sandwich – the soldiers on the beach were boarding her. They'd probably enter through the same hole in the front that I'd used. Musket fire echoed over the water but now sounded muffled. The soldiers were in the hull of the Sandwich, firing at shadows and rats. A powerful yet low explosion broke the night and the musket fire stopped. One of the soldiers must have pulled the trip wire, setting off my last grenade.

That would make them double their efforts to find whoever was on board.

Loud cracking of wooden support beams carried over the water as the giant and proud warship H.M.S. Sandwich surrendered to her fate. She'd taken too much damage from the repeated cannon fire. Beams had been shattered, the sides had been shredded, and her back had been broken. I could see torches now running away from her as the whale of a ship let out her final breath and collapsed in on herself. How many men had she taken with her? How many were still inside her hull, now trapped or dead under tons of wood?

I continued digging into the water with my ore as we pulled farther and farther away from the chaos. My arms burned from fatigue, but I kept going. Shots rang out in our direction as the lookouts spotted us fleeing in the canoe. It didn't take long for us to paddle our way out of the ring of light that the ship provided and into the darkness of the storming night. I crossed over the river, heading to the opposite side, knowing Philadelphia was no longer safe for me.

Oh, I'd go back one more time, but not tonight.

Once we reached the shore on the New Jersey side of the river, I jumped out and pulled the canoe as far up onto the beach as I could. I needed to drag it out of sight but didn't have the strength. I collapsed in the sand, feet still in the water, eyes closed, breathing hard, not caring about the rain that was pounding down on me. I rested there for several minutes until Tallmadge started moaning. His distress forced me to my feet.

In a sudden panic, I reached for my throat, realizing that my night vision goggles were no longer around my neck. I must have lost them in the river while fighting the devil's grip on my ankle. My greatest advantage lost. My ability to walk among the enemy in the dark, like a ghost, without being seen, is what had caused men to fear my name. The goggles made the difference between life and death, victory and defeat, and now they sat useless at the bottom of the river.

The moan of pain and agony from the canoe brought me back to the reason I was standing in the first place. Tallmadge was trying to sit up. Both his hands clung to the canoe sides, and he dragged himself up to a sitting position.

"We need to get you out of the canoe so I can bring it into the tree line," I said. "We can't be here come sunup. They know we fled in a canoe and will be looking along both sides of the river come first light. They'll spot the canoe and send everyone they have after us."

"Agreed," Tallmadge groaned through gritted teeth. "Get me to my feet. I think I can walk."

I pulled him to his feet, and with an arm around my neck, I escorted him to the tree line. I made him as comfortable as possible in the brush and then went back for the canoe. Grabbing the front end, I dragged it into the tree line as well. It seemed out of sight, but I covered it with leafy branches anyway. Then, grabbing my sword and satchel, I made my way back to Tallmadge. He laid on his back, still breathing hard, fighting the pain of his twin brandings and the bruises that covered his body.

"This will help with the pain," I told him, pulling out my last morphine shot.
I gave him the shot and then my last antibiotic shot. His burns would get infected for sure if left to fester. I then gave him one of my canteens and told him to drink deeply, which he did. I hated using up my last morphine and antibiotic shots, but I didn't think he would survive if I hadn't. Like my goggles, those twenty-first century advantages were now gone. He handed me back my canteen.

"Drink the whole thing," I said, handing it back after taking a long swig myself.

The remains of my first aid kit consisted of two bandages, some tape, and half a bottle of pain killers. In my count of my ammo, I still had over forty rounds for my Thompson Contender but only four magazines for my Tec-9. Six rounds per magazine. In truth, I was amazed that I had made my ammo last this long.

"Get some sleep, if you can," I told Tallmadge. "We should be safe tonight. I want to get farther away from shore before sunup."

"Yes, good idea," Tallmadge said in a groggy tone, the morphine doing its job of hiding the pain and making him groggy so he could fall asleep.

Sleep for me was a luxury that I was not given. I needed to ensure that the British didn't start checking the shoreline by torch light to find us. Musket fire continued to rumble in the distance. I was bone tired but grabbed my satchel and trudged back to the riverbank to see what the commotion was about. After all, I was the only enemy around and they weren't shooting at me.

The Sandwich had been utterly destroyed, reduced to a burning pile of timber, having been ripped apart by cannons. It had then been set on fire by the troops who were no longer willing to board her after my grenade killed who knew how many.

The cargo ship that had been tied to the docks offloading cargo had been sunk. Only its mast stuck out of the water. The warship that had held Tallmadge still burned despite the pouring rain. The fire had spread and now the second and third decks were ablaze. Flames sprayed out of the cannon ports. The cannons had ceased firing while the entire crew scrambled to put out the fire. The captain of the burning warship was trying to sail her to shore before she went under, as the Sandwich's captain had done months ago. Muskets fired in the city as if they were being attacked by an invisible enemy. *What were they shooting at?*

Cannons from the shoreline fired at the massive, flaming, three deck warship that was now heading straight at them. It was like a ship from hell, piloted by the devil himself. The lightning and thunder overhead was an awesome sight to behold. A panicked run for shore by the crew to save their ship was misinterpreted as an attack, no doubt from the infamous Pale Rider. The poor misguided souls on shore had no idea what was going on and were shooting at their own sailors, while the crew of the massive warship did not know why they were being fired upon by their comrades. Men on the ship died as cannons ripped through what remained of the ship's hull and the great sails. Men jumped off the great ship, believing it was their only hope of surviving a battle against their own army.

Cannons from the city fired into the tree farther down around the river, killing shadows, downing trees and destroying an enemy that was not only not there, but never had been. Drums echoed throughout the city, calling troops to formation and signaling that the city was under attack. The guards, who only minutes ago had circled the entire city to prevent me from entering it, ran for cover, abandoning their posts, fearing an enemy that must be close enough for the cannons to have opened up. Bells rang from every ship in the river as their captains woke their men and prepared for battle. Trees in the forest continued falling as cannon balls from the city ripped through them, cutting them in half. Small fires erupted in the city – only God knew what started them. Screams reverberated in the night as the civilian population panicked at what they thought was the start of a major battle in the city. It was pure and absolute beautiful chaos.

The burning warship was still being fired upon from shore. Her captain must have realized that the men on shore were firing at her on purpose, trying to sink her. He was being forced to turn away from shore and sail upstream, only to be fired upon by the other ships in the river. The captains of those ships did not know what was going on, only that the troops on shore were trying to sink the huge, fiery ship that was struggling to escape the battle. With no other target in sight, they attacked the only possible enemy that they could see, not waiting to find out why the troops were attacking the beast of a ship. The ship tried to sail out of range, escaping the battle that they never wanted. I could tell it was too late for her. She had taken too many cannonballs to her hull, some of which were already under the water line. Between taking on water from below and being set on fire above, she was doomed. Even as she sailed away, she was sinking deeper and deeper. The captain would have to order his men to abandon ship soon, or they were destined to die with her.

It would take the officers the whole night to get the soldiers under control and discover that the city was safe, that the barbarians were not at the gates. In fact, the only barbarian around was soaking wet, across the river from them, and sitting in the mud while being rained on. And this particular barbarian wanted to get as far away from that shit show as he could.

I needed to clean my weapons after swimming in the river but trying to clean them in the rain wasn't possible. They would have to wait until the storm was over.

"General Clinton is going to shit a brick," I said out loud to myself, while laughter bubbled up in my throat. "Fear and suspicion. Well…That should do it."

I wondered if General Clinton was standing in the rain right now, as wet as I was.

Chapter Fourteen   Old Friends

Initially, I had planned on making a run for it before the sun even came up, but **Tallmadge** never would have gotten far on foot. No, we were going to have to use the canoe, and I needed to wait until things settled down.

The British finally figured out that they were either shooting at one another or at thin air. Once they realized the enemy wasn't attacking, the officers got their men under control. Not soon enough for the warship that sunk in the night as her crew jumped into the river. Several of the smaller warships had gone downriver to the ocean, blocking off any chance of us leaving last night. The storm had passed over us as fast as it had blown in. Now, I stood behind a large willow tree, as the sun's golden rays climbed out of the Atlantic Ocean and leapt over the low New Jersey hills, to show yours truly what laid before me. When I looked across the river, it appeared the sun wanted to show me how badly I was screwed.

Thousands of British troops fell into formation in the fresh mud, as if ready to march. Several dozen horsemen prepared to ride north and several dozen south. Half the soldiers or more from the city fell in with the other troops, also ready to march. Small and large warships alike sailed up and down the river with all hands-on deck, searching for me on either side of the river. Soldiers in two dozen smaller row boats and canoes made their way along the river on both sides. The smaller boats stayed close to shore, searching for any signs of us or our stolen canoe. At least they had waited for morning. They were afraid of missing the spot where we'd left the river for the safety of land. Well, safety was a strong word that really didn't apply here.

"Well, Thomas," I whispered to myself, "you wanted to get under General Clinton's skin. You wanted him pissed off and scared of you. You thought it was funny last night. Why aren't you laughing now?"

The answer was simple. Because I was about to die. I didn't see any way out of this. No strategies, no plan B, nothing. I tried not to think about Annie.

One of the boats carrying six men rowed my way, barely ten feet out from shore. They were still a hundred yards from me but bearing down on the river fast. Five of them wore the bright red uniforms of the British Empire, while the man in front wore brown. This had to be the man, the hunter Clinton had sent for. He was the General's point man on this fox hunt. Another one of my would-be killers looking to make a name for themselves as the man who killed the Pale Rider. The hunter looked familiar, but they were still too far for me to see his face clearly.

As the boat drew closer, the spit in my mouth dried up when I recognized who the man in brown was. *John Brooks.* The sniper who had tried to kill me last year. The last time I had seen him, he had a horse galloping under him and a bullet in his stomach. No, I hadn't shot him. One of his own men shot him by accident, while trying to shoot me in the back. I had dived out of the way, and Brooks took the bullet meant for me. In all fairness, I did kill the man who had shot him. Not because he shot Brooks, but because he'd tried to kill me. He took one of my knives into the chest.

I had given Brooks a chance to live but didn't really think he had much of a likelihood of surviving the gut shot injury. It seems like that was another one of my decisions I now lived to regret. At least I hoped I would continue to live to regret it. The cold temperature of last winter must have slowed his blood loss long enough for him to find a doctor. His official report undoubtedly made his part in our fight seem braver than it had been. If his commanding officer had known how he put his own self-interest above that of the Empire's, he would have been hung. He had allowed me to kill one of his own men for the trade of a horse and a chance to live. He was a coward who liked to kill from a distance, but he was still a man who was, indeed, a good shot.

I couldn't help noticing the extra-long musket in his hands. I had taken the musket Brooks owned when we fought and had gifted it to Jonas. Jonas had later given it to Lafayette. The musket could fire a lot farther than the standard British musket. Lafayette still owned it, and although he didn't carry it very often – as an officer he was expected to rely on pistols and swords – but he cherished it as a gift from Jonas. Brooks evidently found himself a new one. He could shoot that musket as far as I could shoot the Thompson, taking away another one of my greater advantages.

Rubbing my hands over my face, I glanced toward the bushes where I had hidden the canoe to make sure it was well enough out of sight. My heart dropped. The canoe was well hidden, but deep drag marks and footsteps imprinted in the mud led from the water to the bushes. Even the greenest tracker could see the marks. Small, stupid mistakes like this got men killed more often than the big ones. This was not a mistake that a woodsman like Brooks would overlook or let go unpunished. When they got close, he'd spot my mistake, and they would kill us.

Sure, I could take the soldiers out before they so much as got out of the boat, but then what? The other boats would hear and see what had happened, and I'd have all of them after us. No grenades, no cell phone, and no night vision goggles to help me. I did have my bullet-proof vest, my knives, my sword, about twenty-four rounds left for the Tec-9, and over forty for the Thompson. Not enough to fight an army of thousands.

Tallmadge wouldn't be able to run, which left me two choices. Leave him and run on my own or hide him and lead them away from here. As much as I considered the former, I knew the answer before I asked the question. I'd distract and lead them away. I wished Little Joe was here – doing this on foot was really going to suck.

I quickly made my way to Tallmadge, who was awake and moving. The brands on his chest glowed a fiery red and blistered. I didn't envy him those wounds.

"How are you feeling?" I asked.

"Better," he answered. "Would you happen to have any more of . . . whatever you gave me last night?"

"Sorry, no," I said, pulling out my bottle of pain killers.

I dropped two pills into his hand. "Take these. Can you row the canoe by yourself?"

"I can't run, but I can row," he answered, popping the two pills into his mouth without question. He must trust me a lot more than I trusted him. "May I ask why I would need to row by myself?"

"We are out of time," I told him. "They're coming."

"How many?" he asked, trying to stand.

"Looks like all of them. Or maybe only half of them."

His swollen eyes widened. "Half? You mean half of the soldiers in the city? That would be thousands."

"You stay hidden, and I'll lead them away from here," I said, ignoring his comment. "When the chance presents itself, take the canoe and make your way to General Washington. Tell him to attack now, not later. The very minute you reach him, tell him to march. The city will be his for the taking if you both hurry."

"No," he said, shaking his head. "I'll stay, you go to Washington. You can make it there faster than I can."

"Sorry to burst your ego," I said, "but Clinton doesn't care about you. They would kill you without stopping and still chase me. Clinton wants the Pale Rider, and he's sending everything he has to make sure I don't get away again. If I go to General Washington, I'll be taking the British with me. Your death won't help General

Washington, but maybe, if you get to him soon enough, mine will. I'll lead the British towards New York and away from Philadelphia."

Tallmadge's face fell. He was ashamed of the fact that he'd have to hide while I distracted the British, but nodded his head, understanding what I said was true. I grabbed my sword belt and strapped it on as I moved back to the tree line without another word. I left my filled canteen for Tallmadge. He'd need the water more than I. I did take the empty canteen in case I somehow had a chance to fill it.

I moved away from Tallmadge and towards the river. After finding a good thick willow tree to stand behind, partially hiding my body with its drooping branches. I waited for the rowboat to pass me. Brooks held his musket up and his head on a swivel, scanning left to right. I wanted to kill him first, knowing he was the one with the best chance of tracking me. As I feared, he spotted the tracks in the mud and pointed to them, and the boat pulled toward the riverbank.

I withdrew my Thompson and aimed it at Brooks. He was only forty yards from me, too close to miss. As the boat pressed forward in the water, he dropped out of my sight, blocked by the very tree I was hiding behind. I leaned farther out from the tree, bringing Brooks back into my view. I slowed my breathing and gently pulled the slack out of my pistol.

I don't know if Brooks saw my movement when I leaned out, or if my white shirt caught his attention, or if it was some sort of hunter's sixth sense, but as I started squeezing the trigger, his head turned my way and he spotted me. He dropped straight down into the boat as the Thompson bucked in my hand. The unfortunate soldier behind Brooks did a disastrous looking back flip out of the boat and into the water.

Brooks didn't waste a second trying to help the young man that I had certainly killed. Brooks was back up, musket aimed in my direction, butt stock in his shoulder. I pulled back behind the tree as he fired. As his shot boomed out, tree bark splattered and landed in my hair, and the whack of a heavy lead ball struck the tree.

I still had one major advantage over Brooks that I could and would exploit. I could load my Thompson four or five times faster than he could load his musket. Breaking the breach open and letting the spent casing fly out of the chamber, I slipped in a fresh round. After I snapped the pistol shut, I was loaded and ready in a mere few seconds. I envisioned in my mind where the boat was so that I'd instantly be on target when I exposed myself. I leaned out from behind the tree to kill Brooks as unfairly as possible while he was still loading his musket.

As I leaned out and aimed in Brooks's direction, he was already up and aimed in on me, waiting for me to pop my egotistically foolish head out. His men rowed hard in my direction, cutting the distance between us with every oar stroke. I didn't have time to sight in, so I pulled back again as his musket fired with a loud boom and a belch of dark gray smoke.

I thought he'd missed again for a second time, and was ready to count my blessings, until I felt the burning on the top of my right ear. When I reached up to touch my ear, I discovered a quarter size piece of cartilage missing from the top. My hand came away covered with dark red blood.

The bastard hadn't bothered loading his musket. He'd traded it with another soldier in the boat! I'd missed that trick. In the back of my mind, I found it hypocritical of me to be pissed about the fact that he was cheating better than I was.

I thought about trying again but wasted my chance examining my ear, and I knew he'd already traded muskets again and was now aimed in at this tree, waiting for me to make the same fatal mistake. If I had popped out and shot right away instead of checking my ear, I might have killed him. Well, that ship had sailed, and I had lost my chance. The one thing I knew for sure was that I was not sticking my head out again. I could feel Brooks aiming another musket at the tree, waiting for me to pop my head out like a life-size whack a mole. Splashes in the water on the shoreline told me that the boat was getting close.

I had wanted to get his attention and was confident that I had done that, so it was time to run like a fox and let the hounds chase me. That had been the plan, after all, to lead them away from the injured spy who had gotten me into this mess in the first place, so he could make his way back to General Washington.

Pushing away from the tree, I shot forward, breaking into a run. I tried to run the path of least resistance and go around the thick willows, but this wasn't New Jersey in the year 2021. This was 1778, and most of the country was still raw, virgin land. I was forced to push through thick walls of brushes, scratching my face and hands. My sword seemed to go out of its way to snag on every bush I ran through. I couldn't see or hear my pursuers, but I knew I was leaving a trail that a man like Brooks could follow in the dark on his worst day.

I had gotten a little turned around in the thick bushes, and the fact that my sword kept snagging and pulling me to the left didn't help. When I finally busted through the thick man-hating bushes, I found myself back on the muddy bank of the river. Several smaller warships were only two hundred yards away. Men spotted me standing on the bank like a target waiting to be shot and pointed my way. One of the ships disappeared in a field of gray as every cannon on her east side fired, covering the wooden beast in a blanket of smoke. The riverbank erupted in explosions, as cannon balls hit the water, mud, and trees, then exploded like bombs. None of them impacted near me, but running along the bank was not an option I was going to choose. The ship was turning her nose, and the rest of the cannons would be pointed straight at me any second.

As I turned around the way I had come, two soldiers burst from the bushes much quicker than I had. I'd blazed a trail for them, after all. One of the two yelled out that they had me while the other raised his musket. I drew my Tec-9, firing twice at point blank range and killing them where they stood. Movement came from behind where they'd been standing, but I couldn't see anyone in the thick brush.

Doing what I had firmly said I was *not* going to do, I ran north along the bank of the river. Four or five row boats in the river quickly turned my way. The second small war ship erupted in explosions as she fired her cannons. Dirt and sand rained down on me as the cannon balls struck much closer than the first volley had. Between the smoke and the flying dirt, I could barely see where I was going.

Brooks and several more soldiers broke into the clearing where their dead companions lay. I'm guessing their first thought was to shoot me in the back, but as the muddy bank had turned into a killing field of fire, smoke, and flying sand, they ran the way they'd come. Cannon balls didn't ask what side you were on. They killed you no matter what uniform you were wearing.

One of the cannon balls that missed me had ripped through several trees like an unstoppable force of nature. Never wanting to look a gift horse in the mouth, I spun on my toe and jumped over the stump of a tree and the one behind it. The bushes were thick, but not near as bad as before.

I needed to continue north towards New York but had to get out of sight of the ships and their massive cannons. I put the sun at my one o'clock and pushed northeast. The men in the row boats would head to the bank and give chase in a few minutes, but I intended to get as far away from here before they, or Brooks, picked up my trail.

Flashing back to my escape and evade academy classes, I knew of different kinds of traps I could have made using only branches and vines, but they took too long to build and set. Now was the time to focus on the evading away part of the class.

As I ran through the bushes, I was leaving a trail no better than a charging bull. I needed to find a stream to run through or maybe hard packed ground, anything to cover or hide my tracks. I wanted them to follow me north, but now that they were, I needed to lose them.

Drums sounded across the river, signaling the primary force of the army was on the move. They'd head north to get ahead of me. That meant that there had to be a bridge somewhere upriver. Nowhere close by to me that I could see. The river was too wide here for any kind of bridge. British to the south tracking me, a river with warships was to my west, Atlantic Ocean to my east. I had no choice but to keep pushing north. As the British nipped at my heels, my earlier joke about the fox and hounds no longer seemed funny.

As I continued trekking northeast, the landscape started to change. Mud turned to packed dirt, bushes thinned out, no longer forming solid walls of vines. Willow trees turned to ash and pine trees. With the rain that the storm had brought with it, my trail was still easy to follow in the packed dirt. Where was Daniel Boone when I needed him? He'd know what to do. The man had a way of moving through the forest that would put Brooks to shame.

The thought of back-tracking and going south, letting the British pass me, was the only tactical idea I could come up with. Brooks was a much better woodsman than I, however, and he'd no doubt be looking for that tactic. My best and maybe only hope of survival was to keep pushing hard north and hope that I could stay ahead of my pursuers. Not what I would call much of a plan, but it was all I had.

I drove hard throughout the day, turning due north. I hadn't pushed myself this hard since I was in the Royal Police Academy. I filled my canteen at a stream I was lucky enough to find. The stream ran north-south, and I was only guessing that it might lead me back to the river. But it was an educated guess, so it was good enough for me. Wading in past my ankles, I stuck to the freezing cold stream, walking in knee-high water. The sun climbed high above me, warming the day. My lunch consisted of a handful of blackberries that I was fortunate enough to find growing over the stream bank. As the sun sunk in the west, my dinner was the water in my canteen and a lone piece of wet beef jerky that I found at the bottom of my satchel.

The sun disappeared on the western horizon, and the moon appeared from the patchy night clouds. The moon was a sliver short of a full moon and gave off enough light to see by. The higher the moon rose, the lower the water temperature dropped. My feet grew numb from the cold water now that I didn't have the sun to warm me or the shallow stream to walk in. Cold feet were a cheap price to pay for making it harder to track me.

I hadn't seen any British soldiers since that morning when I started my death run. I knew I wasn't even close to being safe. I was only moving slightly faster than those tracking me. My advantage was that they needed to move somewhat slower and make sure they hadn't missed or bypassed the spot where I exited the stream and lose my trail. If Brooks was tracking, they might not need to slow down too much. I had to hope they never bothered looking for Tallmadge. He should have been well on his way to General Washington by now.

If he wasn't, I was going to kill him myself.

The British on the other side of the river and on the ships were my bigger concerns. I had no idea where they were or what they were doing. They assuredly were searching for a way to cross over the river and cut me off. I didn't know what they called it in the eighteenth century, but in my time, it was called a *blocking movement*. No matter what they called it, they'd set up some kind of blocking force north of me. I had been pushing myself hard and moving fast, so I was probably ahead of the foot soldiers on either side. What of the men on horseback? Or on the river? Were they ahead of me? How could they *not* be?

Throughout that day and night, between walking and running, I estimated I covered twenty or twenty-two miles. I was beyond exhausted, and my body clamored to rest for a few hours. With only my light linen clothes, weapons, and satchel, I made sure that I'd put enough distance between the British in their gear and uncomfortable uniforms to rest for a few hours. On the upside of things, my ear had stopped bleeding.

I came upon a huge fallen oak tree that had pulled out its dirt-encased roots from the ground when it had fallen over. The tree was dead, appeared to have blown down years ago, and had fallen with the top half laying across the stream. Cold water rippled freely through the bare branches. A thick layer of bright green moss coated the entire north side of the tree. The south side had no moss and appeared dead and dry, even with the fresh rain that we recently had. The large tree was rotting from the inside out. The tree was exactly what I needed for cover and concealment.

Working quickly, I dug out a cubby hole in the soft ground next to and amid the giant trunk a few feet from the stream. I tossed the dirt I dug out on the north side with my knife and bare hands into the stream as to not bring attention to this spot. Lying down in my hole partially under the tree and fresh moss, I was hidden from the British as well as the breeze blowing from the south that might carry my sweaty scent.

My watch said it was midnight, so I had about six hours before sunup. I closed my eyes.

Final Chance

Chapter Fifteen   A Bundle of Nerves

My eyes shot open in the dark when voices reached my ears. I didn't move, not even to look at my watch, but it was still night. Two different voices spoke, but their words were muffled by the tree I was hiding under.

Large frogs near the water croaked loudly and competed with crickets in the grass. The sudden impact of boots jumping on the top of the tree right over my head, silenced the nearby creatures of the night. I held my breath. Moss broke off and fell on my face. The dirt and grass in front of me lit up in a ring of bright yellow light from the torch that the owner of the boots held. The torch light moved as a pair of black leather boots landed inches from my face. My eyes skimmed upward to a pair of legs in British red pants and led to a British red coat.

The soldier walked forward, holding the torch high in front of his face. A second soldier climbed over the fallen tree and moved to catch up to his friend with the torch. If either man turned around or even looked back, they'd see me clear as day.

"Stay closer to the water, you fucker," the second man told the one with the torch. "We're looking for the spot where he might have cut from the stream."

I moved my head a few inches to see if anyone else was with them. Torch light bounced around on the other side of the stream. They figured out I'd taken to hiding my tracks in the water and were looking for the spot where I may have climbed out. If I stayed here, they'd be ahead of me, with who knew how many soldiers behind me. I may not have been a military tactician, but I did know that I didn't want to get trapped between two forces.

Voices yelling farther back told me that they'd be the first of many to walk over me. They must have been searching for me throughout the night without rest. The fact that I was hidden, and their own exhaustion, were the only reasons I was still alive. Brooks wasn't one of these two men, but I was betting he was nearby. I didn't think he would let others find me first. No, he was in this group somewhere – he had to be. I had bested him once, and he wouldn't let another get the first shot at me.

I needed to move from this hiding space, and I needed to move right now. The next group to pass me might not overlook me so easily.

"*Move, damn you,*" I yelled at myself in my head, convincing my body to cooperate.

I rolled out slowly and soundlessly from my shallow hole, holding my sword against my left leg so that it didn't rattle. Coming up on one knee and drawing my Tec-9, I pushed off with my other foot, rising into a walk. As I stood, the tip of my sword scabbard scraped the ground, and I groaned inwardly. The second soldier spun around to find me standing in front of my log.

Before he had a chance to react, I fired two quick shots into his chest. The *thunk thunk* sound that the Tec-9 coughed out wasn't loud, but in the silent dark night after the creatures and insects had gone quiet, I might as well have been banging a drum. He crumpled onto the ground as his friend spun around, firing his musket without aiming. His round went wild somewhere in the darkness, but it didn't matter because the gig was up. Every British soldier within five hundred yards had to have heard that.

I fired one round into his chest as I ran straight at him. He was face down in the dirt when I jumped over him and turned away from the stream toward the woods. Two shots rang out from the other side of the stream. One round flew deep into the night, but the other struck a tree I was running past. Splashing in the water told me at least two men from the other side of the stream crossed over to this side. A dozen more shots behind me disturbed the night.

"Where is he?" a voice called out.

"Up ahead!" came an answer to the first voice.

"I don't see him!"

"And you won't," Brooks's voice yelled out. "Not unless he wants you to. We aren't chasing some blacksmith or sheep herder, you fool. This is the Pale Rider."

"We're off to your right," a new voice shouted.

Other voices yelled out from the south as the men who'd been behind me were now rampaging through the bushes and around trees to catch up. Looking over my shoulder, I watched several torches dancing up and down through the black of night. The moonlight that had provided some illumination before was now blocked out by the trees. An ever-growing number of unfamiliar voices kept yelling to ask if anyone saw me.

Did anyone see me? Such a stupid question for them to yell out.

If one of them saw me, everyone would know because they would be shooting at me.

The air exploded out of my lungs as an unknown force from my left collided into me. Arms enclosed my body, and I was tackled to the ground by my assailant. I rolled in the dirt with him. The distinct sound of a musket hitting the ground was followed by a grunt from my attacker.

"Over here!" the man on top of me yelled out. "I have him! I have him!"

I brought my pistol up under his chin.

"You already fired that, boy," my attacker said, chuckling.

I grimaced more than grinned when I fired my last shot, and hot, metallic blood sprayed over my face. The top of the man's head blew off, and his dead weight fell on top of me. I had to close my eyes and mouth as blood sprayed out and poured over me. Blind as I was from the dark and his blood, I still managed to push the dead soldier off me. I didn't know how close the others were, so I holstered my now empty pistol and drew my two knives, expecting the fighting to be up close. I wiped my eyes with the sleeves of my shirt and stood up, spitting blood out of my mouth, knives out in front of me. As I blinked my eyes open, the glow of torches moved closer but was still mostly hidden behind trees.

"Where?" a voice called out.

"Shut up, you fool," Brooks's voice yelled in a comically loud whisper. "Just keep moving forward."

I spun around and ran as fast as I could, wishing I still had my night vision goggles as I crashed into one branch after the next. I could stop and fight, but without my goggles, I didn't have a chance of surviving. Much of my rumored skill was a result of my tech. I heard the trickling stream off to my left and turned to make my way back towards it. The compass on my watch confirmed I was still running north.

The sound of men shouting lessened as I pulled away blindly, running at a full sprint in the night, slipping in the mud, smacking into branches, and leaving an obvious trail for everyone to follow. I sheathed my knives as I ran, then stopped behind a tree and withdrew my Thompson. I aimed it the way I had come, but no targets presented themselves to me. Holstering my Thompson, I drew my Tec-9 and reached into my satchel for a newly loaded magazine. My fingers found three of them. I slipped two of them into my front pocket and loaded my Tec-9 with the last. Knowing it was going to be a fruitless endeavor before I checked, I reached into my satchel to search for any additional magazines but found none. I had eighteen rounds left for my Tec-9, and then it turned into a large paper weight. I was going to have to rely on my Thompson more.

With my left hand against the tree, I rested my forehead against the back of my hand, and stared down at my feet, panting hard. I holstered my Tec-9 with my right hand. I needed a plan and couldn't come up with one. My mind was a blank. I was alone, short on ammo, no explosives, and being chased by dozens of soldiers with thousands more on the Philadelphia side of the river. Outnumbered and outgunned, I resorted to my only option. I pushed off from the tree, sprinting north again as a thin beam of light crested the horizon. Daybreak.

Midday came and the sun was high above me. I was starting to stumble as I ran and knew that I was going to drop if I didn't rest soon. Every muscle in my body screamed as I moved, and I'm sure sheer exhaustion was why I couldn't think of a solution or plan for my present situation.

The stream was again off to my left, and I made my way to it. I had been putting it off, but I knew I was going to have to backtrack in the stream and find a spot to set up an ambush. Not for the first time I wished Daniel Boone was with me. He would have been better at this than I was.

The soldiers would follow my tracks so I could predict where they'd be coming from. I knelt in the stream behind some high grass, trying to catch my breath as I washed dried blood from my face. The water was warmer than it had been at night, but still cold enough to make my nuts push up into my stomach. When my breathing slowed, I struggled to regain my feet and made my way down river.

A hundred yards down, I located a spot with a four-foot-high bank. When I stood at the bank, only my head and shoulders were exposed. Two hundred yards from the bank was a clearing that I recognized as having ran through twenty minutes ago. A suggestion of an idea formed in my mind. If I could kill a few of the soldiers as they made their way through that field, it might slow them down. But in truth, I was lying to myself. I was actually hoping to see Brooks. I needed only one good shot to finish the fucker. He was the one tracking me with a singular deadly purpose.

The rest were cannon fodder for him, to make me waste my ammo. If I took him out, I might stand a chance.

The soldiers were closer than I thought. Several of them broke through the trees and into the open field about fifteen minutes later. First, a few soldiers spread out, then a dozen, and then about thirty. The first of them focused on the ground, following the deep, muddy tracks I had left in my wake. They all wore red coats, and none had on a brown coat. Either Brooks wasn't among these men, or he'd taken a coat off one of the men I had killed so that I couldn't pick him out of the group. There was no telling with that back-shooting, spineless, sneaky bastard.

I had my Thompson out, supported by the shelf bank I stood behind. Six 30-30 rounds rested on the ground in front of me for faster reloads. I didn't want to use my Tec-9 but set it on the bank within easy reach in case they got close, and I had to use it. I couldn't wait any longer for Brooks to show himself. The first of the red coats were halfway through the open field.

If you have ever tried to fire a pistol after wading in freezing cold water, you know that the biggest problem is stopping your hands from shaking. With my unsteady sights on the first lead soldier, I slowed my breathing and very slowly squeezed the trigger, letting the pistol buck in my hand. The soldiers turned to face my direction, several of them firing blindly as the lead soldier fell face first in the mud. Some of them ran my way, but most remained in the field like they'd been trained to do.

Not taking my eyes off the men in the field, I broke my Thompson open, letting the spent cartridge fly out as I slipped a new one into the chamber. Snapping the barrel back into place, I aimed in and shot one of the three men running at me. The first crumpled over and rolled in the mud. I had rushed my shot and hit him in the stomach and not the chest, but the results were acceptable. He wouldn't get up for a while, if at all. I reloaded again and shot the next man in line, who flew over heels over head backwards. Adrenaline rushed through my body and my blood flow warmed me. My hands were steadier now that I was in a fight than they'd been a minute ago.

The men in the field fired at me now, not realizing I was too far from their muskets to reach. If they were closer, I'd still present a difficult target with only my head and arms above the riverbank. From my point of view, I had been in this century for almost ten months now and yet I was still amazed at the stupidity of their tactics. To stand straight and tall in the open field while firing at me was nothing less than suicide.

I fired and the third and final man running at me landed on his back, arms sprawled wide. One of the soldiers in the field with a few stripes on his coat took charge, ordering the men still standing to form up into two ranks, the first rank on one knee and the second rank standing. The entire front rank fired on me as the second rank reloaded. The next man to fall was the one giving the orders. When he fell, several of the men in the front rank stood up as if they were going to run. Another soldier stepped out of line and started taking command, yelling at the rest to stay in place. When he had their attention, the second rank opened fire on me while the first rank reloaded.

Their shots were getting closer with every volley, pinging in the dirt yards in front of me, as they gauged how far away I was. My next shot stuck the newest soldier giving orders in the head, blowing most of it off his neck. This time the ranks broke, and twenty-something men raced for the trees behind them. Grabbing the last bullet in front of me, I rushed another shot, trying to take out one more soldier to help the rest with their motivation to keep running. The soldier I shot at fell, but by the cockeyed way he collapsed, I must have only clipped his shoulder.

That all bought me some time to get away. I didn't think any of them were in a hurry to run into the open field again. Even if they tried secretly to circle around, it would slow them down enough for me to escape. I pulled out another 30-30 round from my satchel, getting ready to load it.

The sound of a musket shot rang out behind me as a hammer slammed into my back, knocking the air out of my lungs. I was pushed hard onto the riverbank shelf in front of me. I bounced off the shelf and half fell, and half rolled into the river. I didn't feel the bullet in my left hand escape my grasp, but it was no longer there.

I whipped my head around, trying to figure out what was going on, and found myself laying on my back in the water. I was lucky that it was only six or seven inches deep where I was. It took a second to put two and two together and realize I'd been shot in the back. Pain shot through my body like lightning. My fingers went numb, and I had a hard time controlling them.

About a hundred and fifty yards from me on the other side of the stream, John Brooks and another man rose from some high grass, muskets in hand, and yelled out some kind of celebratory *yahoo* sound. He'd shot me in the center of my back. Did he think me dead? My vest had stopped the bullet, but he'd managed to punch a cluster of nerves hard enough to lock up my body. My legs had a hard time moving, but at least they *were* moving, if not fully under my control.

Brooks didn't bother reloading his musket. Instead, he and the other man waded into the water, crossing the stream at an angle, coming straight at me. He was casually walking, taking his time. He knew he hit me in the center of the back. At that range, a marksman like him could never miss. In most cases, getting shot in the center of the back was a kill shot. My vest had stopped the bullet, but that didn't mean I was going to live through the next few minutes. My Thompson was laying in the water next to my open hand, which still didn't want to obey me.

I could bend my legs, but my fingers still didn't want to work. I flailed at my Thompson, but my fingers were numb and didn't close around the grip. When I finally got them to close, I lifted the pistol out of the water. It took several more attempts to release the breach, but the spent cartridge did finally leap free. The splashing of water was getting closer. I kept an ear on Brooks's footsteps as he got closer as I reached into my satchel for another loose round. Finding one with my tingling fingers, I tried to grab it without luck. I had a hard time wrapping my fingers around the shell. When I finally did, I dropped it. Growling at myself, I shoved the fresh round into the breach and closed the pistol with a snap.

Turning my pistol towards Brooks, I had to concentrate more on pulling the trigger than on aiming. I managed to fire just as Brooks pulled the soldier next to him directly in front of himself. The man stumbled, arms swinging wildly as Brooks yanked him off balance and then dropped straight down into the water as my bullet took him in the side, a few inches under his arm.

Clambering to my feet, I made it to the bank shelf. I didn't know if I could reload the Thompson again, so I grabbed my Tec-9. I spun around to face Brooks, but the man was gone. He had dived into the weeds and tall grass. Not wanting to press my luck, I took off running again.

I knew Brooks well enough to know he wasn't coming after me alone with only a musket by his side. He'd regroup with the other soldiers and build up their courage to come after me again, but they'd come at a much slower pace – knowing I could hide anywhere, ready to kill whoever was in front.

I traveled through the night and into the next morning, pushing myself to the brink of exhaustion. It didn't take long for me to get the feeling in my fingers back. I had been swallowing pain killers like they came from a Pez candy dispenser since Brooks had shot me in the back. It was a fair shot – the group of nerves he hit ached like hell.

Final Chance

Chapter Sixteen   Mother's Advice

The stream didn't connect to the river like I had hoped but did lead close enough that I could hear the rushing water. I paused to take a needed break and sat behind a wide thick blackberry bush, picking large juicy blackberries and drinking water out of my canteen for breakfast while watching for any activity on the far side of the river.

So far, I hadn't seen or heard any soldiers. The river narrowed here, only about fifty feet wide, and the bottleneck caused the water to run faster at this point, forming small rapids. I stood on the bank eating wild berries thirty yards south of a wooden bridge extending across the river.

The bridge was built about ten feet above the waterline and constructed of a log frame with flat boards across the top for a smooth crossing. The logs were cut and fitted into place like a giant set of Lincoln logs I remember having as a kid. The ends had been covered with tar, and ropes were wrapped around the tar and logs to prevent them from slipping out of place. It looked sturdy enough for the British to move across, so I presumed this was the way they were going to come. The other side of the river was clear of British troops for now, but then again, you couldn't move an entire army as fast as a single man could move alone.

I had just popped another berry into my mouth when two men across the river rode over the slight hill on horseback from the south. I shifted deeper in the brush and studied them. The red coats they wore on told me they were British soldiers, and they were heading straight to the bridge north of me. They had muskets slung on their backs. Cavalry swords hung on their hips, scabbards bouncing against the flanks of their horses. But why only two of them? Messengers or scouts? If they were messengers, they might have dispatches I wanted to read. If they were scouts, then thousands of troops could be on the far side of the hill coming this way. It was all academic, because in the end, I needed a horse, and two of them were coming my way, ridden by dead men who didn't know they were about to die.

Bending at the waist to lower my profile, I rushed the bridge, staying as low as I could. When the line of bushes ended, I hurried to a tree next to the bridge, then I waited until the clapping of horseshoes against the wooden planks grew near. I climbed up onto the bridge as the two men on horseback closed in on me.

Stepping out in the open with my knife in my right hand and my Thompson in my left, I decided at the last second to give them a chance to survive. I stood in the way with my arms in the air to stop them. Seeing me standing there blocking their way, they instead kicked their horses into a run, coming straight at me full gallop. The deafening sound of their hooves echoing against the wooden planks made it seem like they were going faster than they actually were. I didn't know if they knew who I was or if they were going to run down anyone in their way, but they came at me full speed.

I threw my knife at the first rider right before I dove to the ground to avoid being trampled to death. I had aimed for the center of his chest, but my knife stuck deep in his right shoulder. He rolled over backwards off his horse, landing on the bridge face down. His musket fell off him and crashed a few feet away. The other rider didn't slow down or look back to check on his friend. I rolled to my feet, shifting my Thompson from my left hand to my right. Bringing my sights up to eye level and thumbing the hammer back, I had to wait for the riderless horse to veer to the right and out of the way of the second rider. I placed my front sight of the Thompson on the center of the rider's back. As my hammer slammed forward, striking the bullet's primer, and the rider fell forward off his horse, striking the ground on his side.

Now, with neither horse being controlled by a rider, they slowed to a walk, unsure where to go. I went after them before they strayed too far. The horses were well trained and didn't run from me. I mounted the first horse I was able to grab. He was solid brown and tame enough to let me on his back without protest. When I returned to the bridge, the soldier on his face hadn't moved. He carried a satchel not unlike mine over his shoulder.

Dismounting my new horse, I picked up the discarded musket and chucked it over the side of the bridge. I was rewarded by the sound of a splash in the water. Then I rolled the soldier over with my foot. His chest moved, but he was unconscious. He looked to be in his early twenties, fair haired, and hadn't shaved in a few days. A pistol was tucked in the front of his belt. I reached down and pulled it out of his belt, tossing it over the side of the bridge, too.

I grabbed the handle of my knife, and he woke up screaming as I yanked my blade free from his shoulder muscles. Ignoring his protest and with a quick ripping sound, I severed the strap on his satchel. The soldier tried to sit up, and I shoved him back down with my left foot. Leaving my foot on his chest to hold him in place, I dug through his satchel. Tucked inside was a piece of what looked like hard candy, a small metal ball with holes in it attached to a thin chain, a tri-folded, two-page letter, and a few biscuits.

I sheathed my knife and then shoved one of the hard, crumbly biscuits in my mouth. I chewed the biscuit, hoping not to break a tooth on it, as I unfolded the document. The sour biscuit was the worst biscuit I had ever eaten, but I was so hungry I was ready to fish out another. The folded document was correspondence from General Clinton. The letter was not addressed to anyone in particular and written in a way that the messenger could have handed it to any commanding officer they came across.

Clinton wrote about spotting General Washington and his Continental army moving north towards New York. Clinton was moving his entire army north, giving up Philadelphia in order to protect New York from Washington and requested New York forces to move south to capture any of Washington's spies or scouts.

Why was Washington moving towards New York? Did his plans change? If I had gone through all this to provide a distraction for him so he could attack New York, me and the General were going to have words.

Glancing down at the soldier under my foot, I gave him my best *I'm not starving. I'm just a mean asshole, look.*

"What's your name?" I asked.

"Wesley, sir," he croaked out while his eyes fixated on the top of my head.

It took me a minute to realize that he was looking at either my scar or the dry blood in my hair. What a mess I must have been, between my old scar, the piece of my ear now missing, and my white linen clothes that now probably resembled the first ever set of tie-dyed hippie clothes, staining dark red on my shoulders to the washed-out pinkish pants. My once-normal looking black boots and black vest, now contrasted even more against the white, pink, and red of my clothes.

"When was Washington spotted and where?" I asked him.

He shook his head no, and I interpreted that to mean he wasn't going to answer. His left hand drifted to the front of his belt. I let him move his hand and waited for him to realize that the pistol was no longer there. Once he discovered his pistol was absent, I put more of my weight on my left foot and onto his chest. He grabbed my boot with both hands. He couldn't dislodge my foot and was too terrified to put much effort into his endeavor.

"Answer me, Wesley," I commanded.

"You don't understand," he wheezed out between breaths and shaking his head.

The young man pissed himself right there in front of me as he laid on his back. The dark red of his pants turned even darker in the crotch with the wet stain of urine. I shifted some of the weight back to my right leg and nodded my head for him to explain. I could tell he was resigned and too afraid to lie to me. I almost felt bad for him.

"I meant that Washington wasn't spotted," he clarified.

I shifted my weight back a little to my left foot for emphasis and waved the paper in the air, as if to say *I read it for myself.*

"It's a lie," he said. "The whole thing is a falsehood. A justification to march his army north."

"Explain," I said, not easing up on his chest.

"General Clinton has sworn that you'll not get away again," he said. So, he *did* know I was the Pale Rider. "He's sending everyone under his command at you. The letter justifies him sending thousands of troops after you and, at the same time, bringing soldiers down from New York to cut off your escape. If you do manage to escape him, then he'll continue to New York, seeking safe harbor from you there. This will all be done under the guise of Washington marching north to New York."

"Why?" I asked.

"I heard him talking," the soldier explained quickly. "He would hang, or worse, live in disgrace, for surrendering Philadelphia to chase one man. Plus, New York wouldn't send soldiers south to search the countryside for you. Washington is heading for New York in the general's official documents only."

"I know the man wants me at the end of a rope, but why would Clinton give up Philadelphia to catch me?" I asked.

Even the most wanted man alive wasn't worth giving up an entire city. At least not one as big and important as Philadelphia.

"There's been talk," the soldier said. "Those who guard the general say that he has nightmares about you. Ever since he found his secretary dead and your knife sticking in his desk. He says that if you could kill the Prime Minister of England, in the king's own palace no less, then what chance would he have of stopping you here?"

They knew that was me as well. Wow, the general and the mad king could start a support group about me.

"To be clear," I said. "Washington was *not* spotted heading to New York?"

"I have no idea where Washington is, sir," he answered.

I took my foot off the soldier's chest and took another bite of dry biscuit.

"Thank you, Wesley," I said. "You should run away now before I change my mind."

The young man was on his feet with his left hand clamped against his bloody right shoulder and running east across the bridge before I had finished my sentence. His sword swung wildly behind him, but I think he'd forgotten that he even had it on.

Sticking the rest of the biscuit in my mouth, I climbed back onto my new horse. I rode hard and fast westward, riding around the entire British force that was marching north along the river. I was far enough west before General Clinton and his troops made their way from the south. Then I circled around south, and the next day headed east for General Washington and Philadelphia. I couldn't believe I had made it out of all that alive.

I rode at a slow pace since I was no longer being chased by the British. I stopped at a creek to refill my water bag, wash down the dust that clung to my throat, and let my horse rest. I was so hungry that I was searching in the trees for a squirrel to shoot. I knew for a fact that they tasted like chicken, so I wasn't against shooting one out of a tree.

A shot rang out and my poor horse crumpled to the ground, but he wasn't dead and was screaming. I dove to the side, landing in the water when another shot fired, the bullet smacking the mud right where I had been merely a second ago.

I crawled to a log, keeping low as to not give anyone else a shot at me. Down the trail I had come from, I noticed a horse tied to a tree. It was the other horse from the two scouts I had ambushed. Two shots rang out, so two red coats must have ridden double on him.

Two more shots echoed the air, and two solid whacks struck the log I was behind, flicking wood chips into the water. The shots came from two different locations. One was to my left, somewhere in the high grass, and the other was straight ahead of me, closer to the horse and among the trees.

My horse fell silent and no longer kicked out or tried to raise his head. I needed a horse, so I crawled forward into the woods. Staying low, I kept hearing shots, but they were still shooting at the log and not me.

I had hung my sword belt over my horse's saddle so that I could wash in the creek, so my sword and Tec-9 were under the dead animal. I cursed under my breath at that loss. I did have my Thompson out and in my right hand, and I knew where the shooter was. I just needed to circle around and come up from behind him.

It was painfully slow going, moving such a long distance while trying not to make a sound. I stood up and moved in closer to the shooter. The ground was mostly dirt and still slick with mud from the rain. Brooks stood behind a tree, aiming at the log I had dived behind. I wanted to get in closer. I wanted to be too close to miss. Moving until I was only ten feet away, I, too, ducked behind a tree.

As I focused on him, Brooks turned and shot without even aiming. His round hit the trunk of the tree next to my face, splintering it. His wild shot was spot on, only stopped by the tree in front of me. I recoiled when he fired, and when I looked again, Brooks was running straight at me. I moved to shoot, and he kicked out with his right foot before I could bring my pistol to bear on him. His boot knocked my pistol out of my hand, and it flew against a rock, clattering behind me. I grabbed one of my two knives, intending to slash his throat. The butt stock of his musket came down into my face, smashing my left eye and knocking me to the ground, the back of my head impacting against a rock.

Stars filled my vision like lightening in a storm, as my left eye swelled shut. I struggled to focus on not letting go of my knife. Brooks took a step back from me, not ready to kill me yet. Like a badly written 1990s T.V. villain, he needed to taunt me and make sure I knew he had bested me, that it was *he* who would have the last laugh.

"I'm sure you're surprised to see me alive, after leaving me gut shot," he said with scorn heavy in his voice, and a smile on his face.

"As I remember it," I grumbled, "I left you on a horse riding to a doctor so you wouldn't die."

"Did you really think I'd make it to Fort Stanwix alive?" He raised his eyebrows high.

"No, not really," I answered with a groan. "I only let you go because I was sure you'd never make it there. But I still gave you the chance."

"At the cost of my friend's life," he snapped, his scornful smile fading.

"You were the one who betrayed your friend for a chance, and a horse," I snapped back. "And how did you survive not being hung by your own command? I'm guessing you lied and made yourself out to be a hero?"

I really didn't give a shit about how or why he was still alive, but I needed to stall and think of yet another plan to get out of this mess.

"I gave an accurate report, based on my point of view," he said. "The only person who could have contradicted my report was the Major. If you hadn't killed Major Campbell, I would have hung. Thank you for that. I knew you'd kill him. You bested me that day, so I knew you'd kill Major Campbell easy enough."

"So happy I could help," I said sarcastically, as I turned the knife around in my hand, preparing to throw it. "But easy wouldn't be the way I remember it."

He stepped forward, ready to butt stroke me again. I guess he was done bragging and wanted to end this. I brought my upper body up and threw my knife at his chest. He swung his musket in reflex and knocked the knife out of the air. Then I kicked out with all my strength with the heel of my right foot and caught him in the right kneecap with a loud crack. Brooks screamed, grabbed at his leg, and fell to his side into the mud. I rolled again and scanned the area.

My Thompson laid in a puddle of water between two rocks a few feet from me, its barrel sticking up. Brooks was using his musket like a cane to help himself stand, so I dove forward, landing a few feet from my pistol. Reaching with my right arm, I grabbed the Thompson by the barrel and snatched it out of the water. I let the Thompson slide through my palm and grasped the pistol grip, swinging my arm towards Brooks as my thumb jerked back the hammer.

Brooks froze in place a few feet from me, his musket raised high like a club ready to smash my head. Brooks's smile deepened as I pointed the pistol at him that had been pulled from the water. Any water-logged flint lock would be useless when pulled out of the mud and water. As he brought the club down, I fired. My round struck him in the right shoulder, and he spun around, landing in the mud face down, away from me. In the back of his shoulder was a hole where my bullet had exited. His shirt was already soaked in blood. A fist-sized bulge under the shirt looked like bone and muscle had been pushed out the back of his shoulder with the round.

I stood up on wobbly legs and fished out another round for my Thompson. Brooks rolled over slowly, taking a deep breath of air, as his face emerged from the mud. With a shaky hand, I broke the Thompson open, let the spent cartridge escape, and loaded a fresh round.

Blood seeped out of the hole in the front of Brooks's shoulder. His right arm hung in a way that told me I had destroyed his scapula. A 30-30 round could do a lot of damage to the human body, especially from a close range. Hell, this gun was designed to take down a deer with its thick bones and powerful muscles. With the primitive level of medical care he had received in this century, he might never use that arm again.

He was done. He was a sniper who would never fire a musket again.

"How?" was all Brooks asked, staring wide-eyed at my dripping pistol.

"Does it matter?" I asked.

"You win," he admitted. "I'm finished. Even if I make it to a doctor, I won't be coming for you again."

"If I let you live, we're done?" I asked, unsure if I believed him. "You won't come after me again?"

"In the name of all that is holy to me, I swear it."

"You should have thought about that last time."

As he opened his mouth to say something, I raised the gun and pulled the trigger, blowing his brains out the back of his head and into the mud under him.

"Like my mother used to say," I said to the dead body of John Brooks. "Fool me once, shame on you. Fool me twice, shame on me."

I stood over him with my one swollen eye, tired all over. Holstering my empty pistol, I pulled out my other knife. Taking a trick from General Washington's bag, I sliced a small cut under my eye, like I had seen him do the first night I'd met him. The blood flowed freely down my face and freed the pressure of built-up blood until I was able to open my left eye again.

The sound of a snapping branch caught my ears, and I turned my head to see a British soldier standing stock still behind high grass.

The soldier looked to be seventeen years old, if that. I doubted that he needed to shave yet. He gripped a musket in his hands, with the butt pulled tight into his shoulder. His eyes were wide, and his mouth hung open. The barrel of the musket was pointed slightly down as if he wanted to shoot me, but an invisible hand held his rifle, stopping him from raising it any higher. As if he knew that he only had one chance to kill me, and if he failed, he was doomed. As if merely pointing a musket at me might cost him his life.

We locked eyes, and fear and dread shadowed his. He knew he was looking at the Pale Rider. Not only had I lived after what had to be a fatal hit to my back yesterday, but now stood in front of him on my own two feet. The Pale Rider who, without mercy or compassion, shot Brooks in the head. Then he saw me talking to Brooks's dead body? Did the young man wonder if I really had the ability to speak to dead people? Not to mention that I had taken out my knife and cut my own face. Blood still seeped from the laceration under my eye. I could not imagine the bloody monster I looked, equal to the rumors of my nefarious, impossible deeds. I stood before him, covered in not only my own blood but the blood of others.

Shifting my body, I squared off with him, giving him the widest target possible. For a minute, I didn't care if he pulled the trigger or not. I was so tired of running, so tired of killing, getting shot and hit and stabbed. How many of my problems would end if he pulled that trigger?

His eyes dropped to the knife I clutched in my right hand, as if it was the scariest thing he'd ever seen. To my surprise, the young man opened his hands, and the musket dropped from his grasp to the ground. He raised his hands slowly in surrender, and he backed away from me. After a few steps, he spun and ran away as fast as he could.

"What the fuck?" I asked myself.

Why didn't he shoot me?

He had me dead to rights, but once again, the name and reputation of the Pale Rider saved me. I sheathed my knife and reloaded my Thompson. I took one last look at Brooks's prone body and considered putting another bullet into him for good measure, then finally decided against it. Not out of compassion or humanity, but because I didn't have the ammo to waste to make myself feel better.

I ached to drop down on my butt and rest right there in the warm mud. Thinking better of it, I exhaled hard and pushed forward, stumbling to the horse that Brooks had been using. I holstered my Thompson and then retrieved my Tec-9 and sword under my horse's body.

I reined Brooks's horse around, heading back to Philadelphia, and made it to the city around noon. The sun was high and blazing. It was a beautiful day with a refreshing breeze from the south. A great deal of Washington's forces camped outside of the city. From the numbers, I was guessing half of his men had made camp. Washington was smart in not wanting to overwhelm the city all at once. I knew the whole army would either be in the city or on the march in the next day or two.

None of the soldiers tried to stop me as I rode through their camp. A few walked or ran up to me, but they either recognized me or didn't want to talk to the crazy, bloody, ragged man. Either way, not a single soldier said a word to me.

I slid off my horse and as I walked him into the city, where citizens and soldiers alike parted for me like the Red Sea. I thought about washing the itching, crusted blood off my face and hands before walking into Independence Hall to report to General Washington but decided against it. This way, the outside of my body matched the mood I was in on the inside.

I tied the horse to a hitching post and walked up the red cobblestones that led to the front door. Two sentries guarded the door, and as I got close, they moved together, blocking my way. There had to be a hundred people in the hall, running around. From outside the closed door, it sounded like the cries of a thousand seagulls.

"Where is Washington?" I asked the sentries.

"You mean General Washington," the soldier on my right said, putting emphasis on the word *general*. "He's in his office with his staff officers."

"But you won't be going in there looking like this," the soldier on my left said, motioning his hand up and down at me. "The general has no time for riffraff. Go beg elsewhere."

I inhaled a deep breath to calm myself. After all, it wasn't their fault I looked the way I did or smelled as rank as I did for that matter. But I needed to talk to General Washington right away and see if his top spy had made it back alive.

I considered a few intimidating words might force them to move out of my way without the need for any delay or violence. I opened my mouth to say something frightening in a low, deep, quiet voice, the kind of voice that forces people to listen carefully in order to hear you and make them understand the mistakes they were making. My father used to call it the *come to Jesus moment.*

Unfortunately for the three of us, my stomach chose that moment to scream its hunger, letting out a loud, long growl that sounded like something between a coffee pot percolating and a moose's mating call. The two soldiers laughed and pointed to my shrunken and noisy stomach. Any chance of reasoning with or intimidating these two mocking fools flew right out the window.

A minute ago, they were two American soldiers guarding Independence Hall and General George Washington, but now they were two obstacles in my way. Their *come to Jesus moment* was going to have to arrive in a different form. I was done messing around.

I stepped forward, bringing my knee up into the balls of the one on my right. As he bent at the waist, his partner reached out for me with his left hand. I grabbed his wrist with my left hand, twisting it, pinning it against his chest, and, more importantly, getting it out of my way so I could throw a quick jab into his nose. Not a hard punch – I didn't want to knock him out. I only wanted to break his nose. His hands grabbed his face as blood poured from between his fingers, and his musket crashed to the ground with a clatter.

His buddy curled into a ball on the ground, holding his family jewels with his musket lying uselessly next to him. I stepped back and then forward again with a hard kick to the center of the bloody-faced soldier's chest. He flew back, crashing not only into the door but through it, landing on his back inside the hall.

Quite the announcement of my arrival.

The room fell silent as a hundred faces of military and civilian dressed men gaped at me. No one reached for a weapon or screamed in alarm. They stood in the entry, waiting to see what I'd do next. No one moved as I turned with authority and stormed up the stairs like a demon with a vengeance. A voice from the back of the room spoke in a whisper that took on a life of its own. *Pale Rider.*

The soldier with the broken nose wobbled to his feet and stepped in my direction. He froze in mid-step when the whisper reached his ears. Ignoring him, I made my way to the office that once belonged to General Clinton and was now no doubt General Washington's. The door was open, and I walked in to the first office. A major sat behind the desk and rose stiffly when I entered. Without waiting to be announced, I shoved past him into the general's office.

Washington dwarfed the large wooden desk he sat behind, back-lit by the light from the window. Lafayette, Hamilton, General Von Steuben, and, thankfully, Tallmadge filled the chairs in front of the General, their backs to me. Everyone in the room wore uniforms except Tallmadge, whose brown pants and brown shirt were of a clean, light cotton. I assumed his burn marks were too painful to wear anything else.

"Thomas," Washington yelped in surprise and jumped to his feet when I walked into the room. "My God man, you're alive."

The men around his desk sprang to their feet as well, facing me with mixed expressions of shock and awe.

"Thomas," Lafayette said. He rushed to me and opened his arms to embrace me in a hug. Well, he started to, until he noticed the thick, crusty blood on my face and shirt. Then he grasped me by the shoulders and squeezed as if it was a hug. His uniform really was too clean to embrace the likes of me.

"So much blood," Lafayette said in a low tone, his smile fading.

"Rest easy, my friend," I told him. "Most of what you see is not mine."

"*Dieu merci*," he said, his smile again gracing his lips. "I told them all you were still alive. I'm pleased to see you. I don't mind admitting that I was starting to worry myself."

I bowed my head slightly at his exuberance. "I'm happy to see you as well, Marie."

"Your face," Lafayette said with concern in his voice. His brow knitted, as if just noticing my self-inflicted laceration under my eye. "Your ear. *Mon Dieu!* What happened?" His fingers moved up to my ear as if he was going to touch it.

"Don't," I said indignantly and slapped his hand away. "Yes, Marie, it hurts, and you touching it won't help."

"It's good to see you, Thomas," Washington said, interrupting my moment with Lafayette. My jaw clenched at his greeting.

"General," I said neutrally, not yet sure if I should be pissed off about being left on my own while they sat here in the city. "How did the battle go?"

"The lack of battle is more precise," Washington said. "The city was ours for the taking. We were told that General Clinton and his army march for New York."

"Yes. My eyes and ears in the city tell me that General Clinton was misinformed that our forces were on the march to New York," Tallmadge agreed.

Washington nodded. "General Von Steuben was quite disappointed. He was looking forward to showing us how effective his training was."

"The General is a fool if he's disappointed about the lack of soldiers dying," I commented flatly. "Just as Tallmadge's eyes and ears are. Clinton went north in an attempt to capture me, not you."

General Von Steuben's face burned red, and he puffed out his chest, obviously insulted by my words.

"Excuse me, Lieutenant Colonel!" Von Steuben yelled his indignation.

Tallmadge stepped forward and opened his mouth to say something I'm sure would be arrogant. I raised my right hand and pointed my first two fingers at Tallmadge, freezing him mid-sentence.

"The condition you see me in now is due to you having to be rescued," I said, "so choose your next words with care."

Tallmadge snapped his mouth closed and stepped backward. General Von Steuben took the opportunity to step forward until my hand swung in his direction, fingers still extended.

Washington, the ever peacemaking diplomat, moved between us and held up his right hand to stop anyone from saying another word.

"Gentlemen, if you would shut the door behind you, I'd like a minute alone with Mr. Nelson."

Washington might have been playing peacemaker, but his voice had a hard edge that left no doubt his request was an order.

Lafayette gave my arm a final squeeze and let go of me.

"I'll send for a doctor," Lafayette said as my stomach growled again. "And some food."

The rest of the men exited the room, shutting the door behind them.

"What profit do you get from insulting General Von Steuben and Major Tallmadge?" Washington asked.

"Any man who hopes for blood and carnage, so he can show off your newly trained army to you, is not only a fool but a sycophant," I said, ire over their presumed insult flaring in my chest. "As for the Major, well, sir, in truth, I don't trust him."

"Very well, Thomas," Washington said, rubbing his forehead with his forefinger and thumb. "In the future, I'll keep him away from you. For now, you look a bloody mess. Go eat, see the doctor, and bathe. Come see me in the morning, and I'll have new orders for you."

I looked him square in the eye and swallowed the cursing insult that was perched on my tongue for him. "No, sir. No new orders. We had a deal, if you remember. I'll be leaving in the morning to oversee the building of our farm. I'll have that letter you promised me."

"Thomas," Washington started, his hand outstretched toward me. Almost begging.

"General," I interrupted him. "I had Clinton's entire army after me so that you could walk into Philadelphia with no losses. You wanted a victory for your men, and now you have it. I have nothing left in me to give."

Washington was quiet for a minute. He took a deep breath through his nose, then nodded his head.

"Very well, Thomas. You are correct. You have done all I've asked and more. Go tend your injuries, eat, and clean up. Come see me in the morning, and I will have your requisitions for labor and materials. You may oversee the construction of your new house and two barns. I'll send word to Martha right away to have Annie and the girls meet you there."

I'll admit, I had thought he'd put up more of a fight to get me to stay. I must really have looked a fright. General Washington stuck out his hand to me.

"It's been an honor to serve under you, General," I said honestly as I grasped his hand.

"No, Thomas. The honor has been mine."

Final Chance

Chapter Seventeen   Three Years Later

October 4th, 1781

I awoke on my plush goose feather mattress and stretched. My arm and leg muscles flexed and tightened as I let out a deep moan. My arm found its way across the bed to discover Annie's side empty. The sun was high in the morning sky and illuminated the entire room through the open windows. The curtains moved as a light breeze blew them around. Annie managed to get out of bed without waking me again. Over and over, I'd told her to wake me, but every morning she let me sleep. She would be downstairs feeding the kids right now. Molly and Regan, now fourteen and twelve, would be getting ready for school. Like most children in this century, that meant homeschooled. Annie was teaching them herself after she fed them and our two-year-old son, George.

Climbing out of the bed, I washed my face to help me wake up. I combed my sun-kissed brown hair that now tumbled my shoulders and tied it into a ponytail. Annie seemed to like it that way. I'd never worn it this long in my life.

My scar was still noticeable, but not nearly as obvious as when I had short hair. My beard had grown in thick and full. I thought it caught too much of my food, but Annie loved it and that's the only thing I cared about. She enjoyed holding my face between her palms as her fingertips scratched my hairy face. I adored her touch, and the beard was a small price to pay for her attention. I dressed quickly in my work clothes. Today was a big day for me and my new company. I wanted everything to go off without a hitch.

I headed downstairs to find my beautiful wife feeding little George. The girls were in the parlor, waiting patiently for their mother to start their math lessons. The smell of fresh baked bread wafted in from the kitchen. It was a scene I never could have imagined in my previous life – a wife, children, a home.

"Good morning, husband," Annie said in her strong Irish brogue.

"Good morning, my love," I said, grabbing an apple off the table. I kissed the top of her head. "Please take it easy today."

"I gave birth to three children already with no problems," she explained, rubbing her slightly rounded stomach. "This next one will be no different."

"Just the same, no heavy lifting if you please," I requested as I headed out the front door.

"As my lord commands," she called out to me as sarcastically as possible.

Stopping at the horse barn, I walked past the first five horses and stopped at my horse's stall. The barn was big enough to hold twelve stalls, but we only had eight of them filled right now. Annie's mare, like her mistress, was pregnant, so we would have the ninth stall filled once the mare gave birth. I patted Little Joe on the neck and held out the apple for him while he bit into it. He pushed his nose into my chest, letting me know it had been too long since we'd gone for a long ride. I made a mental note to ask the girls to play with him when their schoolwork was done.

"I know, buddy," I said to my horse and friend as I rubbed his nose. "I've been busy with the strikers, but we'll go soon."

After spending a little time brushing down Little Joe, I walked out of the barn, heading next door to my work area. It was a solid, red brick building about thirty feet wide and fifty feet long. We only called it a barn because of the wide double doors on the front and the rafters on top. It had been fully paid for by the Continental Congress, so I went all out when I told the workers what I wanted. A large sign in the shape of an arch was fixed to the front of the building above the doors – it read Cain's Strikers.

I opened the two barn-sized double doors and walked into my own personal workspace. The entire foundation of the workshop was paved in with cobblestone. Annie thought it was a great waste of money to pay workers to lay the cobblestones, but I wanted the area clean and dirt free. Her protest ended when I reminded her that Congress was paying for it.

Six different but equally large work benches lined the left side of the building. No two benches looked or were built the same. The work benches were designed for different stages of producing my strikers. Dozens of crates filled with different supplies sat on the right side of the room, stacked up against the wall.

I had spent two years collecting the materials I needed and experimenting with them, trying to get them in the perfect order and amounts. It would be wrong to say I had truly invented the first match, since I grew up with them and was taught how to make them when I was in my twenties. I will say that as far as this new timeline was concerned and anyone alive knew, I had indeed invented them.

I had hired a few men as employees, plus Jonas's family. Jonas's family were candle makers by trade and whose business had been burned to the ground in the confusion the night the British came after me. I felt responsible for their financial loss. To make up for their loss, I paid them to put a coat of wax on every match. The wax protected the matches from the weather and from rubbing together, accidentally igniting. The wax was still a little too thick, though, and the average person had to strike the match twice – once to remove the wax and then again to light it. With a practiced hand, a person could do it in one strike. Most of the workers I'd hired had manned cannons in the war, so they were familiar with working with explosives. Many of the chemicals and supplies I used were flammable by themselves, but dangerously explosive when mixed together wrong.

With General Washington and Benjamin Franklin's help, I secured contracts with Congress for my new stick matches. I called them *strikers,* but in my mind, they were matches. Today was a big day for me because the large wagon that fit easily in the middle of the workroom was filled with crates. Every crate contained hundreds of smaller boxes filled with strikers to be delivered to George Washington's army. The war was all but over, but after the war, the country would still need matches. Upon hearing of the strikers, buyers from Canada and Spain had traveled to our farm wanting to secure contracts with me. My contract with Congress stipulated that I couldn't sell strikers to any other country until the war was declared over. That was Benjamin Franklin's input. The sneaky old fox got over on me with *that* provision.

The workers would show up any minute, and I'd have them hook up the four wagon horses to the large wagon and deliver the merchandise. I stood in the barn, gazing around at my life, and smiled. I had Annie, the girls, George, and the new baby and a business that was finally taking off after three long years. As shocking as it was to admit, for the first time that I could really remember, I was *happy.*

When my childhood friend and boss, Aden, sent me to this century in that blue alien ship, he said that he hoped and wished that I would find the peace I needed. I hadn't found it in my own century, and he seemed to know that I might find it here in this century. He was right, as always. The war was over for me, and I had made a life for myself here. Not only in this place but in this century. I had a good life and a grand future. All I could do was stand around and smile, marveling at not only my happiness, but at how bright my future was.

"You're a hard man to find," the French accent behind me said.

I spun around to face my best friend in this timeline.

"Marie," I called out with excitement and moving towards him.

"*Mon ami*," Lafayette responded, opening his arms for an embrace.

"It's been too long, my friend." I stepped forward for a long hug.

"*Oui*," he said, wrapping his arms around me.

We hugged, then slapped each other on the back.

"Since you're here, I guess the war is over?" I asked as I pushed away.

Lafayette shook his head sadly. "*Non.*"

"*Non?*" I repeated. "The news I hear from the city and every traveler that comes our way is that the end is near. Everyone knows it, except the king."

"*Oui*," Lafayette said, nodding his head. "That is the problem."

"How is that? Please explain, my friend."

"General Washington has General Cornwallis trapped in a place called Yorktown," Lafayette explained. "My countrymen have blocked off all chances of the British escaping or receiving any reinforcements from the sea."

I froze at the name Yorktown. Four years ago, when I was sent here, I was given three missions. To save George Washington, ensure the victory for the continental army at Saratoga, and make sure the battle of Yorktown was won. I had done the first two but didn't see any reason to take part in the third. My actions of the past had already insured a victory at Yorktown. I had completed my mission. It was my time now. My life.

"Then why are you here and not there?" I asked cautiously. "I know you, Marie. You would never miss the big end to this war."

"General Washington requests your help," Lafayette said, his voice low. He knew the profundity of his words.

I sighed and rubbed my forehead with my fingers. "How many men does Washington have at Yorktown?"

"A total of twenty thousand," Lafayette answered. "That includes Americans and French troops."

"And Cornwallis?"

"Nine thousand," Lafayette said.

My brow furrowed as I pulled my finger away. "Twenty thousand against nine thousand? With no hope of reinforcements? What does Washington want with me? Like I said, the war is over."

"Washington has been informed that Cornwallis is probing our lines to find the weakest point," Lafayette said. "Cornwallis is going to mount an attack when he's ready. His whole nine thousand men at one spot."

"Where is this information coming from?" I asked in a tired voice. I already had an idea.

"Tallmadge," Lafayette answered and quickly raised his hand to stop me from interrupting. "Tallmadge still has Washington's confidence. I know you don't like the man, but he's intelligent."

"It's not that I don't like him, Marie. I don't like him, but that's not the point. The point is, I don't trust him."

"I'm afraid Washington does," Lafayette said.

"General Cornwallis will still lose," I said, changing the subject. "Even if he's able to push out of Yorktown, he'll lose most of his men. Washington will chase him down and keep attacking until they're finished."

"*Oui*, that is the General's plan," Lafayette said. "Unless you can think of something better."

"Why would I need to think of something better? Marie, the war is over. We won. You should be happy."

"Nine thousand British troops will die for sure, and Washington is guessing at least that many American and French soldiers. If Cornwallis tries to break out, eighteen thousand men are going to die. The General believes you're the only person to . . . how did you put it that time . . . think around the box?"

"Think *outside* the box," I corrected.

"*Oui*," Lafayette said, raising a hand, pointing his first finger at me. "*Outside* the box. What a strange expression."

I shook my head, not wanting to hear anymore. I had done my job. The Americans had as good as won the war. History had been changed.

"Marie, I haven't been shot or stabbed in three years," I said, as my hand reached up to touch my ear, my finger caressing the half-moon of missing cartilage. "Believe it or not, I've enjoyed people not trying to kill me."

"Thomas," Lafayette said, his voice tight to gain my attention, "the General hasn't asked for your help in three years. I've asked for the General's permission, several times, to come to you and request for your assistance with different military matters. Each time I asked, the General has said no. Each time, the General has said that you've done enough. That you had done your part. Now, after three long years, he wakes up, mounts his horse, surveys the battlefield, and then, without any warning, orders me to find you. I asked him *why*? As you say, Thomas, we've already won the war. He said that in the past he's asked you to kill the enemy, but now he's asking you to find a way to save them."

"Thomas," Annie's voice called out to me from behind Lafayette.

Lafayette turned around and stepped forward, embracing Annie. He looked down at her now protruding stomach, surprised to see her pregnant again.

"Another one?" Lafayette said, pointing to her stomach. "That's wonderful. Congratulations. If it's another boy, I hope, you'll consider naming him Marie."

My wife and friend exchanged pleasantries, then Annie surprised Lafayette and me by dropping her serene smile.

"The answer is no, Marie," Annie said firmly, eyebrows tight on her usually shining face. "You can't have him. He has done enough for this damn war."

"The General needs him, Annie," Lafayette said.

Annie's face shadowed more. "Don't hide behind the General. This has your handwriting all over it."

"This war has gone on too long," Lafayette said. "It's all but over. But tens of thousands of men or more are going to die in this final battle. Thousands of mothers and wives will never see their husbands or sons again. The General wants to prevent that."

"By sacrificing Thomas?" Annie asked, pointing to me.

"That's not fair," Lafayette said. "But *oui*. If need be. But he also has a better chance of surviving than anyone else I know."

Annie was right. I had done enough. The mission was everything, and I'd accomplished it. More than that, I did the impossible and survived it.

"We'll talk about this later," I announced, ending the conversation. "You'll be staying the night, will you not?"

"*Oui,*" Lafayette said. "I go back in the morning. With or without you."

My workers started to arrive and hitch the horses to the wagon in my shop. They knew what they were doing and didn't need my help. The wagon would be on its way within the hour.

Later that night, Annie and I laid in bed. George dozed in his crib near Annie. I was lost deep in thought, considering what Lafayette had said. Annie must have been thinking the same thoughts because she started crying. I turned to her, trying to figure out what had happened.

"I'm so selfish," Annie said, wiping her tears, "yet, you've done enough, Thomas."

I didn't respond. This was one of those times when Annie wasn't really having a conversation with me as much as she was talking to herself. She was trying to convince herself of one thing or another that she really didn't want to admit. She slipped out of bed with a smooth grace for a pregnant woman that always surprised me and looked down into George's crib.

"If you did go back with Marie, could you make a difference?" she asked. "Could you really save all those lives?"

"I don't see how. I don't know if there is anything I can do or not."

"You have to try, Thomas."

"No, I don't."

"We both know you will be leaving with Marie in the morning," Annie replied. "Promise me one thing."

I ground my jaw. She knew me too well. And she was going to ask me to promise to come home safe, and I hated that I couldn't do that.

"Promise that if you can't do anything to save those men, you will come home and not throw your life away."

"I promise," I said. The decision had been made. "If I can help, I will. If I don't think I can make a difference, I'll leave and come straight home."

The next morning, I sat in a chair in our bedroom while Annie cut my hair and shaved my face. I needed to keep the Thomas Cain and the Thomas Nelson parts of my personality completely separate. I truly had become two people. I also didn't want people to know we were the same person. The beard was a great disguise, preventing people from connecting me to the Pale Rider.

Annie had finished, and I washed the shaving cream from my face. Then I dressed in brown pants and a matching brown, long-sleeved shirt. I stood at the foot of my bed, staring down at the chest on the floor. The lock I had placed on the chest was still secured. The only key dangled on a chain around my neck. I took a deep breath and dropped to one knee and stuck the key into the lock. With a hard twist of my hand and a loud snap, the lock separated from itself.

Removing the lock and lifting the lid revealed a brown wool blanket. I lifted the blanket out, under which laid my original boots that I hadn't worn in years. A local cobbler had repaired them back to their former glory, and they felt like new.

I reached back into the chest and pulled out my prized and infamous black leather vest. In truth, it was no longer mine – in a weird way, it belonged to the Pale Rider, not me. A tailor who worked with leather had copied and remade my vest. Trying to explain the bullet proof material inside the leather covering had been the hardest part. The vest now sported two upper shirt pockets and two larger, lower pockets on the front. Though it had been repaired over two years ago, after my last birthday, I had three knife sheaths attached to the center of the vest. Being locked away for so long, the vest still had that new leather smell to it.

Under the vest were two wooden gun boxes. Opening the first box, gun oil attacked my senses. My Tec-9 rested in the box. Three empty magazines laid next to the pistol. Eighteen 9-mm bullets laid in a row. In the other box was my famous Thompson Contender. Twenty-nine 30-30 Winchester rounds laid with it. Every bullet bore a drop of oil to protect it from time and rust.

My hands worked automatically, as if I'd worn the vest just the day before. The shoulder holster was next, followed by me sliding the Thompson into its leather-bound home. My black leather sword belt went on around my waist. A leather loophole in the front of the belt had been specially made for the Tec-9. Three small pockets had also been added to hold my extra magazines. One of the magazines and six of the bullets would go into the Tec-9. The other two mags and twelve bullets fit in two of the three pockets. My one and last original titanium knife slid into its scabbard at my back.

I still felt the loss of my night vision goggles. I really could use them right now, but they resided somewhere at the bottom of a river, or most likely washed out to the ocean. My range finder would also have been nice to have, but it was buried in the woods. I had taken a fall a year ago while hunting and cracked the lens. My biggest advantage had been my cell phone. A library of information and it was lost to me. It had been destroyed when I saved Annie.

My two pistols and my own brain were now the extent of my twenty-first century advantages. The rest were lost to me forever.

I walked over to my dresser and picked up three custom throwing knives that Annie had made for me for my last birthday. The knives slid into the scabbards attached to my vest, as if they had been made for the knives, which they had been. Annie handed me my satchel filled with everything else I could think of. Finally, I placed a small box of strikers in two of my vest pockets.

Molly was practicing the piano as I descended the stairs. She'd been learning the piano for the last year and getting better every day. Annie was rather accomplished at playing the piano and turned out to be an excellent teacher. My chest ached at the sound of the notes drifting up the steps. I didn't recognize what Molly was trying to play, but I was going to miss hearing that racket every morning.

Lafayette was waiting patiently for me. He stood in the main room, peering up at a large family portrait I had commissioned last summer. Even little Joe was in the background, his head over my shoulder. When he turned to look at me, he paled as if he saw a ghost.

"You're still the Pale Rider," Lafayette whispered.

"Please don't start that nonsense again, Marie," I told him. "It took two years of me hiding here before people stopped looking for Thomas Nelson or the Pale Rider. I haven't heard that name in over a year. Promise me you won't mention it again. As far as the army is concerned, I'm just a friend of yours."

"Of course, Thomas," Lafayette responded, his full lips smiling against his whitened face. "I understand completely. You have my word."

Turning my attention to the fireplace, I looked up at my two swords mounted to the wall, crossing one another to form an X. One was English made, a British cavalry sword. It was the sword I had taken off Captain Bonifield years ago. Though it was covered with scratches and nicks, the blade was still as sharp as a razor

The other sword was French made, given to me by King Louis XVI, and one of the last two French Musketeer's swords ever made. Not a single blemish tarnished the weapon from tip to handle. It was also my most prized possession. After all, how many people could say that they were given a real Musketeer sword by the king of France? How many people owned a real Musketeer sword at all, for that matter?

I reached and grabbed the British sword, the one I was more accustomed to using. Sliding the sword into my scabbard was the final piece that transformed me. I had to admit reluctantly that I did feel like the Pale Rider again. Despite what I'd told Lafayette, I was the Pale Rider.

Little Joe stood outside the door next to Lafayette's horse, saddled and ready to go.

"Don't fret, Thomas," Annie said. "I will handle everything here until you get back."

I gave her a slight smile. "I know you will. You're better at bookkeeping than I am, anyway. The guys know what to do. All you need to do is make sure the deliveries go out on schedule."

Annie handed over George to me, and I gave my son a last hug and kiss before handing him back to her, trying to imprint the memory of him so I'd not forget a single thing. Reagan curled up on the couch, crying silently. She was afraid I wouldn't return and was afraid to say goodbye to me. When I walked over to her, she jumped up and buried her face into my stomach, clinging to me. I had to blink back hot tears that suddenly flooded my eyes. I wanted to promise her I'd return, but I couldn't give her a promise I wasn't sure I'd keep. It might reassure her today, but if I didn't return, my broken promise would cause psychological trauma. I kissed the top of her head and asked her to help her mother.

Then I turned to Annie. She didn't blink back the tears that streaked her face, but she didn't sob. Her face was stoic, ready to be strong for our family. I loved her even more for showing such strength when she must have felt so vulnerable. I kissed her and stroked her face, but again, didn't promise I'd return. Instead, I vowed to love her always.

After a last kiss from Annie, Lafayette and I climbed onto our saddles and rode off for Yorktown.

Final Chance

Chapter Eighteen   One Last Favor

October 18th, 1781

We rode into camp after midday. Cannon fire boomed all the way down the line surrounding Yorktown, though the line was still too far away for the cannon balls to land deep in the city. French ships also took turns firing at the city from the ocean outside of the harbor. The British troops, for their part, returned fire as best they could. From what I had seen, the carnage was at a minimum. The cannonballs did little more than churn up dirt and keep the American and French armies from marching directly into the city.

Washington's forces were closer to the British-held city than Lafayette had indicated. Empty trenches stretched out in rows fifty feet apart. The scene told a story of how the Americans had moved closer day by day, digging new lines for protection while they planned on moving closer again the next day, even in the stormy weather that turned much of the camp and surrounding areas to mud. Another three, maybe four days and the Americans would be close enough that the cannons would lay waste to the city. That's when Cornwallis would be forced to act, one way or another.

I quickly learned why Lafayette had laughed when I made him promise not to tell anyone I was the infamous Pale Rider. As we rode among the men, it turned out that three years wasn't long enough for the soldiers to forget about Washington's assassin – the man with the scar on his head, two pistols, and the famous black vest. Men pointed and called out *the Pale Rider!* The chant picked up and grew louder as we moved deeper into the camp. A cheer went out and carried down the line like wildfire.

Great, I thought. How many years will it take for people to forget about me this time? Seeing the smiles on their faces filled me with dread. I didn't think I was going to do much more than maybe bring up the morale of the men. The weight of their expectations and hopes pressed down on me like a ton of bricks.

As we rode up towards an oversized white tent, General Washington and four officers of his command staff, hearing his men's cheers, stepped out. A dozen horses stood tied up in front of the tent. The first of them was a large chestnut horse that I recognized at once.

"Thomas," Washington greeted me with a tight smile and head nod.

I played nice with the general. "General, I see you still have Nelson." I tipped my head toward the very horse that I'd given him four years ago.

"Yes," Washington answered, shouting over the cheers of his men. "He turned out to be a fine mount for warfare. Nothing frightens him."

Washington was forced to raise a hand over his head, signaling for quiet from the crowd.

"Is it true, General?" one of his men yelled. Another faceless voice yelled out, "Is it really him, General?"

Instead of answering, General Washington strode up to me and patted my horse's neck.

"I see you still have Little Joe," he said. "Step down and come inside. It's good to see you, Thomas."

I didn't respond that it was good to see him, because that would have been an obvious lie. Climbing down from our horses, Lafayette and I then tied them up next to the other mounts. One of Washington's officers named Benjamin Lincoln walked up to me with his hand extended.

"Thomas," Lincoln greeted. "It's good to see you, my boy."

"Benjamin," I responded. "I haven't seen you since Saratoga. How have you been?"

General Lincoln liked me but hated it when I called him Benjamin, as if we were equals. As always, he pretended not to notice my over-familiarity, and we shook hands.

"So, the Pale Rider returns?" Lincoln asked.

"Not my idea, General," I answered with my lips tight. "But it seems so."

We followed Washington and his generals inside the massive tent.

"Thank you for coming, Thomas," Washington said. "You look good."

I didn't waste time on pleasantries. "I don't know what you think I can do, General. But I'm here at your request."

"Straight to it, huh?" Washington said. "Same old Thomas. Very well. Follow me if you please."

I followed Washington out the back flap opening of the tent. As I stepped through the flap, it was like stepping into a movie theater where the movie was already playing. Cannons fired, men ran about with cannonballs and barrels of gun powder under rumbling gray skies. Washington swept his hand to the thousands of American and French soldiers in front of us and the large city of Yorktown beyond them. He moved his hand to point at an open spot on a slight rise of earth.

"Two weeks ago, I came out to that very spot," Washington said. "I looked out over the city and the miles of trenches between here and there. I envisioned the battle to come. The victory that I could describe step by step. How we would decimate them with cannon fire from both land and sea until they were forced to surrender. In my mind, Thomas, I saw Cornwallis ordering his men to push out. I didn't know if he'd move to the left or right flank, but he'd push out on one of our flanks. We'd wipe them out man by man with cannons then muskets as they tried to escape us. It was in that moment that I knew the war was as good as over."

Peering out over the field, I saw readily that he was correct. The British were trapped, pinned in, pinned down, outnumbered, outgunned, with no hope of supplies or help. They had no chance of surviving except surrender. From what I'd heard about Cornwallis, though, *surrender* was not in his vocabulary. Lafayette told me that Cornwallis had never lost a battle. Men like him would rather die before they recognized defeat.

A hundred small fires burned in the city. Black plumes of smoke rose up from where soldiers burned the dead to prevent diseases. This was a true siege in all its horrific glory.

"As I considered the battle to come, I became afraid," Washington continued, looking out at the battlefield.

"Afraid?" I asked with a touch of surprise. "Of what, General? Victory?"

"Yes," Washington answered, locking eyes with me. "As I thought of the victory, I found myself smiling."

"And?" I asked, still confused.

"And then I remembered something a wise man once told me. Any man who hopes for blood and carnage so he can show off his newly trained army is not only a fool, but a sycophant."

I bit my tongue. He was repeating some of the last words I had spoken to him three years ago. Gazing around at his army of young men, many of whom would die in the days to come, I knew he was right. I nodded my head in defeat and resignation.

"I'll fight to the last man, Thomas." Washington's voice was hard, borne of war and death. "I'll kill every British soldier down there and throw away as many of my soldiers as necessary to win this war. But I'll not throw away one life more than necessary.

My God, Thomas, we must try to save these men. Too many boys have died in this justified but bloody war."

Washington again pointed towards the city, moving his arm from left to right, covering the entire British army.

"And what about those men, Thomas?" Washington asked. "They're the enemy now, but they were once our brothers and might be again. Most of them are only boys. Sent here by a King they don't know, to fight in a war they don't understand and have even less interest in. Are we to send them back to their mothers, wives and children in boats or in coffins?"

I had a new understanding of Washington and why he behaved the way he did. A sour ball of shame filled me. Up till now, I thought I had done my share. That there was nothing I could do here except stand in line and get shot. Washington noticed my eyes drop away from his, and he knew by appealing to my sense of humanity he had me. I wasn't the monster of rumor and gossip.

Following him back into the tent, I laid eyes on a new member of our group. Tallmadge stood in front of a table with a map on it. The map was clearly Yorktown and the surrounding area. Tallmadge wore a wide smile on his face.

Washington must have noticed a subtle change in my expression. He stopped and turned around to face me. His hand touched my arm as he leaned in to whisper in my ear.

"Easy, Thomas," Washington said. "I know how you feel for the man, and I know what I promised you. But we need him still."

"Thomas," Tallmadge greeted, his smile unfaltering. "It's good to see you. How are your new strikers coming?"

He was letting me know that he'd kept up on current affairs and knew about my business. I wasn't sure I cared for that.

"My spies tell me that Cornwallis is planning on pushing through one of our flanks," Tallmadge continued.

"And?" I asked.

"I've convinced the General to move two out of every three men from the center to our flanks," Tallmadge continued. "If

Cornwallis tries to push out of either flank, he'll meet heavier than expected resistance."

I studied the map. "What if he doesn't push out on one of the flanks?"

"Of course he will," Tallmadge countered. "It only makes military sense, and my agents confirmed it."

"So, you have him all wrapped up in a nice little bow, do you?" I asked, shooting him a sidelong glance.

"Yes," the master spy answered with confidence. "But it's irrelevant, because we're going to prevent him from pushing out."

"Let me guess, Tallmadge," I said, pointing to him. "You have a plan."

Tallmadge dipped his head. "Yes. Indeed, I do."

He pressed on the map with one bony finger. Three red circles were marked on the map in the city. His fingers pointed to one circle, then slid to the second one, and then up to the third.

"I've located where they are keeping the majority of their black powder," Tallmadge explained. "You'll make your way under the cover of darkness and blow up these three locations. It's my belief that once the three largest stockpiles are gone, Cornwallis will be forced to surrender."

"Just like that, huh?" I asked. "I'll cross hundreds of yards of open battlefield in the dark. Find the three stockpiles of powder and blow them up. Then walk back as easy as I please. Without being captured or killed?"

"Well, yes." Tallmadge cleared his throat. "I've seen you do the like before."

Not for the first time, I wished I hadn't rescued him from that British ship.

I tilted my head at the map. "Just target those locations with cannons."

"We've been trying to do just that," Washington interjected, "with no results. Our cannons aren't close enough yet. They will be in a few days, but then again, this will be over, one way or another before that."

"What's this?" I asked, pointing to an X on the map.

"We believe that is a group of buildings where Cornwallis resides," Tallmadge answered. "Same problem. Our cannons can't reach that part of the city yet."

"You're convinced that if I blow up these magazines, Cornwallis will surrender?" I asked.

Tallmadge stood straight and tucked his thumbs into his belt. "I'm sure of it."

Looking back down at the map, I pointed to the top corner of the paper.

"What's this?" I asked, pointing to a fancy handwritten capital T.

"Nothing," Tallmadge said, with a dismissal wave of his hand. "I put my mark on all my maps, so I know that they're mine."

My mind flashed back to three years ago. Captain Brant had left that map for me to follow him when he kidnapped Annie. A map with a capital T on it, just like this one. Or at least I *thought* it was at T. I hadn't paid much attention to it at the time, and it was three years ago. But where did Brant get the map? Brant was from Quebec. Someone locally had given him that map. Up until this second, I had always assumed that person was General Clinton.

My jaw tightened and my hands clenched into fists. If Tallmadge had given him that map and had helped the man who had been called The Monster, he'd pay for his part in Annie's abduction. He'd pay with his life.

The shame I had felt minutes ago was replaced by anger. I found my hand moving towards my knife and had to stop myself. Too much depended on me figuring out how to end this war without costing tens of thousands of lives. Tallmadge would have to wait, but I'd have a conversation with him about his part in Annie's kidnapping when I was done with the business at hand.

Focusing in on the mission, I looked back down at the map, searching for the best way into the city and marking the three circles and the X in my mind. While I had no intention of going after the powder magazines, I also wasn't going to voice my real plan out

loud. I'd just come up with it and hadn't worked out the details yet.
Reaching over, I ripped off the corner of the map with the capital T
written on it.

"What are you doing?" Tallmadge yelled.

He moved forward to stop me until I lifted my face and
locked eyes with him. He froze in place, then took a step back.

"I'll be back," I said to General Washington as I shoved the
paper in my pocket and strode out of the tent.

Lafayette followed me, and we mounted up on our horses.
We rode along the line of cannons where the air was thick with
acrid smoke. Men hunched behind their muskets, watching for any
target to shoot. I didn't see any way across the open field of death.
If I traversed it at night, the distance was still hundreds, if not a
thousand yards of open field constantly fired upon by cannons and
muskets. Dead bodies rotted in the open, picked at by carrion birds.
The large scavengers had no fear of the musket fire blasting around
them. I couldn't help but notice how fat the birds were. Every now
and then, one exploded in a shower of feathers as someone took the
time to kill one. Even the carrion wasn't safe from death on this
field.

"How far will these fire?" I asked Lafayette as I pointed to
the largest of the cannons.

"They'll make it to the city," he said. "The outskirts, at
least. Maybe the first hundred yards into it. We've destroyed all the
buildings that they can reach from here. My countrymen have been
drubbing the city from the water. The center of the city is still safe
for a few more days. We'll be moving our cannons closer tonight
under the cloak of darkness. That will give us the ability to level
more of the city."

So much death and destruction. There was no way across
this kill zone. The only people not being shot at were the . . .

I smiled. "I got it, Marie. I know how I can get over there.
I've got to talk to Washington. He needs to send a message, and
then I need to go to your field hospital."

Chapter Nineteen   Good Guys Wear White

An hour later, I marched to the wide-open field, pulling a horse by the reins. A litter was attached to the horse's back, dragging behind us. Two lines dug into the ground behind me as the litter poles left a trail marking my path. Musket rounds impacted the ground near me, but never so close that I thought someone was trying to hit me. Cannonballs crashed into the earth, but never where I was.

I wore a large, thin, white coat that I nicked from the hospital, and I matched the real litter-bearers out in the field who were searching for wounded soldiers. British, French, and Americans searched the area in front of their camps and the killing grounds for comrades in arms. I made a point of checking men who I knew were dead, as if I believed they might have yet lived. I wanted everyone to see me looking for the wounded.

I had traveled a few hundred yards with cannon and musket fire impacting the ground, showering me with dirt and debris. About halfway between the British and American camps, I stopped checking the American soldiers and began checking the British soldiers. I found a dead soldier who hadn't been dead long and rolled him onto the litter. I needed a body to justify me entering the British camp.

I lurched forward when a low moaning sound sent a shiver down my back. I swept my gaze across the grass and found a young man in his twenties lying face down. I might have overlooked him as being dead if he hadn't moaned. As I rolled him over onto his back, I readily saw the giant spread of blood staining his chest. Opening his shirt, I noticed he had several pieces of wooden shrapnel embedded in his chest and shoulders. A cannonball must have destroyed a beam or wooden blockade that the young man was hiding behind.

I rolled the dead soldier off the litter and dragged the wounded one onto it. Don't get me wrong – I would have cut his throat if he'd stood in my way. But he wasn't in my way. In fact, he was done fighting. The war had used him up and spit him out. His death wouldn't gain me anything. Maybe saving his life might help me earn back some of my lost soul.

I grabbed the reins hanging under the horse's mouth and moved towards the British lines. Men who were firing the cannons and those with muskets seemed to go out of their way not to hit anyone in white. It made sense, seeing how tomorrow anyone of them could find themselves wounded in the dirt, praying that someone like me would come looking for them. Even the enemy was safe as long as they wore white coats.

When I made it to the British lines, I followed the other litter-bearers. An inn had been transformed into a makeshift hospital. A large angry woman emerged from the inn, yelling at the litter-bearers and directing us where to place the men based on how badly they were injured. Half of the men were ordered to place the injured outside in the dirt against a low stone wall. It was apparent that these men were hurt too badly and unfortunately left there to die. This would later be known as triage, but for now, as this nurse saw it, she was making sure that the doctors spent their precious time trying to save men that were savable.

No wonder she was angry. She was the one who doomed men to die so that others might live. This should not have been her responsibility.

The shrapnel in the man's chest didn't appear too deep, and the woman giving orders must have agreed with me, for she ordered me to lay the soldier down inside the inn. Another man dressed in white came over and helped me lift the soldier out of the litter and carry him inside. Bloody cots were crammed into almost every open space in the front entry, and most already held broken bodies. I found an empty bed. The sheets were covered with crusty blood from the man who had previously lain in it. I tried to make the young soldier as comfortable as possible. Grabbing a dirty, abandoned coat from the floor, I tucked it under his head. A bucket of water sat on a table. I wouldn't call it clean water, but it was water just the same. With a tin cup, I scooped up some of the dirty liquid. Lifting the soldier's head, I put the cup up to his lips. His eyes fluttered and he sipped at the water, then drank it down. Who knew how long the injured kid had been out in the field?

I rose and walked out of the inn and noticed my horse and litter were gone. I didn't need it anymore. It just surprised me that someone would have taken it so quickly. I hoped it was one of the litter-bearers and that they were putting it to good use. Most likely not – the horse was probably pulling a cannon right now.

I walked deeper into the city as if I was randomly strolling down the street. In my mind, I was trying to determine my present location on the map and where I was headed. One thing I knew for sure, I wasn't looking for the three powder magazines. Tallmadge wanted me to blow up the powder, so that was the last thing I was going to do. It may have been a sound plan on the face of it, but Tallmadge knew more than he was saying. For all I knew, he was hoping I'd blow myself up. No, I had an altogether different target in mind.

As I walked through the city, the British soldiers didn't seem to notice me. It wasn't that I was invisible – more like no one was willing to look at me. I kept my hat on low and the collar of my white coat turned up high. No one wanted to talk to the men who went out and collected their wounded or dead companions. Litter-bearers were men who, for one reason or another, couldn't fight. This was their only ability to help in the war effort.

After a few turns, I came across five British soldiers marching alongside three imprisoned American soldiers and a French soldier. One of the British soldiers was a lieutenant, with a sword and pistol on his belt. The four soldiers had bayonets attached to their muskets and marched behind their prisoners. The prisoners' hands were tied together in front of them. I wondered how many prisoners the British had here and followed the group at a distance.

The group headed towards the destroyed section of the city. Most of the houses and buildings had been leveled by cannon fire and it was completely absent of any people. The group marched down a wide street that led to a dead end. That must be where they kept the prisoners under guard. I turned the corner and froze where I stood at the scene before me, realizing in a fell swoop that I would have to act out of necessity and not choice.

This wasn't a brig or holding cell area. The dead end was nothing more than piles of rubble where houses used to stand. About twenty dead bodies laid in a neat row. The four prisoners were forced to wear blind folds and line up facing the British soldiers who aimed their muskets at the prisoners. The officer had his sword out and raised.

This wasn't an alley. This was an execution area. A place to kill the prisoners and not have the stink bother the British.

I didn't realize what I was doing until my pistol was already in my hand and firing. *Thunk thunk.* My pistol coughed out rounds on its own. I shot the first two in the back, dropping them onto their faces before anyone knew what was happening. The officer was the first to twist around and see me. He was also the first to take two rounds to the chest. The last two soldiers spun and raised their muskets at me. I dove into a roll over my shoulder as they fired their muskets. They missed, but one must have been close because dirt and stone flecks flung up into my face.

Firing my last two rounds, I killed one of the men. The first round struck him in the shoulder and the second hit him in the chest, launching him off his feet. My Tec-9 then locked back on an empty magazine. The last soldier charged me, screaming, rifle held high and bayonet coming fast. Pulling my sword, I parried the bayonet and musket to the side, bringing my sword down low as the soldier passed me. I swept my blade against his leg as he passed, and it bit deep into his thigh. He screamed again. He spun on his good leg to face me as my sword came back high in the air, slicing through his throat with a spray of blood. He grabbed his throat as his knees buckled and he dropped down and fell forward onto his face.

I sheathed my sword, reloaded my Tec-9 with one of my last two magazines, then picked up my hat that had fallen off my head during my roll. The four prisoners were still tied and blindfolded but huddled on their knees as if to hide from whatever was happening.

"You can take the blindfolds off now," I called out to them.

One by one, the blindfolds came off and they stood up, staring at the grisly scene before them. I dusted myself off with my hat as I approached them. The men remained where they stood, taking in the carnage. I cut one of the men free and gave him my knife to free his friends.

"Are you alone?" one of the men asked. Some of their surprise must have come from the fact that I was by myself.

"Yes," I said. "Gather up their weapons and find a place to hide. Don't try to make it back to your lines. Hide in one of these destroyed buildings. Wait for the Continental army to take the city."

Taking back my knife, I turned to walk away.

"*Monsieur,* wait!" the Frenchman called out. "Are you him? *Cavalier de la mort?*

I paused. "What? Who?"

"The Pale Rider?" he asked again. "Are you he?"

"Yes," I said reluctantly.

"Is General Lafayette with you?" he asked, looking around with eyes full of shining hope.

"Sorry, no," I told him. "But he's coming. Hide in these buildings and wait for him. If I need any help, I'll know where you're at."

I walked away as they gathered weapons. I wasn't worried about anyone having heard the musket fire. It was an execution area, after all.

As the sun started to droop in the sky, I made my way to where the large X had been marked on the map. A lot more officers milled about in this part of the city. Most of the commotion seemed to focus around three buildings, two stories high. Sentries guarded the front entries. Plenty of soldiers stormed up and down the street, sometimes entire platoons marching one way or the other. A dozen horses were tied off in front of the center building.

I didn't think I was going to get more than one shot at this, so I had to watch and wait. I entered the tailor shop directly across the street. The shop had been emptied of the owner's belongings and turned into housing for quartering soldiers. Bedrolls lined the floor. At least thirty soldiers slept on the floor though all the ruckus. Heading up the steps, I came to three doors on each side of the hallway.

I reached for the second door on the left, where the room would have windows facing the street. Opening the door without knocking, I stepped in to find three soldiers lounging in chairs, eating at a small round table in the middle of the room. A lantern hung on a hook, and a blanket covered the window. The soldiers froze in place, staring at me. One actually froze with a piece of chicken halfway to his mouth.

"Get out, litter-bearer," one of the men growled with disdain dripping from his words. "No room for you here. Find elsewhere to sleep."

The thought of sharing a room with one of the men who walked among the dead was too much for him.

"It's bad luck to be around white coats," one of the other men said under his breath. "You smell like death."

He had a point. The white coat I had on did stink. I wanted the room to myself anyway, so if it was the white coat that bothered them, then I'd take it off. I closed the door behind me and pulled off my coat, letting it fall behind me, my black vest now more than visible. They might have known who I was right away, but if not, my intentions became clear when I dropped my hat onto the floor and pulled out one of my throwing knives.

All three men stood up and rushed forward. The first of my three knives flew from my hand to strike the closest man in the chest. I didn't have ammo to waste and there wasn't enough room to draw my sword. I pulled another throwing knife with my right hand and my hunting knife with my left. The soldier on my left moved for his musket leaning against the wall. The soldier on my right grabbed a shovel that was lying on the floor. The soldier with the shovel lunged forward, meeting me halfway. Ducking under the shovel that was trying to take off my head, I swiped my knife at his leg, making him jump back. I then swiveled towards the one with the musket. As the musket came down towards my face, my knife went up, biting into the wooden stock. The soldier had a two-foot-long bayonet attached to the end of the barrel, and he pushed forward, hoping to run me through. Pushing the musket to the side with my knife, I forced his bayonet to my right to pierce his partner in the side.

Turning my body left, I threw my knife with my right hand, impaling the musket soldier in the eye. It sounds like a hard target, but from four feet away, it was an easy throw. The soldier stumbled back, slamming against the wall. I spun back around in time to catch the shaft of the shovel that was coming down for my head. I followed through by stepping in close with my left foot and slamming my knife into his rib cage, just below the spot where the bayonet still protruded. The musket soldier was dead and the one with my knife in his ribs dropped the shovel and collapsed to the floor. He coughed out some blood and then paled and became still. I retrieved my three knives and shoved the dead men into the corner.

The door didn't have a lock on it, so I pinned one of the chairs under the door handle to ensure no one could walk in on me. I blew out the lantern and pulled the blanket on the window to the side, letting me see outside and the street below. I moved another chair next to the window, so I'd at least be comfortable while I waited. Picking up an uneaten chicken leg from one of the plates on the table, I went ahead and ate while I waited.

When full night came, the streets were covered in darkness, the only light coming from the low-burning fires around the city. I remained in the same spot, staring out the same window. The cannons continued to explode in the distance but sounded louder. They'd moved closer, maybe another fifty yards, hitting buildings deeper in the city. The buildings in this area of the city weren't in danger yet but would be in another two or three advances. I was running out of time.

A soldier on horseback galloped down the street, yelling. He rode up to the building, sliding to a stop, horseshoes grinding against cobblestone. He carried a satchel and shouted for General Cornwallis. Several soldiers pointed to the center of the three buildings. Now I knew where the General was staying. I just needed to figure out how to get in there. The buildings were blacked out with curtains or blankets, so I couldn't tell if any of the rooms had lanterns lit inside. Otherwise, the whole street was dark, as if a blackout order had been given.

Shoving my hat back on my head, I picked up the three powder tins from the floor and tucked them in my satchel. Then, grabbing the lantern off the peg, I left the room. I crept down the stairs, heading out the back door and into an alley. Once I made it to the street, I skulked around the block, sticking to the darker areas. I found another alley that led to the back of Cornwallis's building. Two attentive sentries guarded the back door.

Then a rumble of thunder sounded over the cannons, and I held my breath, waiting to see if raindrops would follow. If I was going to do this, it would have to happen before another storm came on full force.

I needed to hurry and couldn't worry about my ammo count, so from the shadows, I drew my pistol and shot each of them one time in the chest. They tumbled silently to the ground. Taking out the three tins of gunpowder and the last of my medical tape from my first aid kit, I taped the three tins to the lantern. With one of my own handmade strikers, I lit the match with one hand, then lit the lantern wick. Turning the tiny wheel, I unrolled more of the wick, making the flame to blaze higher. As an afterthought, I traded magazines so that I now had a fully loaded six-round magazine in the pistol, plus the one bullet still in the chamber from the last magazine. My last magazine now sat in one of the pockets on my belt, with my last three bullets in it.

Ten rounds to end a war. It seemed impossible.

Looking both ways to make sure I was still alone in the alleyway, I threw the lantern as hard and as high as I could. The shattering of glass and whoosh of fire exploded in the night sky. In the darkness of night, the fire on the roof could be seen from miles away.

I made my way around the alley and then back down the street where I could watch Cornwallis's building. Three loud booms boomed as the gunpowder in the tins exploded. The fire on the roof grew bigger and made for a great signal. The building was made of brick, so there wasn't any chance of it burning down. I estimated the fire would burn itself out in a few minutes.

General Washington didn't have any cannons close enough to reach this area, but the French in the harbor did. The French ships could sail in closer at night if they had a target to fire at. And I had just given them a target to fire at. That is, assuming Washington's message had been received by the French captain.

No sooner did I have that thought then twenty-four cannons began firing off as one from the harbor. I ducked low, hoping not to get killed by friendly fire or brick shrapnel. A cannonball ripped through the roof of the tailor shop I had been in minutes ago and exploded inside the shop. Then one of the front windows on the first floor of Cornwallis's headquarters blew out as a cannonball smashed through and blew up. Several cannonballs flew over the rooftops, impacting with the buildings behind Cornwallis's building. The building to the right took most of the damage as the ship's aim was off a slight margin. The first and second floor took direct hits. Men raced out of the three buildings, and I tensed. I hadn't seen Cornwallis yet.

Soldiers ran in different directions in a shouting panic as cannons from the city firing back at the French ship. The roof fire had burned itself out, and the French no longer had a clear target. I knew the French sail out of the harbor by now to a safer distance and avoid British cannons. The French volley on Cornwallis's building was the total sum of help I was going to get.

The last of the British soldiers sprinted out of the building, not wanting to wait for another cannonball to come flying through a window. Then Cornwallis himself ran out of the building. He was with a group of British officers, surrounded by soldiers. Cornwallis's officers clutched armfuls of paper and maps, trying to save what they could in case the building was destroyed.

I ran down the alley and up the steps to the back door. Opening the door, I peered in but didn't see anyone left in the building. I raced down the hallway, heading to the stairs. I took the stairs two at a time to the second floor. Several smaller rooms were to my left and one big room to my right. That had to be Cornwallis's office. The single door opened inward and stood wide open.

Pulling out my Tec-9, I held it high as I slowly stepped into the room, searching for anyone who might have stayed behind. The room was empty. Several large couches and lots of chairs. All the windows were covered with blankets. A large, dark wood desk sat at the far end with room for others to stand around. Papers were scattered all over the floor where they'd been dropped during the mad dash to get out of the building.

I didn't see anywhere to hide, so I hid in the only spot in the room that I could think of – behind the open door. I pulled the door open as far as it would go and stood behind it with my Tec-9 in my right hand.

The cannons went quiet, and the only sounds I heard were horses galloping and men yelling outside. When the soldiers were certain the attack was over, they started filing back into the building. Boots pounded on wooden floorboards. Footsteps sounded on the creaky stairs. Lots of footsteps. Not for the first time, I questioned a plan of mine that sounded good in theory but might have lacked something in the execution.

Men walked into and across the room. I tried to count how many men entered the room by their footsteps and different voices.

"Washington has figured out the location of my headquarters," a voice hollered. "Captain, find me a new location. This will be our last night in this one."

That had to be Cornwallis because the captain ran out of the room. *Clomp, clomp, clomp* went his boots as he rushed past me. I stood in my hiding space for a few more minutes to ensure no one else was coming in.

"We'll push out tomorrow night," Cornwallis was saying, "here in the middle of the enemy's lines."

"In the middle, sir?" another voice asked. "Not on the American flanks like we talked about?"

"No," Cornwallis answered, his voice rough and edgy. "Washington has spies, and he'll know by now that we're planning something. We've seen the Americans and the French weakening the center to fortify the flanks. We'll push out here," he said, thumping a finger against the map.

"Will they not see us moving our men, General?" the same officer asked.

"We'll leave men manning the cannons and enough to support them," Cornwallis said. "It'll mean leaving a thousand men behind to be killed or captured, but we'll still have seven thousand to push out with. Then we move south where we can get supplies and reinforcements."

This maniac is going to drag out this war. Some people just didn't know when they were done for.

I needed to make my move now while they were distracted. Peeking my head out from behind the door, I took note of four soldiers on their hands and knees, muskets on their backs, picking up papers off the floor. Cornwallis stood behind his desk and pointed to a map, with six officers leaning over his desk, looking down.

I slowly pushed the door shut. There was a long skeleton key in the lock. I turned the key, and the bolt locked in place with a loud click. The room fell completely silent and every head turned my way. The closest soldier on his hands and knees shifted to rise when I stepped forward and kicked him in the ribs. He spun in the air and landed hard on his back.

"Don't move," I said, raising my pistol.

"Get him, you fools!" Cornwallis yelled.

The three soldiers on their knees rose and brought their muskets straps over their heads. My first shot sailed past the soldier on his back and struck the second soldier in the head. Firing what they thought was my only shot emboldened the others. The officers stood in place, letting the common soldiers do the work. The last two soldiers brought their muskets with bayonets to bear. They both rushed at me, and I fired a well-aimed shot into the next soldier's face, and he fell onto his stomach, dead.

The last soldier was only a few feet away from sticking me, and I was forced to fire off three quick shots into his chest. His momentum kept him going as I swept to the side like a bullfighter who almost got the horns. His bayonet stuck an inch into the door, and he bounced off the door with a loud impact, already dead. The soldier on his back rolled to regain his feet, or was trying to until I kicked him again, this time in his face, knocking him out.

The officers finally realized that they needed to take action themselves. Five of the officers drew their swords while the sixth was pulling the hammer back on his flintlock pistol. One round to the bridge of his nose dropped him at Cornwallis's feet.

The youngest two officers charged first. My last round took the one on my right in the shoulder. He dropped his sword but was still standing. I released my Tec-9 and grabbed the musket stuck in the door. I yanked it free and swung it around, hoping that the soldier I had killed had loaded it. Pulling the trigger, the musket bucked in my hand harder than I expected. The gun powder smoke from the flash pan spewed in the air in front of my face. The soldier that was in front of me was now on the floor, holding his stomach.

Smoke settled into my eyes and was momentarily blinded. Taking a step backwards, I blindly threw the musket across the room, hoping to hit one of the officers. The crash of the musket hitting the floor indicated that I'd missed. Blinking my eyes and clearing my vision, I drew my sword and titanium hunting knife. The three officers were already coming at me fast before I realized they'd moved. The injured officer had retrieved his sword up with his left hand. Someone was trying to open the door behind me from the hallway, fighting the locked handle. My shots had all been silenced, but that last musket shot had not. The entire building was going to be up here soon.

One of the officers reached me before the others, and I blocked his sword from piercing my stomach, then side stepped around the couch, trying to keep it between me and the others. I didn't want to have to fight four at once, even with two blades. Two officers went around the couch one way and two came at me from the other. I charged to my right, swinging my sword for the first one who blocked my swing easily enough, but was forced to step back and to the side at the same time. When he moved out of my way, he left the already wounded officer alone. The wounded officer made a clumsy, left-handed swing for my head. I ducked under his awkward attack and ran past him, slicing my knife across his inner thigh. He crumpled to the floor, and I could see blood soaking his pants in a fast bloom. Since femoral artery is a relatively unprotected artery running along the inside of our thigh, it's rather simple to slice through. Most of our arteries are in our arm, neck, or deep inside our body – places that we humans protect. The femoral artery, being so close to our balls, is one we should protect the most. At least this officer should have. He was out of the fight, and unless he put a tourniquet on his leg in the next thirty seconds, he'd be dead.

My blade still dripping, I spun back around to face the room and my attackers. I ignored the pounding of fists against the door and shouts of men wanting to come in. Two of the officers came at me together while the third bent down to pick up one of the muskets on the floor. I didn't want to risk throwing my knife with my left hand, so I was forced to throw my sword. I had done this once before in a duel in France, but not with great accuracy.

This time, my accuracy had improved, and my sword blossomed from his chest. He stared down at his chest in disbelief, dropping the musket with a clatter and grasping the hilt of my sword as if to yank it out. His legs were wobbly, then gave out on him as he fell to his knees, then to the floor on to his side. The two still moving in on me, both stopped and watched their fellow officer in twin masks of horror and shock. It always amazed me how gentlemen in this century were fine with killing one another but always saw it as cheating if you didn't kill in some kind of socially acceptable and traditional way.

Then they turned back to me to find me holding a large knife and without a sword. Switching the knife to my right hand and bending my knees, I was ready to spring in any direction. I waited for them to come at me, but they hesitated, neither wanting to be the one to move first.

"What are you waiting for, you fools?" Cornwallis screamed again from his hiding spot behind his desk. "Kill him! Kill him now, you cowards!"

With encouragement from their general, they ran at me as one. I leaped to my right, throwing my knife in midair at the nearest officer. My knife struck his chest, but he stumbled forward and as he fell to the ground, his sword went through the thick thigh muscle of my left leg. I stumbled backwards with a good six inches of steel sticking out the back of my thigh.

Breathing through the shocking pain, I drew my Thompson, and the last officer froze in his tracks. Panting, we both faced each other and knew he was going to die, but then someone in the hallway had thrown their body at the door, trying to break it open. Turning, I fired dead center at the door, putting a hole in it. I was rewarded by the sound of a body falling to the floor.

The officer in front of me didn't squander his opportunity and leaped forward, sword slicing downward over his head. Instead of backing up, I stepped forward on my good leg, closing the distance between us, and blocked his sword with my Thompson. His blade bit deep into the belly of the cherry wood frame of my pistol. Reaching out with my left hand for the hilt of his sword, I wrapped my fingers around his right hand, holding the sword and his right arm high in the air. I released my Thompson and rotated my body to my left, then brought my right fist up in a powerful uppercut to his right elbow. He screamed in pain as the sound of his elbow snapping echoed through the room. We stared at his elbow, now bent backwards in the most impossible and sickening position. His hand opened, and he dropped his sword, which I gladly caught in midair with my right hand.

Bringing the sword up into and through his stomach, he doubled over in a death curl, and two feet of curved steel shot out of his back. I shoved the soon to be dead man forward, and he crumpled to the floor, still bent over, eyes open.

From the hallway, another body collided with the door. That lock was not going to take much more of this punishment. Thank God they were using their shoulders and not their boots. Taking a painful step back, I bent over and picked up my Thompson. Hot blood ran down my leg and into my boot, and I tried to ignore it. I faced General Cornwallis, the only other man in the room still breathing.

He'd picked up the flintlock pistol from the dead officer at his feet and aimed it at me. He'd been waiting for a clear shot where I wasn't dancing around or behind his officers. I opened my mouth to say something when a cloud of smoke erupted from the barrel of his pistol. I never heard the shot, then I was suddenly on my back. I felt nothing at first, but then my chest throbbed like I had been hit by a car. But I was breathing, so I was still alive. My vest must have stopped the lead ball, but not some of the kinetic energy that came with it. My ribs were going to be black and blue, and at least one might have been broken.

General Cornwallis raced for the door. I grabbed one of my throwing knives from my vest and threw it as his hand reached out for the key in the lock. These were well-made throwing knives, and I had spent a good amount of time practicing with them since Annie had gifted them to me. My knife went through his hand easily enough, and he yanked it away with a cry, as if he'd been bitten by a snake.

He stared at his hand and the black handle sticking out the back of it. His mouth was opened silently but in rage or pain I wasn't sure. He reached again for the key, but this time with his left hand.

Fool.

I threw again and my second knife impaled the palm of his left hand, with the blade sticking out the back this time. From my semi-prone position, I pulled out my last knife, and he froze in place.

Another body impacted with the door, but this time the door frame emitted a loud moan and crack of wood. The frame didn't release the door fully from its grip, but it was only a matter of time before it would.

"Tell them to stand down," I ordered in a hard tone.

Cornwallis glanced at me and then the door, uncertain of what to do.

"If that door opens, you die," I told him, pulling my arm back, ready to throw my last knife.

"Hold!" Cornwallis yelled to his men. "Don't come in here!"

"Sir?" a voice on the other side of the door questioned.

"I said stay out, damn you!" Cornwallis screamed.

"Yes, sir," came the reply. "What do we do? Are you hurt? What are your orders, sir?"

"Do nothing," Cornwallis said in a calmer voice as he stared at his two bloody hands. "Just stay there and wait."

"Turn around," I told him.

Cornwallis looked down at me. "What? Why?"

"Turn around now," I said in a harder tone.

Holding his two injured hands up in front of himself, Cornwallis slowly turned to his left until his back was to me. Slipping my knife back into its sheath, I reached over and grabbed my Thompson. I reloaded the Thompson as quickly as I could while still on my back. I then slowly and painfully stood up on my good leg, using the couch for leverage. The sword sticking out of my leg was cutting into my muscles every time I moved. When I wasn't moving, the heavy hilt was still pulling down on the far end and up on the tip. But if I extracted it, the blood loss would be substantial. Best to leave it in for now. My teeth were clamped shut with pain.

Hopping on one leg while trying to hold the sword still with my left hand, I made my way to one of the chairs in the room. Flopping down hard on my butt, I extended my wounded leg, hoping to prevent any more damage.

"Who are you, sir?" Cornwallis asked slowly.

I leveled my gaze at him. "I am the bringer of death."

All his blood drained from his face. "Washington's assassin," Cornwallis whispered.

"I prefer the Pale Rider," I answered.

"I never believed the stories. So, you are here to kill me?"

"If I need to."

"If?" he asked, his eyebrows high on his pasty forehead.

I waved my pistol towards the couch. "Sit down."

Cornwallis moved to the couch, still holding his bloody hands in front of him.

"Now what?" he asked.

"Who is next in command after you?"

"Brigadier General Charles O'Hara," Cornwallis said.

"And where is he?" I asked.

"I ordered him to take command of the harbor when the French ship attacked."

"Order the men in the hallway to call for Charles, a bottle of whiskey, and a doctor," I ordered.

Cornwallis yelled towards the door, ordering his men to find a doctor and General O'Hara. Then, after a hard look from me, he added the bottle of whiskey.

Twenty minutes later, a soft knock came at the mostly broken door. Using a musket as a cane, I limped to the door, the sword still sticking out of my leg and a blood trail staining the wooden floor. I let the doctor into the room, then closed the door as best I could. He sported a black doctor's bag and a bottle of whiskey. After I shoved a chair under the doorknob, I sat back down in my chair. I had the doctor work on my leg first, while I kept my gun on Cornwallis.

I took a drink of whiskey straight from the bottle, while the doctor cut my left pant leg off. Cornwallis's face regained some color at his obvious joy in my pain as the doctor withdrew the sword out of my leg. I hissed and gripped my thigh as he worked. To his credit, the doctor pulled the sword out fast in one powerful move and didn't try pulling the weapon out slowly. It bled, but not as badly as I'd expected, so I had to hope the blade missed major veins and arteries. I didn't think doctors in 1881 knew about disinfectant, so I poured whiskey onto the entry and exit wound.

Once the doctor's questioning expression left his face, he put six stitches in the front of my leg and five more in the back. He wrapped a dirty bandage tightly around my leg. It looked like he might have used the bandage on someone else before me, and that idea made me cringe on the inside. I poured more whiskey on top of the bandage for good measure, hoping it'd help prevent infection. He noticed me holding my ribs and directed me to lift my shirt.

I didn't know what Cornwallis would think when he saw his bullet hadn't ripped a jagged hole in my chest, but I complied and removed my vest and shirt. If anything, it would only add to the rumors of the Pale Rider. Once my shirt was off, I was rewarded with a sight of purple and black bruises covering the area the size of a grapefruit. There was nothing to be done about it, but after probing my ribcage, the doctor declared none of my ribs were broken.

The doctor then turned to aid Cornwallis and removed my two knives from his hands. I rose stiffly and collected my weapons. While the doctor bandaged Cornwallis up as best he could, I retrieved my sword and knife from the bodies of the British officers, as well as my Tec-9 from the floor. I reloaded my Tec-9 with my last three rounds. When the doctor announced he was finished, I let him leave, and the door was pinned shut with the chair again.

"So, what's your plan, young man?" Cornwallis asked. "Why am I still alive?"

"When General O'Hara gets here, you'll order him to surrender your army to General Washington," I told him.

"I will do no such thing," Cornwallis stated with obvious indignation. "You and your master, General Washington, can both go to hell."

I let a sly grin cross my lips. "Oh, I have no doubt we will, General. But you'll scout the way for us if you don't order O'Hara to surrender in your name."

"You'll kill me either way," he stated as a fact.

I shrugged. "If you order your men to surrender, I'll have no reason to kill you. Otherwise, I'll kill you in some grotesque, tortured manner and leave your body for O'Hara to find. Then I'll go after him and have him order the surrender instead of you. Your death gains nothing for you or your king. I'll have your surrender if I have to kill every officer in Yorktown."

I was bluffing as best I could. Between my injured leg and ribs, I had no expectations of surviving this encounter if he didn't agree. I didn't even have a plan to escape this room. My only chance was to secure his surrender.

Final Chance

Chapter Twenty   The End of a War

It was well into the morning of the 19th when General O'Hara was finally located and brought to us. General Cornwallis conceded to my threats and ordered O'Hara to surrender. I imagine seeing me live through a direct musket shot and kill off nearly a dozen soldiers and officers in front of him was enough to convince him that the Pale Rider rumors were true.

Cornwallis ordered O'Hara to announce that Cornwallis was too sick to enter upon the field and surrender himself. I noticed Cornwallis told O'Hara to surrender to the French and not to Washington, but I didn't care who they surrendered to. That was Washington's problem, not mine.

It took the whole wet, humid morning for the British soldiers to be informed, organized, and lined up. We sat in the room and watched the British march out of the city from the window. The British soldiers seemed as happy about the surrender as the Americans. They wanted to live long enough to sail back home and be with their families.

As the city emptied of soldiers, Cornwallis and I stepped out of the room. Soldiers had left two horses tied up outside for us, as I had ordered. I limped pretty badly, but with the sword removed from my leg, I was able to walk down the stairs and mount up on the horse.

With Cornwallis in front, and me right behind him, we rode slowly out of the partially destroyed and abandoned city. I instructed Cornwallis to head toward the execution area. He either was surprised or pretended to be when he saw all the dead bodies. He swore he knew nothing about what had been going on. The three Americans soldiers and the French soldier came out of their hiding spots when I called for them.

"Let's go home, boys," I called out.

With the four soldiers walking behind us, we rode slowly across the open, muddy field. American and French soldiers parted their ranks for us. My four new friends were treated as heroes as their fellow soldiers shouted out to them. It seemed that these four had been written off as dead already. Walking out of Yorktown with the Pale Rider and with General Cornwallis as your prisoner had to score these guys some major points with their companions.

We rode up to Washington's tent to find it empty, except for a few soldiers. The soldiers pointed to a big shit show several hundred yards off – the surrender ceremony where O'Hara would surrender his sword to Washington. Not that I wanted to be a part of that, but I wanted to report to Washington right away and be finished with all this. I left Cornwallis with my four new friends in Washington's tent. I might have also told them to help themselves to the general's food and alcohol. I also made each of them promise not to hurt the General unless he tried to escape.

I reached the ceremony in progress. Dozens of American, French, and British officers sat on their horses. Thousands of American and French troops surrounded them, watching intently, almost in disbelief, and proud to one day be able to tell their children that they were here when it happened. I had to admit, I too was proud to be a part of the end of this long, bloody war.

The British troops were about four hundred yards away, marching single file. They never bothered to stop and kept marching past us. Their drummers and pipers played a tune I'd never heard before. It had a steady rhythm to it and sounded nice. Lafayette sat on his horse next to General Washington. He was the first to notice me and smiled widely, pleased and mildly surprised that, once again, batter and broken though I might be, I'd made it. He waved me over to where they waited. I rode up between Lafayette and Washington. I wasn't trying to get between the two. I just didn't want to repeat myself.

"What's that tune they're playing?" I asked Lafayette.

Washington turned his head, noticing me for the first time.

"It's called, *The World Turned Upside-down*," Washington answered me. "It's about a hundred and fifty years old and quite popular. Strange how you've never heard it."

I let the comment slide by without response.

General O'Hara sat atop his horse and galloped to the gathering of officers by himself, not mandating that his lower officer share in the shame. He withdrew his sword and offered it to General Rochambeau, the commander of the French forces. General Rochambeau shook his head and pointed to General Washington.

With a look of sour disappointment on his face, General O'Hara rode up to Washington. His gaze fell on me and he froze in place, eyes wide. Washington looked from O'Hara to me and back to O'Hara.

"General Washington, I'm afraid that General Cornwallis is not feeling well and has ordered me to present my sword to you," O'Hara stated, holding out his sword with one hand on the blade and the other holding the handle. His voice cracked as his eyes kept flicking my way.

O'Hara, by himself in his bright red uniform, sitting on a black horse alone, was such a vast and pathetic contrast to Washington, who wore his bright blue uniform and sat tall and proud on his chestnut horse Nelson, surrounded by dozens of officers. It was such a visual metaphor, contrasting the difference between the two armies that were on the field.

General Washington pursed his lips, displeased, and like General Rochambeau, Washington shook his head from side to side and pointed to General Benjamin Lincoln.

"If Cornwallis is going to send his second in command to offer his surrender, then he can offer it to my second in command," Washington said loud enough for everyone to hear.

"It's not his fault, General," I said under my breath. "Cornwallis really was ill."

"Ill, you say," General whispered as he turned to face me again. "What ails him?"

"He had two of my knives in him at the time," I quipped back with a side smile. "He's under guard in your tent as we speak."

Lafayette slapped his own leg. "I knew this was your doing! Tallmadge kept saying that the British were getting ready to break out. Right up until O'Hara offered to surrender."

"Where's Tallmadge?" I asked in a tight voice, and I scanned the crowd for the man.

"Let it go, Thomas," Washington commanded, tired of the subject. He removed his hat and fanned himself with it. "I know you don't like the man, but you must let this go. Leave the man be."

I held up the small piece of ripped map.

"The piece of map you tore off Tallmadge's map?" Washington asked. "What of it?"

"The capital T, marking it as his. Captain Brant had a map with the same mark on it. I restrained myself and waited until this mission was over, but I'll be having words with him, General."

Washington paused for a few seconds of thought, then placed his hat back on his head. "I'm sorry, Thomas. The man is gone. He left this morning, right after a lone British soldier started waving a white flag."

I'm sure he did. The double agent.

"Left?" Anger built in my voice. "Where did he go?"

"I can't tell you, Thomas," Washington said again. "I still need him, and I've a feeling I know what kind of words you wish to have with him. He's on a different mission for me now. Your conversation will have to wait for another day."

"Very well, General," I said. "But know this, next time I see him, you may need a new spy master."

"I will pass that along to him," Washington said, holding his hand out for the piece of map I still held. "And Thomas, if I find out he helped Brant in any way, I'll have his head myself."

I openly folded the map and stuck it in the inside pocket of my vest.

"Sorry General," I said, as I padded the outside of my vest. "I'll be keeping this for myself."

He bowed his head for a moment, again as if weighing something he was impelled to tell me. "And speaking of Brant . . ."

My hands clenched into fists at his words. His tone . . . something was wrong.

"What of Brant?"

"One of my officers near the Quebec border reported that Brant returned home. He was seen by a group of soldiers heading north."

My entire body clenched.

"What are you saying, General?"

Washington shrugged. "Maybe nothing. Maybe a rumor. You should know how rumors grow, Pale Rider."

I didn't answer but touched my vest pocket again.

"But if he is alive, he's no longer working with the British, for obvious reasons, and since you nearly killed the man, I doubt he'll come looking for more."

He might have doubted it, but I didn't. Was I going to be looking over my shoulder, and that of Annie and my children, for the rest of our lives?

Washington's arm extended toward me again, but his hand rotated from palm up to palm to the side, wanting to grasp something. I understood the meaning and stuck my hand out, grasping it in a handshake.

"I'll find Little Joe, and then we'll be heading home, sir," I said, as I let go of Washington's hand. "Don't forget about Cornwallis. He's still in your tent," I called out behind me as I rode off.

Washington nodded his head and gave me a wave of his hand. Lafayette rode with me and led me to Little Joe. When I dismounted, so did Lafayette. I stuck out my hand, and he slapped it away. He stepped forward, and we embraced like brothers.

Brothers who knew they might never see one another again.

Chapter Twenty-One A Visitor

I had tucked my new son, Little Marie, into his crib for the third time. He learned quickly that I'd pick him up if he cried and held out his arms to me, though Annie told me over and over not to. He didn't try this with Annie – he was too smart for that. Annie reclined in bed, waiting for me to get undressed and join her when a knock came at the door.

Annie's face paled as she looked at me. Grabbing my Thompson from under my pillow where I had taken to keeping it, I seized the lantern and went down the stairs. The knock came again, but this time it was more of a pounding. The little hairs on the back of my neck stood on end.

Who would be coming around here this late at night?

I hadn't lived this long by answering the front door in the middle of the night, so I set the lantern down and moved to the back door. Opening the door as quietly as possible, I stepped out into the night air. I moved quickly around the back of the house to the side. I slowed to a walk as I approached the front and peeked around the corner. A man stood at my front door wearing a brown cloak. He carried a satchel over his shoulder that resembled mine. His hood was over his head, hiding his face. He was a stocky guy, and though I couldn't see his face, I could tell it was a male.

He banged on the door again with his left hand and held his lantern with his right. He was now beating his fist against the door in a panic. I walked up quietly, side stepping the bucket on the ground that I didn't need to see to know was always there. The girls always left it there, never quite putting it onto the porch where it belonged.

The man's hand froze in midair when I pressed the barrel of my Thompson against the back of his head.

"Who are you, sir?" I asked in a harsh voice, "and why are you banging on my door this time of night?"

"I'm looking for Thomas Cain," an oddly familiar voice answered.

"Turn around slowly," I ordered the man.

His lantern shook in his hand, and I took a step back as he started to turn around.

"Jake," I said with wide-eyed surprise.

Jake Mendoza was about forty pounds overweight and had to be pushing fifty years old. He was Aden's private pilot, the man who brought me here in the alien ship, and he was supposed to be in the twenty-first century.

"What are you doing here?" I asked.

"We need to talk about Aden," Jake told me. "Can you put the gun away?"

My chest clenched. I was in shock and had forgotten about my Thompson. I didn't have my holster on, so I shoved it down the front of my pants, the worst thing one can do with their weapon. Then I moved quickly and gave Jake a hug.

"Why? What's going on with Aden?"

His eyes looked at me pleadingly. "Aden needs your help. He's stuck in the year 1814, and I need you to rescue him."

"Come in," I said, unlocking and opening the door.

We walked into the house, and I closed the door behind him.

The End

Final Chance

Excerpt from Aden's Chance, the next book in the exciting Second Chance series!

Chapter One   New Orleans

August 28, 1814

Chauncey perched in his makeshift chair – a wooden shipping crate he found on the docks and set on its side. He sat in front of an old decrepit table in the back of a shack he called home when he was not on ship and at sea. Chauncey didn't have a last name, or at least not one that he knew of. His father had been a pirate, and his mother a whore.

Chauncey was born and raised in the same house of ill repute that his mother had worked in until she was killed by an angry drunk who accused her of pinching his purse. Chauncey was all of twelve years old at the time, but old enough to stick that drunk lecher in the back with a large kitchen knife, killing him not mere feet from his own dead mother. Without his mother working for their keep, the owner of the brothel kicked Chauncey out, and he was forced to grow up on the streets of New Orleans, stealing and begging.

Once he was old enough, he signed on for a new life as a sailor for a privateer. It didn't take long for him to follow in his unknown father's footsteps and turn to the faster and more rewarding life of piracy. He presently sailed with Captain Burlington, a man known for his violence and ruthlessness. Chauncey was by far smarter than Captain Burlington. By all accounts, Chauncey should be captain of his own ship with Burlington answering to him. Chauncey was born a small, starving child, and although he grew tall, he was always thin and sickly-looking. He could use violence as long as it didn't involve a fair fight, but he learned long ago not to rely on brawn he didn't have. He survived by his wits and cunning. He was a planner, always looking for a good deal and fast coin. He was sure that, last night, he'd finally found it.

Chauncey studied the unconscious man on the floor. He laid on his side in the fetal position, facing away from Chauncey. Chauncey had placed him there, then tied him up. This man was a stranger in New Orleans, and strange in other ways. Captain Burlington had told Chauncey to find more crewmen for the ship, so Chauncey and a few others went down to the docks to find a few healthy-looking drunkards they could talk into joining Burlington's crew.

Chauncey had spotted the man on the floor and one other, in one of the taverns. Chauncey was watching them to see if they were drinking or not when he overheard them speak. They spoke English but talked in an odd dialect. Chauncey's eyes narrowed at the fat purses they each had and the peculiar gun the one on the floor had under his cloak, almost hidden out of sight. Chauncey and his friends jumped the two men on the docks with the plan of killing them, but the other, older stranger got away. Chauncey had knocked this man out with a cudgel, and now that he had questions for the man, he hoped the man would wake up soon, if at all. He had killed a man once accidentally by hitting him too hard in the back of the head, and he had to hope that wasn't the case this time.

Chauncey's mates were pleased to split the purse and the few items that they grabbed from the man, but not Chauncey. He knew there was more to be had. A lot more. The man's satchel, sword, knife, and powder horn now sat on the rough table in front of Chauncey. He turned the stranger's odd-looking pistol over in his hands. His mates had made off with the man's fine leather boots, thick black vest with its large brass buttons, and his heavy brown cloak. They would have no doubt given all the items to Captain Burlington as gifts for his forgiveness in returning without the men for his crew. The coins they keep for themselves, forgetting to tell the captain about them.

Chauncey shifted his gaze from the man on the floor to the pistol in his own hand as he turned the pistol over, looking at it from all sides. It was made entirely of steel except for the wooden grips on the sides of the handle. There was no wooden frame to hold the barrel. This was the first pistol Chauncey had ever seen without a wooden frame. It had a cylinder that rotated as the user pulled the hammer back. The hammer, barrel, and trigger were the only parts of the pistol that Chauncey recognized for what they were. He had pulled the trigger to see if the pistol would fire again without priming, and it had. That's when he figured out that the six chambers spun around, each holding a preloaded shot. He discharged the pistol five more times before it stopped firing. For the life of him, he couldn't figure out how to load the pistol. He had found two dozen small brass containers, each less than an inch long and holding what appeared to be lead inside of them. They were the same type of containers as were in the cylinder. Chauncey knew value when he saw it, and this strange weapon was worth a king's fortune to any army.

He also knew an unreputable man known for selling information to both the British and the French. Tomorrow, he would find the man and ask him to set up a meeting with representatives from both countries. Once Chauncey described what he had to sell, they would come. They would come with gold or promissory notes because neither country would want the other to possess such a weapon.

He would sell the pistol to the highest bidder and that country could mass produce it, and in no time at all, find themselves with the most powerful army in the world. No army would be able to stand against a force armed with weapons such as this. None of that mattered to Chauncey, who would be so rich that he could go anywhere he wanted with his own ship.

Chauncey wondered if this design could be used to build a better rifle – a rifle that held six preloaded shots. This weapon would change warfare. One man could kill six with a weapon like this. Why had Chauncey never seen or heard of this weapon before now? And what was this man doing with it? Who was he to possess a weapon that Chauncey had never even dreamed of?

Look for Aden's Chance, coming soon!

Excerpt from Book 1 *Chain and Mace*

Descended

Most people seem to believe that angels do not have free will. The truth is that they do. Angels in heaven chose to follow God, just as those in hell chose to follow Satan. When an angel chooses to follow the Lord but breaks one of his commands, he is cast out from heaven, but not all are cast to hell. These angels are known as Fallen Angels. But where do fallen angels go?

August 18

David fled down the grassy hill as fast as his legs could carry him, looking over his shoulder every few seconds. He was breathing hard; his heart pounded in his ears, and he was so tired. *Where were they? What were they?* They were behind him a minute ago, and now they were gone.

He remembered how they silently came out of the darkness, these strange men, *no not men, they were too big*. Animals, or a kind of creatures, *but they walked on two legs, or some of them did.* Monsters? He tried to think of an argument against using that word but could not. They grabbed Jake, his cameraman, by the throat. Jake hung in the air by that giant hairy hand or paw that shook Jake like a rag doll. There were three of them, that much he was sure of. The first one stood about six and a half, maybe seven feet tall, the biggest bear David had ever seen, but it wasn't a bear. Bears didn't grab people by the throats. He thought perhaps they were wolves. They did look like wolves, but wolves don't walk on two feet.

They must be men in costumes, David thought. After all, that was the reason he was out here in the first place.

His editor had sent him and Jake out to investigate reports of a type of new religious cult. Well, they sure as hell found the cult, or the cult found them. Poor Jake was overweight at least by forty pounds. How could any person just pick up a two-hundred-and-thirty-pound man by one hand? Maybe they were on drugs, PCP, or something. David had done a report earlier in the year about how strong people can get when they are whacked out on drugs. They had heard rumors about a motorcycle gang in the area, maybe they had something to do with this. David's thoughts were interrupted by the rock he tripped on. He fell to the ground and fought to stay conscious as he rolled forward on the grass, the metallic taste of blood filling his mouth.

Kathy! His mind suddenly went to her. *What would Kathy do if he died here?* Crouched in the dirt, he decided he would live. He had to find a phone and call the police, and it was his most unfortunate luck that he dropped his cell phone when he ran. *Maybe a pay phone at a gas station?*

David forced himself to his feet and looked behind him, up the hill that he had fallen down, but it was too dark to see if anyone was still there. He must have run a mile by now. David had played high school football years ago, and he always kept himself in good shape. He thought he could move with decent speed, but these guys were faster. By God, they were fast. It was almost as if they were playing with him. David thought about his cat and how she would pounce on the bugs she would find in the house, only to let them go, then pounce again.

"Stop thinking and just run," David said to himself out loud. He turned to run but was stopped by the very large hand that grabbed him by the back of the neck

Chain and Mace – Book 1

Final Chance

About the Author

Michael Roberts is a Police Officer in Southern California. He also served in the United States Marine Corps for seven years. This is his third book in his Alternate American history series, inspired by the Hamilton Broadway show. He lives with his family, including his wife, Michelle Deerwester-Dalrymple, a published author herself.

Also by the Author:

Alpha Team Paranormal Military Series:

Chain and Mace – Book 1

Chain and Cross -- Book 2.

Second Chance American History Military Time Travel Series:

Second Chance – Book 1

Another Chance Book 2

Final Chance Book 3

Aden's Chance Book 4

Made in United States
North Haven, CT
15 April 2022